The Secret of Gaspard

A Jake Moriarity Novel

R.G. Ryan

Dream Chasers Media Group, LLC

PROLOGUE

The warehouse sat in seclusion at the end of a narrow, nondescript road outside of an equally nondescript French, mountain village. The locals—that is, the ones who actually paid even the slightest bit of attention to such things—had been told, and for the most part believed, that the warehouse had been abandoned for years and was owned by persons of dubious character whose identities were better left unspoken. It was the way of things. And as for the trucks that appeared in the wee small hours of the morning when, as Frank Sinatra had once sung, "the whole wide world was fast asleep," well, that was none of their concern.

Only six people in the world knew what the rundown building housed, and two of those would be dead before nightfall.

This too, was the way of things.

Four men stood in the center of the warehouse just outside a freestanding room in the exact center—a room that appeared to predate the surrounding structure by several decades. The illumination from their cell phones cast spectral shadows that appeared and then vanished quickly into the surrounding darkness. Their voices, when they spoke, were muted, the conversation truncated. Were they inclined toward such folly, they would have noticed that the air they breathed was redolent with the smell of old axle grease, motor oil and rubber mixed with the more piquant odors of strong solvents and something unidentifiable...something dark and dying.

One of the men drew deeply on a cigar that had begun its life thousands of miles away in a rundown, Cuban tobacco shop. He savored the richness of the taste, holding the smoke in as long as possible and then exhaling only to breathe in the heady aroma once again. He was an interesting man—a man two of the other three feared more than the combined power of their respective governments. It would never be said of him that he was wealthy, for based on the standards used by the global financial community to assess wealth no viable measurement existed.

In short, his assets were immeasurable. Even he had no idea what he was worth for it had never been important. He did what he wanted, *when* he wanted and answered to no restrictive moral or ethical standards. Though Persian by heritage, he claimed neither religious nor state affiliation. He was now as he had always been—a lion untamed and unbound by the world's conventions. Or so he believed.

He cleared his throat, a signal that he wished to speak.

"I am not inclined to discuss this situation endlessly. I came here expecting to have my wishes carried out. Now, if that is a problem for any of you, please be honest with me."

Holding his phone up for illumination he sought and held the gaze of each man in the tight circle.

Having satisfied himself that he had their attention, he continued, "This has been an unusually profitable arrangement for all of us and I am quite sure that no one wishes to see it terminated. But, that is the way of the world, my friends. Everything eventually comes to an end. Such is the case with the situation confronting us at present."

One of the others indicated a desire to speak, which was granted.

"I understand all of that," he said with a deep, German accent. "But why do we have to kill our partners? Have they not been fiercely loyal to us?"

The Persian, for that is how he was known, took another

long pull from the cigar, blowing the smoke purposefully in the speaker's face.

"Fiercely loyal? Come now, my friend. Surely you don't expect that to be a viable consideration. Loyalty is fleeting at best. During my rather long life, I have seen even the most 'fiercely loyal' people turn completely against each other for an amount of money they deemed irresistible. Loyalty is something that is bought and sold, having no intrinsic value in and of itself."

The German started to reply only to be stopped by the man next to him laying a beefy hand on his shoulder.

"In Russia, we value loyalty. We value it so highly that we are willing to pay dearly for it. Have you given any consideration to simply upping the compensation to our French and Belgian friends in order to assure their continuing considerations?"

The Persian smiled condescendingly.

"How simple you make it all sound."

"But, it is the epitome of simplicity. You pay them and they keep their mouths shut and their loyalty intact."

The fourth man, who had turned his back to the group while staring at the room in the center, turned slowly and spoke with an authority nearly equal to that of The Persian.

"With most men, that would be true. But these are not most men." The man's Asian features revealed nothing of what was transpiring in his mind. "These are men who have developed a conscience. And in our line of work, my friends, there is nothing more dangerous than someone with a conscience."

The Persian once again made eye contact with each man.

"So then, we are in agreement?" He waited for each man's affirmation before saying, "Good, it is settled then. Gaspard Ducharme and Maxim Fournier must die today. "

The other men agreed and they walked shoulder-to-shoulder through the darkness of the warehouse toward exit doors manned by a small army of security personnel. Once outside, each man was hustled into their own idling, highly armored SUV that sped off into the moonless night, their passing undetected by any, save the creatures of the night.

CHAPTER 1

Y ou gonna finish that?"

The hopeful query came from my best friend and neighbor, Aaron Perry, as he sat across the table from me casting a lustful gaze on the remnants of my chocolate croissant. In spite of the fact that some people *still* have problems believing that a black man and a white man can be truly close, Aaron and I have been best friends for longer than most people have been married. It just works for us.

I picked up the precious piece of pastry and held it to my nose, sniffing luxuriously.

"I'm not sure if I'm going to finish it. But my hesitation isn't driven by a lack of quality on the part of the croissant, for I assure you that it is one of the most flaky, buttery, succulent croissants I have ever had the pleasure of consuming. Rather, it has to do with a recurring issue I have had of late."

"Oh, do tell?" Aaron intoned.

8:00 a.m.

It was a beautiful morning. The pungent salt air, underscored with just a hint of French honeysuckle, was crisp and smooth, the temperature...predictably perfect. We were sitting on the street level patio at *The Good Mood Café*, an oceanfront breakfast spot that had become a favorite during our stay at Gaspard Ducharme's family villa in Villefranche-sur-Mer, just east of Nice, France.

The villa was large—like, twelve bedrooms large.

And old.

Gaspard told me that a good-sized section of the north-facing wall was left over from the original structure that dated to the fourth century.

As a way of saying thanks following our rescue of his kidnapped daughter Simone six weeks earlier, Gaspard had granted us open-ended residency at the villa and had flown all five of us from the US on his private jet—a Gulfstream 650, which, for the record, is a *very* nice airplane. That, plus a quite generous cash amount, was more compensation than I had ever hoped to receive.

And when I say *generous,* I'm talking, like, six-figures generous.

In response to Aaron's sarcastic rejoinder, I said, "Here's the thing, my friend: while I dearly love pastries—especially those of French origin—I find that I can no longer eat one per day with impunity."

He chuckled.

"So you sayin' that your waistline is beginning to expand?"

It was a tragic and yet inescapable reality.

"Either that, or this climate is making my clothes shrink!"

He reached across the table and snatched the remnant off of my plate.

"Then I'd be doing you a favor by eating the rest of this?"

My sarcastic reply was interrupted by the sound of running feet. I turned to check out the disturbance and saw my niece Cassie, her best friend Muriel, and my soon-to-be-adopted daughter, Vanessa jogging toward us looking ever so stylish in their carefully chosen running attire. Well, Muriel and Cassie's attire had been carefully chosen. Vanessa however, as was her custom, simply threw on whatever was within reach and somehow made it work.

She told me once that it was a dancer thing.

Bending over with hands on her knees, Cassie waved a greeting to our server—a young man whose relentless, yet futile attempts to gain Vanessa's attention were the subject of much discussion among the girls—and stared at the piece of pastry in Aaron's overly large hands.

"Are you gonna' eat that?"

He gaped as if she had uttered blasphemy.

"Am I going to...what you think, girl? Man my size has to keep his weight up somehow. Besides, this is a mercy gobbling."

Muriel—her luxurious mane of fantastically red hair pulled back in a ponytail—frowned, pulled up a chair and sat next to Aaron, giving him a quick kiss on the lips.

"Mercy gobbling?" she repeated. "What does that even mean?"

He gestured in my direction.

"My boy Jake here is gaining weight and can no longer consume the frighteningly large quantities of carbs that have been the staple of his diet for the past couple of decades. Out of the goodness of my kind and generous heart, I have agreed to step in and mercifully gobble whatever he leaves uneaten."

Vanessa shook her pretty head.

"I have no idea what you just said."

I said, "Allow me to interpret: Aaron is still hungry and wanted the rest of my croissant."

"Oh. Then why didn't he just say that?"

"That's *exactly* what I said," Aaron countered.

"Maybe you should let me taste some of it so I can have a better frame of reference," Vanessa suggested, batting her eyes fetchingly.

Yes, I said "fetchingly."

I have no explanation.

Aaron's eyes widened in horror.

"You asking me to share the remains of Jake's pastry?"

She nodded enthusiastically.

"Girl, you new to the family, so I'ma give you a pass just this once. But you should never, ever, try to get between a man and his necessary food."

Cassie slapped his broad and beefy back.

"It's a third of a croissant! And by the looks of things, you're not starving. Give her a bite. In fact, give me a bite too. No...on second thought, you should buy croissants for all three of us."

Aaron glanced at the croissant portion; looked each of the girls in the eye and then stared at me with that helpless expression all men come to eventually when they know they are hopelessly outnumbered and defeated.

I shrugged and said, "Hey! Don't look at me."

He sighed and summoned our server.

"Garçon, three—no, four more of these delectable croissants, s'il vous plait."

After we all shared a good laugh, Cassie told us excitedly that Michael had called her earlier. That would be Michael Harvey, her fiancé, aka Charleston Hawthorne to his millions of readers. Michael is one of the most successful novelists in modern history and treats my niece as if she were the most precious thing on earth.

Probably why I like him so well.

"So, what did he have to say?" I inquired.

She beamed.

"His Australian book tour wrapped up early due to a couple of cancellations, so he's coming tomorrow to spend a few days with us and check out some locations for his new book. I already cleared it with Gaspard."

The news was met with predictable enthusiasm by all.

I said, "Be good to see him. It's been too long."

"I know! I haven't seen him in over a month. With the number of dates on his book tour this past year, he might as well be a rock star or something."

"You're right," Aaron said. "Boy's been on the road more than me."

"Speaking of which," I asked. "When are *you* leaving?"

Aaron is Michael's counterpart in the jazz world. Even at the relatively young age of thirty-eight, Aaron is a multiple Grammy award winner with a fiercely passionate international audience whose numbers are legion.

Aaron glanced at Muriel, his fiancée, and said, "Muriel and I were just discussing that last night. Looks as if I'll be leaving sooner than planned. Simone called and wants me to play on the final track of her album and Gaspard agreed to fly me to LA on his jet...tomorrow."

The physical injuries Simone Ducharme had sustained during the kidnapping had healed quickly, but the emotional trauma ran deep. Nevertheless, being the trooper that she was, her return to the recording studio had come less than a week following her rescue. Her belief was that music would heal the trauma much more quickly than therapy. As it turned out, she had been right.

As for my own rather serious injuries, six weeks after the ordeal and a little over three weeks at the villa found me feeling better and more relaxed than I had in years.

Muriel said, "And I'm going with him."

"Will you be coming back when you wrap up the recording?" I asked.

Aaron gazed at me for a moment without speaking.

"Well, you know, that kinda' depends."

He was referring to the call I'd had the week before from Zack Hastings, the Assistant Director in Charge of the Los Angeles FBI office. During the call, Zack informed me that Gaspard Ducharme was the subject of an ongoing investigation by the FBI and several European law enforcement agencies. Evidence turned up in the investigation seemed to indicate that he was up to his eyeballs in a decades old enterprise involving the smuggling and selling of rare and priceless art stolen by the Nazi's during World War II.

I hadn't told the girls about it for the simple reason that I didn't believe it myself and was unwilling to take any action until I had more information.

I inclined my head.

"Yes, well, I'll have to let you know."

Cassie, from whom I'd never been able to hide a single thing since she had become my ward at the age of seven, said, "Okay, spill it! What's going on between you two? I keep seeing these knowing looks being passed between you like there's some huge secret you don't want the rest of us to know about."

I replied, "Maybe that's because there's nothing certain that we can talk about."

"Tell us what's uncertain then."

Muriel and Vanessa each voiced their encouragement...well, their demands that we do just that.

"Okay, okay." I blew out a long breath of air. "So, it seems that our friend, Zack Hastings, believes—along with others in the European law enforcement community—that Gaspard Ducharme may be involved in selling art pieces stolen by the Nazi's during the Second World War."

Vanessa raised her eyebrows in surprise.

"Gaspard? There's no way! He's one of the nicest, kindest men I've ever met."

"And the most generous," Muriel added.

"I know," I said with another sigh. "That's the same problem I'm having. And to complicate the issue, Zack wants to fly over here and have me arrange for a sit-down meeting with Gaspard so they can get this all out in the open and have a frank discussion about the charges he may be facing."

"Charges!" Cassie exclaimed, "I thought you said they just suspected him of wrongdoing."

"Well, technically that is true, but Zack's thinking is that if they threaten Gaspard with the possibility of charges being brought that he may give them the other players in exchange for immunity, or something."

Cassie was shaking her head.

"You can't possibly be thinking of agreeing to that...can you?"

I glanced at Aaron who turned his eyes away as if to say, "You're on your own, bro."

"I'm in a tough position, Cass. I have a professional responsibility to the FBI and, therefore, have to be sensitive to their wishes."

"But what if their wishes compromise your relationship with the Ducharme family?" Muriel queried. "I mean it's not just Gaspard that would be affected by this. You've got Simone to consider as well."

An incontrovertible fact that Aaron and I had been discussing exhaustively for several days.

"Yes...there is that. And believe me when I say that it is a serious consideration."

"So, what are you going to do?" Vanessa asked quietly.

"I don't know, sweetheart. I really don't know. If, in fact, Gaspard has been profiting from the sale of stolen art, it's criminal activity and he needs to answer for his crimes. On the other hand, if it turns out that he has been an unknowing pawn in a larger criminal enterprise, then we need to know about that. The simple truth of the matter is that art stolen by the Nazi's is being sold at a tremendous profit to those selling it and we know for a fact that this has been going on for decades. It needs to stop and the art returned to its rightful owners."

Cassie asked, "And who *are* the rightful owners?"

Aaron said, "Mainly survivors of the Jewish families the Nazi's stole the art from and ultimately murdered in the Holocaust."

We were all quiet for a few moments as the seriousness of the situation began to sink in.

"Ah, my friends, I thought I would find you here."

The greeting came from the last person on earth I wanted to see at that moment.

Gaspard Ducharme.

CHAPTER 2

T o their credit, the girls received Gaspard as if we hadn't spent the past ten minutes discussing his name in conjunction with criminal activity. They greeted him warmly and affectionately—hell, Aaron and I did the same. If you want to know the truth, it was nearly impossible to dislike the guy. He was just...well...genuine, which, in light of the potential charges against him seemed profoundly ironic and incongruous.

Gaspard Ducharme was a good-looking, stocky middle-aged man of average height with thick, gray streaked hair worn in a stylish European cut that framed a kind and deeply tanned face whose lines indicated a familiarity with laughter. He carried himself with authority, only without the air of condescension and arrogance found in many wealthy men.

After kissing each of the girls on the cheek, he said in his heavy French accent, "It would appear that our fair city is agreeing with you."

While one of his ever-present bodyguards commandeered a chair for him from an adjoining table, Vanessa replied, "I don't ever remember being this happy and carefree, Mr. Ducharme."

"Please...call me Gaspard. Mr. Ducharme is far too formal."

"Okay, Gaspard."

He glanced at each of the three girls.

"You are all lovely flowers brightening the garden of my life."

Cassie said, "Ah, but it is *you* who brighten our lives, Gaspard. Thank you for your generous hospitality. Your villa is breathtakingly beautiful."

"If I had another six months to explore," Muriel added. "I don't think I could discover all the architectural wonders let alone exhaust your amazing collection of art."

"Yes, yes…it is an exceptional place and I am quite fortunate to be its owner and curator. So you are comfortable? Is there anything you need?"

Aaron laughed.

"You mean besides the 1897 Steinway grand piano; unobstructed views of the Mediterranean; Paris trained chef and lavishly appointed sleeping quarters?"

"So, I will take that as a, 'no?'" Gaspard replied around a laugh.

Vanessa said, "I haven't eaten this well in my entire life. I'm actually considering giving up dancing and becoming… what was that word you used yesterday, Muriel?"

"A gourmand?"

"Yes! A gourmand."

Gaspard engaged in another few minutes of small talk with the girls before asking if he could speak to Aaron and me privately. We excused ourselves and walked slowly down the narrow street in the direction of his waiting, custom Land Rover with his bodyguards trailing behind us.

Once there, Gaspard suggested we sit inside, so we climbed into the back while he occupied the front passenger seat.

Turning worried eyes on us he said shakily, "My friends, I need your help."

His breathing was suddenly shallow, his face coated with a sheen of perspiration and his eyes darting around like someone expecting trouble at any second. I noticed that the bodyguards had positioned themselves at either end of the vehicle and seemed to be on high alert.

I replied, "Okay. Tell us what's going on."

He sighed and wiped his forehead with a trembling hand.

"It is a long story—long and quite embarrassing, if you must know."

"Why don't you start at the beginning?"

He laughed mirthlessly.

"If only I could. But I fear there is not time for that. So for now may I simply say that my life is in danger and...I will not live to see tomorrow's sunrise unless...well...that is just the problem. The men who seek my life are quite formidable. So much so that I do not know if even your substantial skills are sufficient to save me."

I wasn't sure what was going on, but I decided to take a gamble.

"Is this about the art you have been brokering—the art from a cache stolen by the Nazi's in World War II?"

He gasped audibly and began to sputter.

"C'est impossible! How could you know this? No one has been told. Not even Simone or my closest associates! I need to know how you have come by this information."

I didn't want to get into the looming FBI investigation, so I simply said, "Have you forgotten that I am a consultant with the FBI, Gaspard?"

He took a moment to process that.

"Are you saying that the FBI has known of this?"

I glanced quickly at Aaron who indicated that I should go ahead and tell him.

"Let's just say that some of the art you have had moving through your company over the past couple of years has aroused suspicion. And let me quickly add that this is information that has only come my way in the last few days, so it's not like I've been here as a plant or anything. I hope you believe that."

He gazed into my eyes for several seconds before saying, "I have no reason to doubt you, mon ami. None whatsoever."

"That means a lot to me, Gaspard. And for our part—and

I think I speak for all of us—we have no reason to doubt you either."

"Good. And, for the record…things are not as they seem. I don't have time to explain everything now, but when I do, you will understand. For now, please trust me."

"Done! Now, how can I help you out of your predicament?"

He quickly glanced toward the front and then the back.

"It is as I have already said. The people I have been working with want both of us dead!"

"Both of you?" Aaron asked.

"Maxim Fournier—my partner in Belgium—and me. The order has been given and I have just learned that the men who seek our lives are already on the move. I do not know what to do."

I said, "Well, at least you have your bodyguards."

He leaned toward us.

"You do not understand, Monsieur. Against these men my bodyguards are nothing. Less than nothing."

Aaron asked, "If that's true, then what can we possibly offer that they can't?"

"You beat Yves *and* Jean Luc Barreau. No one has ever done that before. Please believe me when I say that it is no small thing."

Suddenly something told me that we needed to be moving.

Immediately!

"Gaspard, we need to go to the villa right now. Don't ask me to explain it. We just need to go. Have your men drive you there and we will be along shortly with the girls. Once you arrive, get into the most secure place you can find."

"But—"

"Go. Do it now!"

I bounded out of the door with Aaron right behind me and began running toward the girls, where they still sat around the little bistro table completely ignorant of the drama that was beginning to unfold.

When they saw us running, all three stood quickly, their faces registering concern.

"What's going on, Uncle?" Cassie asked.

"We need to go to the villa right now!"

Vanessa started to ask why, and as I cut her off I saw two men walking up the narrow street right toward us. I knew their kind. I had been dealing with such men for most of my adult life.

I glanced at Aaron.

"Here we go."

We had done this so many times that there was really nothing that needed to be said. He turned toward the girls as if asking them a question and I started to walk across the street in front of the men. Right as they arrived in front of our table, Aaron turned and pretended to stumble, reaching out to grab one of the men for support. But instead, he dragged the man to the ground and locked him up in some form of martial arts mumbo-jumbo. Before the other man could react, I tapped him on the shoulder and then tapped him a bit more forcefully on his chin. He went down like one of those lawn blow-up figures that had just had its power cut off.

The cafe owner came running out shouting in French, wondering if his favorite American customers were in need of assistance. I assured him that we were fine and that the altercation had been caused by inappropriate comments made by the men toward the ladies. He glowered at one man who was writhing in pain from a dislocated elbow and the other who was out cold and not moving. He shook both of our hands and smiled knowingly.

Chivalry was not, in fact, dead.

We clandestinely searched the men and confiscated two 9mm handguns along with two extra magazines.

Spoils of war and all that.

The girls were totally confused, but played along like champs. And when the guy who had been out finally came around, Cassie leaned over and reminded him very loudly in French that what he had said to her was not the way a man talked to a lady. Muriel and Vanessa agreed and added a few more comments that were quite disparaging of the guy's manhood before walking away playing the role of defamed maidens to the fullest.

I squatted down and glared at the groggy dude.

"You speak English?"

He just stared at me and tried to spit, but his mouth was so dry nothing came out.

"I'll take that as a yes. Do yourselves a favor...back off while you still can."

Clutching his elbow the other man said, "I do not know what you are talking about, you crazy American!"

Aaron leaned down and grabbed the guy by his injured arm causing him to howl in pain.

"He's talking about Gaspard Ducharme."

The guy with the knot on his jaw from where I had hit him blinked rapidly a few times. A dead giveaway that he knew exactly what we were talking about.

I leaned toward him.

"Just so you know, we are better than you are. Hell, we're better than anyone your bosses can send against us. So like I said, back off! Otherwise..."

I shouldn't have done it, but I was ticked off and often when I get that way emotion gets the best of me. Basically, I punched him again. Well, I wanted him to get the point and couldn't really think of a better way to do it.

The few people seated around us on the patio stood and applauded and the owner actually gave us a salute.

We waved goodbye and hurried to catch up with the girls who waited in a tight group about twenty feet away.

As we got closer Muriel said, "Okay, is someone going to tell us what's going on?"

We started walking quickly toward where I had parked the Range Rover Gaspard had made available for our use.

"Long story short...Gaspard *has* been brokering art. But, he says that things are not as they appear and that when he has time to explain, we will understand. At the moment, however, for reasons unknown, something has happened and his partners want him out. All the way out."

"As in dead?" Vanessa asked in alarm.

I quickly glanced behind us—we were still in the clear.

"Yes. Him *and* Maxim, his Belgian partner."

Muriel said, "And when is this killing supposed to take place?"

"Sometime today, which is why I need you girls out of here."

Cassie started to protest but I cut her off.

"Listen, these guys are not playing around. We're talking hundreds of millions—maybe billions—of dollars at stake. The kind of men Gaspard is involved with do not take losing their money lightly."

As we climbed into the SUV, Muriel asked Aaron, "And what are you going to do?"

Aaron looked at me and sort of shrugged his shoulders.

"I'm pretty sure Simone would rather have me help her papa stay safe than play on her record. So I'm staying to help Jake."

I shook my head and started driving toward the villa.

"I don't think that's a good idea."

"Why not?"

"Because this is at a different level than what we've dealt with in the past."

Ten minutes later, we arrived at the gate. The guard—an affable fellow whose name was Rémi, and who manifested unabashed affection for Cassie—saw us, gave us a quick greeting and opened up.

As we drove hurriedly through and then down the long driveway, I said, "I'm calling Zack Hastings immediately and requesting he send in backup."

I pulled around in front of the impressive entrance as

Cassie asked, "Can he do that?"

We exited and started walking toward the side of the house.

"Well," I said. "He can't commission FBI agents to come riding in like the cavalry, but he does have European operatives who work with the agency much like I do."

Muriel stopped walking.

"What about Michael, Cass?"

Cassie looked at her watch and swore under her breath.

"He's already on his way. Too late for him to turn back."

That presented a logistical conundrum. It wouldn't be fair for Michael to go to all that effort to see Cassie and then discover that she had left before his arrival.

We arrived at the side entrance that led into the villa's expansive, dine-in French country kitchen.

Before going inside, I said, "Okay. Here's what we'll do. Aaron will take Muriel and Vanessa back to the States on Gaspard's plane just as planned and Cassie, you'll stay with me until Michael arrives, at which time he will just have to take you somewhere safe."

Nobody liked the plan, but there wasn't much else that could be done.

We opened the kitchen door. What I saw sent tendrils of ice snaking through my veins.

Gaspard's bodyguards were both on the luxuriously tiled floor, dead from what appeared to be single gunshots to the head.

CHAPTER 3

Motioning the girls to stay behind us, Aaron and I both pulled the confiscated guns from our waistbands. With Aaron covering me, I bent down and checked each one of Gaspard's bodyguards for a pulse.

Dead, but only just.

I turned to face the others and spoke quietly.

"I'm almost certain that whoever did this has abducted Gaspard and is gone, but we need to find the household staff and clear the premises to make sure. Aaron, get on the intercom with Rémi and inform him as to what has happened. Tell him to stay put until we figure something out."

"On it!" he replied quickly moving to the wall phone and dialing the code that would ring the guardhouse. After listening for a few seconds he pulled the phone away from his ear.

"No answer. Maybe these guys are better than we thought."

Just then Rémi—a thirty-something man of below average height and boyish good looks—burst through the kitchen door causing us to spin toward him with our weapons ready to fire.

Breathing heavily, he threw his hands up.

"Non! Non! S'il vous plait, do not shoot me!"

Aaron told him to put his hands down.

"We're not going to shoot you! Why did you run in like that?"

He glanced at his dead colleagues and crossed himself.

"It is because they told me to."

I glanced at Aaron before saying, "Who?"

Eyes nervously cutting back and forth between me and Aaron, he answered, "The men...the ones who took Gaspard."

"You saw them? Gaspard was with them?"

"Oui. When they came past I saw him."

"And how did they get past you?"

Rémi shrugged.

"Eh...bigger guns and more of them?"

Aaron was shaking his head.

"So, let me see if I understand this. After we passed your guard shack, drove up the driveway, entered the house and found the bodyguards, at some point the men who killed them *and* abducted Gaspard drove past—"

He cut Aaron off.

"No, Monsieur! They did not drive. They walked."

"Walked?"

"Oui, Monsieur. There were four of them—well, five counting the boss, that is."

I didn't like it.

"So, four men walked past you with Gaspard?"

He bobbed his head vigorously.

Cassie asked, "How did we not see them?"

Rémi explained, "They came around the other side of the house after you had passed and were walking very quickly, almost dragging poor Gaspard."

I still didn't like it.

"And why didn't Gaspard try to cry out or alert us that he was being taken?"

Wide-eyed and innocent, Rémi shrugged again.

"He had...eh...tape over his mouth and one of the men had a gun to his head." He shook his head somberly. "He looked very frightened."

Muriel cocked her pretty head to one side and wagged her finger in Rémi's direction.

"And how do we know that you weren't in on it?"

Vanessa added, "That's exactly what I was thinking."

"Yeah," Aaron said. "How did they even get past you in the first place unless you were in on it?"

At first he appeared to be offended, then hurt, but that quickly turned to righteous indignation.

"Je ne comprends pas! I have done nothing wrong!"

Aaron said, "We're not saying you did anything wrong, Rémi. It's just that your story doesn't seem...well...plausible."

Rémi started babbling in rapid-fire French with Aaron answering back just as quickly and the girls adding their proverbial two-cents worth.

I whistled loudly.

I'm talking *really* loud.

Like, borderline hearing damage loud.

It's a gift.

When I had everyone's attention, I said, "Look, there's time to sort this out later. Right now Gaspard is missing, we don't know where the household staff is, and whoever did this is getting further away by the second. "

Cassie pulled a Smith & Wesson .380 BodyGuard from an appendix holster clipped to the waistband of her pants. It was one of two firearms we had brought with us on Gaspard's private jet, the other being my ever-present Ruger LCR .38.

She said, "I'll take the girls and look for the staff."

With that, they hustled out of the room calling out for Anna, Louie and Maria—the cook, the groundskeeper and the maid.

As they left I quickly turned to Rémi.

"So, how *did* they get in without you seeing them?"

He shook his head slowly and replied, "They must have come over the wall in back. There are places where heavy forest...eh...grows right up to it—places that do not appear on the video monitors. If not that, then...I do not know, Monsieur."

"Okay, I'll buy that. Did you see whether or not they got into a car or SUV?"

"No, Monsieur. They told me to run and, as I said, they had many guns. So I ran just as fast as I could."

"And did they give you a message to deliver?"

He swore impressively in French while slapping his forehead.

"Je suis stupide! I almost forgot. Yes! They said to tell you that if you try to follow or try to...eh...rescue Monsieur Ducharme that they would kill all of you...beginning with the girls."

That last bit stopped me cold! Why would they mention killing the girls if whoever was behind this didn't know who we were? And how could they possibly know who we were unless there was some previous connection?

I thought quickly.

"The playing field has changed drastically. I don't think we have time to implement our earlier plan."

The girls came back into the kitchen with the three missing staff in tow.

Cassie explained, "They were tied up and shoved into a utility closet close to the garage."

Vanessa asked, "What should we do now?"

I glanced at the two dead bodyguards.

"Rémi, I need you and Louie to take your two colleagues into the game room and wrap them in sheets until we can properly honor their deaths."

"You do not wish to contact the authorities, Monsieur?" he asked.

"Not just yet."

He nodded curtly.

"We will do as you wish."

I turned to Cassie.

"As far as Michael goes...what time is he coming in tomorrow?"

"Well, the only flight available was on British Airways and it stops in Singapore and then London. But I just realized that when we talked earlier I hadn't factored in the time change. He won't be here until noon day after tomorrow."

"Okay. That's actually good news. Hopefully we'll have this behind us by then. With that in mind...you will need to stay here with Rémi and the girls." I thought for a second. "Rémi, besides your personal firearm, does Gaspard have any guns in the villa?"

A smile slowly found its way onto his face.

"Oui, Monsieur. Many guns. Many, many guns."

Aaron said, "You mean like hunting rifles and stuff?"

He glanced down at his fallen comrades; crossed himself once again; smiled, and said, "Follow me, please."

Leading us across the kitchen and through the dining room we walked down a short hallway and entered Gaspard's private office. Walking behind the desk to a bookcase, Rémi reached up and touched a spot on an upper shelf right in front of a book on the South Pacific Islands. And in a scene straight out of a spy movie, the bookcase slid aside to reveal an inner room approximately fifteen by thirty that was lined ceiling to floor with an array of exotic weaponry that would rival most law enforcement armories. I'm talking assault weapons, grenades, flashbangs, body armor...the works!

"This room," he said, "is completely self-sustaining."

"So, it's a safe room?" I asked.

"Oui, Monsieur. There is food and a dedicated water supply sufficient to support a half-dozen people for one week along with a restroom and shower there in the back. There are communication devices linked to backup batteries and a generator if the batteries fail. There are also satellite phones and discrete Internet service. I assure you, Monsieur, that we will be completely safe here should the need arise."

Cassie and Muriel had already begun perusing the cache of weapons and had chosen handguns that suited their fancy. Something you should probably know about those two: they are each absolutely lethal in their own way. Highly skilled MMA fighters, they are also expert level shooters. I watched as Vanessa approached a nickel-plated .357 magnum pistol with a six-inch barrel. She hefted it, sighted down the barrel and picked up a box of ammunition.

I said, "Do you know how to use that?"

"Oh, I get by. I mean I'm not at Muriel or Cassie's level, but from what I hear," she paused and smiled broadly. "Neither are you."

I returned the smile.

"You're on to me."

"From the very start," she replied with a wink.

I huddled everyone together in the center of the room.

"Okay, here's what I think should happen next. Aaron and I are going after Gaspard. I mean we have to. It's not even open for discussion."

Everyone responded in agreement and understanding.

"You girls will stay here with Rémi and the staff. You should set up a watch schedule, probably in four-hour shifts. I don't see the need right now to shelter in this safe room, but keep it open so you can get here in a hurry if need be."

Cassie asked, "Do you think they'll come back?"

"Well, once they figure out that we're on their tail, I don't see how they can't. These are dangerous people, and you can't take them lightly. As I said, the stakes are very high. And high stakes make ruthless people even more cold-blooded than they already are."

"We understand, Uncle. Just do what you have to do and don't worry about us. Besides," she slipped her arm through Rémi's. "We've got Rémi guarding us. We'll be safe, won't we, Rémi?"

He blushed and replied enthusiastically, "Mais oui, belle mademoiselle."

Aaron and I spent the next several minutes procuring tactical vests, body armor and an array of weaponry that would have made a SWAT team proud.

As I removed my shirt to slip into the body armor, I saw Vanessa staring open-mouthed at my bare torso.

"My God, Jake. The scars..."

Glancing down at the crisscross pattern stitched across my skin, I said, "Impressive, huh?"

"But, there are so many."

I put on the body armor, buttoned my shirt over it and completed the ensemble by slipping into a tactical vest.

"Yes, there are. And every one tells a story."

She asked hesitantly, "Will you tell me those stories sometime?"

"Of course I will, sweetheart. But be warned...some of them are not so nice."

She grinned.

"Well, the things I've already lived through were 'not so nice' either. I think I can handle it."

We fist bumped.

I noticed that Aaron was having a hard time finding body armor that fit his 6'4", 260lb frame.

"Don't the folks who make this stuff know that the people wearing their products are quite likely to be burly men?"

Muriel was laughing.

"And what is so funny?" he asked.

"Oh, I was just thinking about all the women in the world who would just die to see the *sexy* Aaron Perry with his shirt off."

"Yeah," he countered sarcastically. "It's a real thrill, isn't it?"

She moved close, buried her face against his chest and purred, "For some of us more than others."

He gently moved her away and said, "Come on, now. We gettin' ready to do deadly work here. Ain't got time for none of that passion stuff."

Looking up at him she batted her eyes seductively.

"Really? No time at all...sugar?"

He looked at me with a helpless expression.

"Hey," I said. "Don't look at me."

CHAPTER 4

We reassembled in the utility room just off of the villa's five-car garage. It housed Gaspard's Range Rover Sentinel he had driven earlier, plus a new Sport SVR model that would top out at around 160 mph. There was also a classic Alpha Romeo sports car identical to one I had once owned and a Maserati GranCabrio.

Apparently, Gaspard Ducharme was a man who enjoyed great cars.

I decided to go with the Sport SVR even though the Sentinel was armored.

In my experience, speed is more important than armor.

Aaron and I each carried a duffle bag containing several hundred rounds of extra ammunition. From Gaspard's impressive collection of firearms we had chosen several: A Sig Sauer P226 Tacops .357 pistol with four twenty round magazines for both of us; a suppressed HK G36 and Standard DP-12 tactical 12-gauge shotgun with sixteen round capacity for Aaron and an HK416 for me. All quite sophisticated...all consummately lethal.

All in all, we had every reason to be confident in our mission.

The only problem was, we had absolutely no idea where to even start looking for Gaspard.

Aaron said, "So, what now?"

"Well, we load our tactical gear into the Range Rover...and..."

As my sentence trailed off, his eyebrows rose in question.

"And what?"

"I don't know."

Rémi cleared his throat.

"I may be able to help, Monsieur."

Turning toward him I said, "I'm all ears."

He looked to Aaron for translation.

"He means that he is listening very carefully."

"Ah, oui. Bien sûr. Well, as I was saying, Monsieur Ducharme, he goes to the country on...eh...the other months, yes?"

Aaron suggested, "Every other month?"

"Yes! Yes! Every other month."

I asked, "Do you know where he goes?"

Rémi frowned in confusion.

"Oui, Monsieur. It is as I have told you. To the country...he goes to the country."

He was staring at me like I was an imbecile.

"No, I mean a location. Do you know the *location* he goes to?"

"Yes...no...that is, I know but I am not supposed to know...I mean, Monsieur Ducharme would be very displeased with Rémi if he knew that I knew...no?"

Vanessa frowned in bewilderment.

"What the heck did he just say?"

Cassie offered, "I think he means that he isn't supposed to know, but he does."

"Know?" Muriel asked.

"What?"

All three girls looked at me with confused expressions.

"Okay, Rémi," I said. "Give me the location. I'm pretty sure Gaspard won't mind."

His eyes widened with a sense of revelation.

"Ah, okay. Rémi will...eh...draw you a map."

He produced a pen and a small notebook from the pocket of his blazer and began meticulously sketching a map of dubious accuracy that would have made a cartographer weak in the knees, but it was better than nothing. After pointing out and explaining a couple of tricky elements, he proudly presented it to us receiving in return glowing praise from all, as well as a quick hug from Cassie, which caused his earlier blush to extend clear to his hairline.

I folded the map carefully and tucked it away within one of the tactical vest's numerous pockets.

I pulled Cassie away from the group and said quietly, "Listen, I'm going to try to check in with you regularly, but you know the way these things go sometimes. If you haven't heard from me by this evening, you need to get Zack Hastings involved because it will mean...well...you know what it will mean."

She nodded solemnly, dropping her gaze.

"I hate this, you know!"

"No more than I."

"You're wrong about that! When you go off on these missions you're immersed in the experience while we're..." she gestured at the other girls, "...left behind wondering if we'll ever see you again." Her voice broke. "That's hard, Uncle. That's very, very hard."

She was right. I knew it and she knew that I knew it. It was a dynamic that had been in play since men first started going off to face conflict and leaving behind women and children who loved and cared about them. It is a monumentally unfair thing to ask, and yet it happens with monotonous regularity, because the world is filled with broken, evil people seemingly dedicated to imposing their will and inflicting pain and destruction on those they deem weaker than themselves.

Somewhere in the recesses of my ecclesiastically dysfunctional brain, a scripture untethered itself and sprang into my consciousness. Something about a people robbed, plundered, enslaved, imprisoned and trapped and basically being fair game with no one to protect them. It was a truth that had driven me since my youth.

It drove me still—drove me to be the exception...the protector.

I pulled Cassie close and embraced her as the father I was —the only father that she had, in reality, ever known.

"I love you, little girl," I said, using the term of endearment I had always reserved for her and her alone. "And you're right...it *is* hard, and beyond hard it's unfair. But this is what I do—what I've always done—and I will keep doing it until I no longer possess the physical and mental skills to do so."

I felt her nod slightly against my shoulder.

"I know that. It's just that this time feels different. It's...I don't know...it feels more risky, I guess. Besides, I'm not convinced you're completely recovered from your injuries from six weeks ago." She sighed. "I don't know what I would do or how I could go on if something were to happen to you."

I leaned back and caught her eyes.

"Nothing is going to happen to me."

"But I feel like you're in danger."

Holding her gaze, I quoted one of my favorite, fictional TV characters, "'I am not *in* danger, Cassie...I *am* the danger.'"

She smiled.

"Okay, Heisenberg!"

Returning her smile I added, "I'm serious."

"I know you are. And I believe you. But, please, be extra careful this time."

I wanted to explain to her that being "careful" didn't get you very far. Truthfully, it has been my experience that those who place caution ahead of action rarely come out on top. And lest you think that I'm advocating reckless abandon, let me assure you that I am not. In my line of work, you can either be safe, or dangerous.

Long ago I chose to be dangerous.

CHAPTER 5

They hadn't treated him badly—his captors. They were more or less indifferent, as if Gaspard Ducharme wasn't of sufficient interest to warrant attention on any level, be it positive or negative. Sitting in stony silence and sandwiched between two bulky, Asian men in the back seat of a Mercedes sedan, Gaspard contemplated the strange reality that had bullied its way into his otherwise orderly world.

He was going to die.

Probably not torturously, but his former partners in the cartel had made it abundantly clear that he would pay for his sins with his life.

And what had he done that warranted this sentence of death? Betrayal. Plain and simple. And if there was one thing he had learned about the men with whom he'd been dealing, it was that betrayal was met with swift and often brutal justice. No one walked away.

No one!

Glancing toward the Asian man in the front passenger seat—the one he had figured for the leader of this efficient four-man death squad—he said in French, "Where are you taking me?"

He stared at the back of the man's shaved, scarred head waiting for an answer, but it was as if he hadn't even spoken.

Switching to English, he continued, "Excuse me, but I don't speak Japanese. I have only English, French or Spanish."

Silence.

"If you are going to kill me, do you not think I at least deserve the common courtesy of knowing where my sentence is to be carried out?"

This time the man turned slightly toward the rear and answered in a heavy Japanese accent, his voice low and of the consistency of broken glass ground under metal rollers.

"You ask for courtesy, Ducharme? If it was courtesy you desired, perhaps you should have thought more clearly about the consequences of your actions before you took them."

Even though Gaspard realized that this man was merely an executioner and completely out of the decision making loop, he nevertheless felt compelled to offer an argument.

"It is not as you think it is."

The man chuckled darkly, an entirely unpleasant sound.

"I do not get paid to think, Ducharme. I get paid to carry out orders. They say to kill you? I kill you. They say to dress you up and take you out for a fine meal? I take you to dinner. They say to torture you? Well, I'm sure you get the picture."

All too clearly!

"But, Monsieur, do I not at least get the chance to offer a defense? To offer an explanation as to why things were perceived the way they were?"

The man turned so that his back rested against the door and stared through eyes that seemed devoid of everything one would associate with life. It chilled Gaspard to look into those eyes, for in their tenebrific depths he saw the onrushing specter of his death.

The man's lips twitched.

"I know nothing of this. I only know that orders have been given. It is nothing personal, Ducharme. It is my job. It is what I do—what I have been doing for longer than I care to remember, actually. But I am good at it and flawless in my, forgive the term, execution."

Gaspard tried to take it all in, to comprehend the inevitable certainty of his demise. No! It couldn't be. He had come too far, worked too hard and had far too much to live for to simply surrender like a proverbial sheep to the slaughter.

He had to try something.

"I assume you are being paid well for this task?"

The man stretched the kinks out of his neck as he continued to stare.

"I assume this question is rhetorical and, therefore, not intended as a serious query."

"Monsieur, whatever you are being paid to kill me, I will double—no, triple the price if you let me live."

The man made eye contact with the other three men in the car. They chuckled as if sharing a private joke.

He said, "Do not insult me—insult us! We are professionals and we conduct our business in a professional manner. What do you think would happen if we started accepting bribes from those we are tasked with taking out?"

"Taking out? You make it sound as if I am a piece of rubbish to be casually disposed of!"

"It matters not to me what you think. In a short while from now...you will never think of anything...ever...again."

Gaspard's heart was pounding. He could feel his blood pressure rising. He started to think that he might be in danger of having a heart attack before dismissing the notion as being profoundly irrelevant.

He suddenly blurted out, "Jake Moriarity is coming for me, you know."

That got the man's attention.

His gaze narrowed.

"Jake Moriarity? What do you know of this man?"

"He is a guest at my villa. He saved my daughter's life six weeks ago. He works with—"

"I know who he is!" the man said, cutting him off. "But even if it is as you say, what makes you think Moriarity will help you?"

Gaspard sensed a change in the atmosphere inside the vehicle. Subtle, but it was there. Jake's name had produced an unmistakable tension among the four men and he had to at least try to exploit it.

"Because we discussed just such a scenario not fifteen minutes before you abducted me."

The man pulled a cell phone from his pocket and dialed a number.

When the call was answered, he said something in slowly articulated Japanese that ended with, "Jake Moriarity." He listened for a few seconds, and then ended the call.

"Was that your boss?" Gaspard asked, his voice trembling in spite of his efforts at control.

Ignoring his question the man spoke to the driver, the only Frenchman of the four.

"Change of plans. We are to go to the country and wait there for further instructions."

Gaspard said incredulously, "You are taking me to the warehouse?"

Piercing him with an icy gaze, the man replied, "I suggest, Monsieur Ducharme, that you stop talking now. You are giving me a headache and headaches make me irritable."

With that, the man turned around and faced the front leaving Gaspard once again staring at the back of his head... wondering if he would see another sunrise.

CHAPTER 6

While Aaron and Rémi finished loading the gear into the back of the Range Rove,r I went over last minute instructions with the girls. Because I remained unconvinced as to Rémi's integrity, I told them to basically mistrust everything he said and everything he did until they felt he had proven himself.

Cassie said, "I don't know, Uncle. As smitten as he appears to be with me, I have a hard time believing that he is anything other than what he appears to be."

"Well," I replied, "while that may be true, I would feel better if one of you were watching him all the time."

Muriel was nodding.

"No, I get it. Remember, Cass, we've been fooled before by a guy who was by all appearances 'smitten' with you and just 'looking out for my well-being.'"

Cassie frowned in disgust, as if having just bitten into an apple and found half a worm.

"Paul Morgan! Ugh! I still can't believe that I was naïve enough to fall for that bastard's lies."

"You're not alone."

Paul Morgan, was, and is a loathsome, vile creature. Were one to equate him with a cockroach, the cockroach would suffer by comparison. When Muriel and Cassie were sixteen and eighteen respectively, he trafficked them for sex in Seattle, Washington. So torturous had the experience been, that had I not rescued them...they would both be dead. As for why I didn't kill the man when I had the chance, well, that is one of many things that keep me awake nights.

Vanessa glanced toward Rémi.

"Look, I don't think we have to be mean to the guy, or anything. But since we've all experienced just about the worst that men have to offer, I agree that we should sort of keep him at arm's length."

I said, "That's all I'm asking you to do. We're family. He's not. He may be the greatest guy in the world, but these are incalculably wealthy, ruthless men we're dealing with here. And, trust me, almost anyone can be bought if the price is right."

The three girls looked at each other, a steely resolve glinting in their eyes.

Cassie said, "Remember that old song by *The Who*, Muriel?"

Muriel smiled.

"Won't Get Fooled Again!"

"You're damned right!"

As I turned to go, Vanessa caught my sleeve.

"Jake?"

"Yeah, sweetheart?"

She stared somberly into my eyes as a mist covered her own.

"No more scars, okay?"

I hugged her and whispered, "No more scars."

I repeated the process with Cassie and Muriel.

Aaron came over and we all stood in an awkward silence, no one really wanting to initiate the separation. But it had to be done. Time was slipping away.

As Aaron hugged Muriel he said, "Call Lonnie. Tell him what's up but to give us some time before he tells Simone."

"But it's her dad. She should know," Muriel argued.

I said, "Yes, she should. But if Lonnie tells her that Gaspard is missing, the first thing she's going to want to do is come over here. Believe it or not, the safest place she can be right now is in the studio."

Aaron nodded in agreement.

"Look, all I'm saying is to give us the rest of today before notifying her."

Muriel glanced at me.

"And let's say you get this solved within the next twenty-four hours. How would you feel if Cassie had been taken and no one told you until after the fact?"

She had a good point.

Aaron and I stared at each other for a few seconds before I said, "All right. Tell Lonnie to fill Simone in on what's happening, but to also tell her that under no circumstances is she to come to France. We're on it and plan to have Gaspard back by this time tomorrow."

Cassie asked, "And what if you don't?"

"If we don't, then there's no good reason for her to be here."

"Look," Aaron argued. "I know how artists work. Lonnie tells her what's up with her dad and the recording sessions will come to a screeching halt!"

Rémi, who had been standing by listening quietly, requested permission to speak.

"I know Simone since she is jeune fille." His eyes grew misty as he continued, "She was always ma trésor...eh...my treasure and I her bon ami. I call her. She is tougher than you think. You go now, Monsieur Moriarity...find the boss. I will take care of everything here. Do not worry about Simone *or* your girls."

Something had changed in the atmosphere as Rémi spoke. The love and concern in his voice; a certain look in his eyes...something. All of a sudden, my previous estimation of the man had been radically altered. I made eye contact with my three girls and a silent understanding seemed to pass between us.

Muriel said, "That seems like a good solution to me."

Aaron and the girls agreed.

I offered Rémi my hand.

"Thank you, Rémi. We really appreciate this."

He shook my hand and stood up taller.

"It is my pleasure, Monsieur."

I slapped Aaron on his beefy back.

"Okay, let's do this."

"Heard that," he replied.

We climbed into the Range Rover, started it up and drove away without another word. We had to. It was just too hard to perpetuate the goodbyes. In the rearview mirror I saw all three girls wiping tears from their eyes.

I jerked my head toward the rear.

"You'd think we were going off to war, or something."

Aaron glanced in his side mirror.

"Yeah, well, we just might be." He was silent for a few seconds before adding, "You got a feeling about this one, Jake?"

I did. And it wasn't good, but I wasn't about to tell him that.

"Oh, you know. Just the usual."

"So, should I start worrying now or wait until we getting all shot at and stuff?"

I pretended to weigh the options.

"Definitely wait. I mean they could hear that we're coming after them and give Gaspard back to us out of sheer terror."

"Could. Doubt it though. Figure they'll put up at least some fight."

Rémi had run on ahead and had the gate open by the time we reached the end of the driveway. He saluted smartly as we passed and then we were off.

CHAPTER 7

Comparing the map Rémi had drawn with the map program on my phone, we figured out that the most likely destination was somewhere around a small, mountain village called Castellane. Then again, it could have been Toulouse. So, we decided on Castellane. Because of various road construction projects, our GPS insisted that the fastest route would be via A8 through Nice, Cannes, and then onto Route de Draguignan toward Tourettes and eventually into Castellane. Once in Castellane, the GPS information would have to give way to Rémi's cartography. Based on his description, it seemed that the last part of the journey would be on narrow, rural roadways that were often "unimproved," which was code for, "buckle up, 'cause it's going to be a rough ride."

We rode in relative silence as we navigated the traffic in and around Nice, but once we were past Cannes and headed up into the high country, I said, "So, let me ask you this question."

"Ask."

"Why do you keep doing this?"

"What?"

I gestured.

"This! Going with me on cases."

Aaron smiled broadly.

"Why, it's because you need me, sugar."

"No, I mean seriously. Hell, Aaron, every time you go out with me you risk being injured...or worse."

"I know that."

"Then why do it?"

"Well," he started and then paused. "Besides the fact that I'm a highly trained former member of the US Marine Corps, I suppose it's because I enjoy it. It's so vastly different from the boring world I live in."

Desperate to escape the gangs that ruled his neighborhood in Compton, California, Aaron enlisted in the Marine Corps at the age of eighteen. He was one of the few recruits who qualified for something called the National Call to Service Program, which allowed the enlistee to serve two years of active duty and then an additional two years in active reserves. However, once he was through boot camp and his superior officers had figured out just how gifted of a musician he was, he spent most of the next fifteen months playing with the All Star Marine Jazz Band and touring the United States.

I laughed and said, "Boring? Do you have any idea how many people would kill or die to live in your world?"

"I don't mean 'boring', boring. I meant that my world is predictable. Ordered...everyone playing by the same set of rules."

"But I thought the big thing with jazz is that there *aren't* any rules."

"Yeah, well, that's true. But apart from the music, it's limo ride to the airport; hustled through security to the plane; hustled off the plane to another limo; straight to the concert venue; sound check; meet and greet; concert; catered meal afterwards; limo to the hotel—and, for the record, you almost never know the hotel's name; grab a few hours sleep and the next day start the same damn thing all over again. Not that I'm complaining, mind you. But there is a particular monotony to it all. Out here with you though, I never know from one minute to the next what's going to happen. And I love it! I absolutely love it."

"Well," I said. "I love having you along, bro. The times you aren't with me leaves me feeling sort of naked and unprotected."

He turned and said, "I got your back, Jake. Always have...always will. You can count on that."

"I do, Aaron. More than you'll ever know."

"We need to change the subject before you pull over to the side of the road and suggest we hug it out or something."

Simultaneously we said, "Ain't nobody got time for that."

We laughed.

I mean why not? We were funny guys.

CHAPTER 8

We pulled in to a little village called Montauroux—a concoction of syllables and consonants that defied my limited abilities of French pronunciation. Actually, all of the names escape me because I can't really speak French other than to order basic culinary necessities in restaurants and inquire as to the location of the public conveniences. Anyway, we drove carefully down one of the narrow streets until we spotted a sign for *Le Meilleur Boulangerie,* which Aaron informed me translated as, *"The Best Bakery."* It advertised *Jambon Beurre,* or the classic "Parisien" sandwich consisting of ham and butter on a baguette. It had long been Aaron's favorite and during our stay had become mine as well.

Addictively so.

On the one hand it was only 11:00 a.m. and we couldn't really afford to take the time to stop, but on the other hand, since we didn't really know where we were going or what we were going to be facing once we got there, the stop was justifiable if for no other reason than figuring some stuff out, and taking a bathroom break.

Besides, we were hungry.

And hungry men can't think clearly.

Ask the women who live with them.

We parked, found a table in the shade and placed our order with an adorable young lady who recognized Aaron almost immediately and nearly fainted when he agreed to a "selfie" photograph with her. I was always amazed at how gracefully and amiably Aaron managed his celebrity. He made that young woman feel as if she were the most important person in the world. And honestly, for him...in that moment, she was. Besides the fact that he is quite simply unparalleled in his abilities as a jazz pianist, his intimate interaction with fans is the thing that sets him apart from almost every other performer. Of course it also helps that he has become fluent in the languages of the European nations that are home to his largest constituency of fans: France and Germany. There is something about being able to converse with your fans in their own tongue that is intensely endearing.

The waitress trotted off to place our order leaving Aaron shaking his head.

"What?" I asked.

"Oh, that. Straight up honesty here, bro...I just don't get the whole fan thing."

"You mean to tell me that you never had a musical hero? That you were never a fan?"

"'Course I was. But that's different."

"Want to explain that?"

"Well, the men and women I was fans of were legends."

"So are you, my friend," I replied with a smile. "So are you."

He waved his hand dismissively.

"Come on now, Jake. You know what I'm talking about."

"Yeah, to a point. But what you seem to miss is that to your fan base, you are no less significant than some of those 'legends' that captured your heart and your imagination as a young man."

He seemed to consider my words.

"Well, maybe. But I still don't get it."

And he never would because my best friend is a humble man, literally incapable of owning his own celebrity or his own importance in the jazz community.

Apparently having expedited our order, the waitress returned with sandwiches, beverages and the bakery owner who was also a fan of Mr. Perry. Greetings were exchanged, more photos taken, food eaten and the beverages consumed. All told we were there no more than twenty minutes and were ready to be on our way, a sad occasion for our waitress who informed us that we couldn't leave until her mother got there —yet *another* Aaron Perry fan. He tried to explain that we absolutely had to be going, but the waitress, whose name was Nanette, did all but hold him in his seat until he agreed to stay a few more minutes.

He consented.

He always does.

Five minutes later Maman arrived with two of her neighbors in tow who were, you guessed it, also huge fans of the famous jazz musician. More greetings were exchanged, along with motherly kisses and selfies, by which point the other patrons, having perceived that a major celebrity was in their midst—even though most had at best a marginal knowledge of who Aaron was—decided to get in on the occasion. As this was going on I stood off to the side completely ignored by the fawning masses. Which suited me just fine, by the way. I've never cared much for attention. And to be fair, neither does Aaron.

After another ten minutes had passed, he very patiently explained that we absolutely, positively had to be going causing the waitress and her mother—apparently his new best friends—to bid him a reluctant adieu. To say that young Nanette was smitten wouldn't be overstating the case. Think film reels of girls encountering Elvis or The Beatles back in the day. Yeah, like that. The only thing she didn't do was scream.

However, her grip on consciousness at one point did appear to be tenuous.

She walked us over to the Range Rover, gave Aaron a fierce hug and then kissed him full on the lips. He graciously accepted the affection, along with a hastily scrawled phone number on the back of a drink coaster. As we drove away Nanette was still standing in the middle of the road, hands clasped to her quite lovely chest, and weeping.

CHAPTER 9

Once we were on our way, Aaron held up the drink coaster.

"Dude, if I had a dollar for every one of these I've gotten over the years..."

"I bet you've had a few," I replied with a laugh.

"You have no idea."

"You ever follow up on any of them?"

"What 'chu think? Sometimes on the road the nights get very long and all you want is someone you can pass the time with."

I pulled to a stop behind a tiny car stopped at a round-about, or traffic circle, the driver seemingly unable to comprehend what to do. After thirty seconds or so, I tapped the horn lightly.

"So, do you do that a lot?" I asked.

"What, hook up with random women? Hell no! I mean I'm not a monk, but I'm not stupid either. I'm going to guess that over my entire career I've called maybe half a dozen or so."

The driver of the tiny car waved an apology and sped off.

"And how did that work out?"

He chuckled.

"You asking me if I got busy with the ladies?"

"Not necessarily, although that would be an interesting tale."

Sighing deeply he replied, "This right here is something that people seem to have the hardest time understanding."

"What's that?"

"The fact that you can be a normal, healthy adult male with normal adult male appetites and still not want to, well, to use an archaic, Biblical term, 'spill your seed' indiscriminately."

We passed a field off to our right with a tractor patiently and methodically turning over the fertile ground.

"And are you saying that you did not?" I asked.

"That's exactly what I'm saying," he said while punctuating his answer with slap to the dashboard. "Like I said, there have been times when the chemistry was right, but those were few and far between."

"Seems to me," I mused, "that most people would have a hard time believing that."

"You got that right! But remember, I was married for most of my career. Those ladies I referenced came *after* the breakup."

Aaron had gone through a terrible divorce several years before, precipitating a nuclear winter that had settled suffocatingly over the emotional landscape of his life.

I said, "But I'm betting that even though you were married people still couldn't believe that a person with your status was capable of fidelity."

"Right again! It's like...like...since no one seems to have any self-control anymore—and especially those who enjoy celebrity status—they can't believe it when someone else does. And then they resent the hell out of you for it."

"And then came Muriel."

Muriel and Aaron had carried on a quietly smoldering, yet unrequited love affair for a couple of years before surrendering to the inevitable and openly declaring their affection for each other. That had happened nine months ago although it seemed as if they had been together far longer.

"Yes," he replied as a smile flowed over his features like sweet honey. "Never met anyone like her."

"Nor will you ever again. She's exceptional."

"Yeah," he agreed. "A 'keeper' as my momma says."

"Does the age difference ever come up?" I asked.

"What, between Muriel and me? Nah, man."

"Yeah, I didn't think so. For some people, thirteen years would be weird, but given that Muriel is such an old soul, it kind of evens things out."

"Yes, indeed."

We had cleared Tourettes and were passing through a heavily forested area when our quietly amiable conversation was suddenly interrupted by the appearance of a threat. This came in the form of a large sedan racing up from behind and positioning its front bumper mere inches from the back of the Range Rover.

"We've got company," I said.

Aaron turned and looked out the rear window.

"Looks like there are three...no, four burly men whose expressions indicate that they most likely bear us some ill will. Want me to shoot them?"

"Not just yet."

He glanced at the speedometer.

"This a V8 turbo?"

"Over five hundred horsepower and zero to sixty in 4.5 seconds," I answered.

Aaron grinned broadly.

"Well, then...let's see what this bad boy can do."

CHAPTER 10

In street racing parlance, I floored it. The sleek SUV took off like a proverbial shot out of a proverbial cannon leaving the sedan momentarily in the, well, proverbial dust. I'm not sure what our pursuers expected, but from what I could see of the driver's face through the rearview mirror...it wasn't this.

I said, "Unless that Mercedes is sporting an AMG setup, there's no way they can keep up with us."

Aaron was still turned around in his seat watching them.

"I'm thinkin' no, 'cuz he's not gaining."

"And I'm still increasing my speed."

Even though the road was narrow and winding, we had the good fortune of being on a long straightaway, but that was going to change soon as I could see the beginning of another series of curves coming up ahead.

Aaron turned back to face the front.

"Gonna have to slow a bit for these curves. Think he'll catch us when you do?"

"No. I actually test drove one of these a few months ago when I was thinking of trading mine in for a newer model. It corners remarkably well for an SUV. Almost like you're driving a car."

"Just the same..." Aaron said as he reached into the back seat and dug the G36 out of the duffel bag. "Best be prepared in case those jokers decide to get frisky."

I braked softly entering the first curve, and the SUV handled it like a champ. Checking the rearview I could see the Mercedes overcorrecting and nearly spinning out.

I jerked my thumb backward.

"I don't think we have anything to worry about from those guys."

Aaron had taken up a permanent vigil and was sitting with his back against the passenger door.

"Dude's not much of a driver."

I maneuvered through several more turns before coming to another straightaway.

I said, "Wave goodbye," and punched it again.

The supercharged Rover's powerful engine roared and we began pulling away from the hapless driver and his outclassed sedan.

Aaron suddenly sat upright.

"Dude's leaning out the window. Got something in his hands...looks like..."

A shot pinged off the rear roof.

A quick glance in the side mirror revealed the rear passenger on the driver's side sighting in with what appeared to be a large caliber scoped rifle of some sort.

This was not good.

"It's gonna suck if he's lucky enough to land a direct hit!"

I thought about initiating evasive maneuvers, you know, like weaving back and forth in a serpentine pattern...stuff like you see in the movies. But as anyone who has had any real-time experience with an active shooter will tell you —and especially one armed with a powerful rifle and sophisticated scope—it's really only a matter of time before he finds range or gets lucky. Either way it spells bad news. So I did the only thing I knew to change the playing field, so to speak.

"Hang on!" I shouted to Aaron while cranking the steering wheel hard to the left and putting the amazingly stable Range Rover into a sideways slide that eventually resulted in a complete 180º turn and a reversal of direction.

Aaron observed, "Looks like that defensive driving

course you took last year finally paid off."

"Time will tell," I replied as the surprised occupants in the Mercedes jetted past.

Before they could react to what was happening, I did another one-eighty, which now put me in the enviable position of being the pursuer instead of the pursued.

I said, "Put a few rounds through the trunk. Let's see how they like being shot at."

Aaron grinned and lowered the side window.

"Be my pleasure."

There aren't many people who can pull off firing a G36 out the window of a speeding vehicle. But being the exceptionally strong individual that he is, my friend managed nicely. Using the Rover's side mirror as a brace, he stitched a line of bullets across the rear end of the Mercedes, shattered the rear window and, as an added bonus, somehow managed to blow the right rear tire as well.

I slowed my speed and watched as the driver once again overcorrected, which sent the heavy sedan skidding off the road and into a ditch that was deep enough to render the car immobile. As we drove slowly past the wreck, Aaron kept the G36 pointed at them and then for good measure shot out both the left front and rear tires causing the car's four occupants to dive for cover.

I thought about stopping and making an effort to gather a bit of intel from the boys, but since we had already raised a considerable ruckus it seemed as if that would be pushing our luck. So we drove away. I mean two high-powered cars speeding down a normally quiet country road was enough reason in itself for someone to have already alerted the local authorities that all was not well in their neck of the woods. But when you added a running gun battle to the mix, the "flics" or cops were almost certainly on their way.

CHAPTER 11

I rolled my window down and listened intently for any sounds of police pursuit, but heard nothing.

I said, "Do the police here use sirens when responding to a disturbance?"

"Yeah, man. Kind of that alternating, high-low two note thing."

"I don't hear anything. Do you hear anything?"

He stuck a finger in his ear and waggled it around dramatically.

"If by 'anything' you mean a pronounced ringing in my ears, then, yes...I do."

"I was talking about sirens."

"Even if there were sirens, there's no way I could hear them due to the one note symphony going on in my head right now!"

I surveyed the passing countryside.

"Actually, I can't see anything remotely resembling a residence, so maybe nobody heard anything."

"Think you might be right. I don't see anything either," Aaron replied, keeping his eyes trained toward the rear.

My phone rang. It was Cassie.

I put it on speaker and answered, "What's up, little girl?"

"Well, Rémi just got off the phone with Simone."

"And...?"

"And it didn't go well."

I pulled the SUV off the road and under the shade of a large canopied tree, where I parked and rolled down the windows. The air was mostly calm, disturbed only by an occasional and illusive breeze that seemed to dissipate as quickly as it materialized. There and gone, not unlike my understanding of what we were up against.

I said, "How well *didn't* it go?"

I could hear Rémi speaking rapidly in French in the background and Muriel telling him to slow down.

"Simone's naturally quite upset and worried," Cassie answered. "They had a huge argument about her dropping everything and coming over here."

Aaron said, "And how'd that work out?"

"Bottom line—she's not coming. But she isn't happy about it."

"No. Can't imagine that she would be. She fall apart like I said she would?"

There were loud voices in the background prompting Cassie to seek a more private place for the conversation.

"Okay. That's better. And no, she didn't fall apart. She's just angry and wants a crack at the guys who took her dad."

I asked, "What did Lonnie say?"

"Well, I talked to him after Rémi finished with Simone. He's in an awkward position, you know? The label is putting tons of pressure on him to finish this album, but at the same time he understands the emotional trauma this is producing in Simone. He actually told her she could come home if that's what she really wanted."

"And she chose to stay there on her own?"

"Not exactly. I think Rémi sort of pulled rank on her and forbade her to come."

"Rémi has that kind of influence?"

"Well, yeah. He's her uncle...on her mother's side."

Aaron's eyes widened.

"What?"

"You heard me. Rémi is Simone's uncle. He's worked for her father since he was a teenager and is one of his closest confidants. It seems he is pretty well fixed financially on his own and works here as a guardian of the gate, so to speak, and caretaker of the estate out of a deep sense of loyalty to the family."

I said, "Well, I guess that settles the question of whether Rémi can be trusted."

"Right? Anyway, from what I could pick up of the conversation between him and Simone, it was quite evident that she has a ton of respect for him and basically did what he told her to do even though it wasn't what she wanted."

"Wow. Who knew?"

"Her only condition was that she be kept updated on an hourly basis and that as soon as her dad is found, the family jet be sent to bring her home."

"Sounds reasonable. Anything else?"

"That's it for now. How about you? Any developments?"

Aaron said, "Just had to ditch a car full of large, ill-intentioned men. But it weren't no 'thang. All is well."

"So, business as usual?" she asked with a laugh.

"Pretty much."

"That's what I thought. Okay, then. Call me as soon as something worth reporting comes up."

I picked up the phone and took it off speaker.

"Absolutely. And Cass?"

"Yeah?"

"I love you, little girl."

"I love you too, Uncle. Be careful."

"Always."

I ended the call and tossed the phone back onto the center console.

Aaron mused, "Simone's uncle. Didn't see that one coming."

"Makes me wonder what else we won't see coming."

I thought for a second.

"We have to go back."

"Go back?"

I said, "We need to go back to where we left those guys."

I tossed Rémi's map to Aaron.

"Something tells me we're not going to get anywhere with this. I was stupid to not take one of them with us when we had the chance. It's only been about ten minutes. No way they've gotten that car out of the ditch."

"Maybe so, but last time I checked, they was all heavily armed *and* dangerous! They not just gonna volunteer to come peacefully."

"I know. But we've still got to do it."

"Okay, then how do you suggest we pull this off?"

"Well," I hedged, giving myself time to think. "How about this: we go back as fast as we left. Maybe they'll be too occupied with trying to get the car out of the ditch to be on the lookout. Maybe they won't have their weapons on them."

"That's a whole lotta' maybes, bro. I'm just saying."

"I know, but I've got a feeling about this."

"Well then...let's go," he said while tossing the useless map into the back seat.

I grinned and made a U-turn pointing the SUV back in the direction we had just come. I stopped grinning when I realized that my "feeling" could just be wishful thinking and that we were very likely heading right into something very nasty.

We'd soon find out.

CHAPTER 12

Gaspard stared through the front windshield in total confusion as a small airport came into view.

"An airport? I thought we were going to the warehouse. Where are you taking me?"

The man with the scarred head turned slightly and said, "I told you. To the country."

"But...this isn't the country."

He laughed his horrible laugh, "I didn't say *which* country, now did I?"

Gaspard squinted through the side window and saw a twin turbo prop idling on the tarmac.

"We can't be going far if we're going in that. So where? Germany? Portugal? England?"

"You'll find out soon enough. For now, you'd do well to keep quiet."

The car came to a stop and the man got out, walking quickly toward two men standing near the aircraft. It seemed to Gaspard that a financial transaction was being discussed. The two men appeared to be resistant at first to what his captor was offering, but a large handgun suddenly pressed tightly against one man's forehead caused them to agree quickly.

The scarred man, for that is how Gaspard had come to think of him, came back to the car and ordered everyone out. The two Japanese men who flanked Gaspard pulled and pushed him out of the rear seat, shoving him roughly toward the waiting aircraft.

"There is no need to be so rough!" Gaspard complained.

The scarred man waved the two goons off and took him by the elbow.

"Please excuse my colleagues' insensitive behavior. Usually we treat those we are assigned to terminate with much more dignity."

And then he laughed as he purposefully tripped Gaspard, sending him sprawling onto the tarmac.

Gaspard landed with all his weight on one elbow, which now throbbed with pain.

"Why was that necessary? Am I not being cooperative?"

The man leaned over, grabbed Gaspard's injured arm and jerked him to his feet.

"Ducharme, let us get something straight between us. I am going to kill you. Whether the process is long and painful or quick and painless is entirely up to you. I told you that you would do well to keep silent. This is just a gentle reminder that I mean what I say. Are we clear?"

Gaspard nodded slowly, "Perfectly."

"Good," the man said with an evil smile. "We can now move forward without this regrettable violence. I do so deplore violence. It makes me...sad. Yes. That is it. It makes me sad when it has to be employed. But it appears that I can now kill you without further violence."

The man was crazy. Either that, or he was pathologically cruel, a possibility that Gaspard had to allow as being just as likely.

"You will have no further trouble from me, Monsieur. That I promise."

The scarred man slapped him on the back collegially.

"I knew you would see things my way. Now, let us be going. This flight is costing my employer a lot of money and, as they say, time is money."

He guided Gaspard into the passenger area behind the cockpit, helped him into a seat and buckled him in as if he were the flight attendant and Gaspard a paying customer.

"Barcelona," the man said, seemingly apropos of nothing.

"Excuse me?" Gaspard replied.

"You asked where we were going."

"We're going to Barcelona? But, why?"

The man stared hard at him as if deliberating whether or not to answer.

He finally said, "It seems as if a...wrinkle has developed in what was otherwise a very well thought out plan...and we need to improvise somewhat in order to keep to our schedule."

A smile crept slowly onto Gaspard's face.

"Jake Moriarity is coming after me."

The man snorted, "Whether he is or isn't is of no concern to me, for by the time anyone determines where you are...you will already be dead."

With that he slipped up into the co-pilot's seat and buckled himself in. The cabin door was secured by one of the attendants and the plane immediately began taxiing.

"Why Barcelona?" Gaspard whispered to himself.

CHAPTER 13

We were going about 160 kph, or 100 mph as we approached the scene of the wreck, so I had to slow down considerably in order to make a turn. Aaron had climbed into the back seat right behind me and had the window down with his G36 locked and loaded, as they say.

Aaron said, "What you gonna do should we encounter any of the fine, local constabulary?"

"We won't."

"How can you be so sure?"

I wasn't, actually. But I was definitely hoping, praying, banking, counting, etc. that we wouldn't.

As we came around the turn, I could see three of the four men lying on the ground under the shade of a tree about twenty feet away from their wrecked car, while the fourth —whom I recognized as having been riding "shotgun"—was pacing in the roadway while talking on the phone. They didn't seem to notice our approach until I screeched to a halt right by their car.

The man on the phone performed a rather comical juggling act as he tried to hold on to the phone, while at the same time attempting to draw his gun. He wound up dropping both onto the ground, with the gun skittering several feet away from him. He thought about going for it, but Aaron was already out of the car and shouting at them in French to toss their guns behind them and put their hands up. I did a U-turn, parked and exited the Range Rover and was walking toward the man in the road with my pistol pointing at him, when one of the guys under the tree made a move to draw his weapon. But, after Aaron fired a burst that tore up the ground in front of him, he seemed to reconsider his choices and tossed the gun backwards over his head.

I stood in front of the man in the road, who was still casting occasional longing looks at his gun.

"Aaron, how do you say, 'Don't even think about it?'"

He shouted the command and the man locked his eyes on my pistol and stood still. I asked him if he spoke English and he nodded his head slightly.

"Good," I said. "Because you're coming with us."

His eyes grew wide.

"No, Monsieur, that is not possible."

"Oh, but it is. In fact, it is not only possible, but it is necessary." I jerked the barrel of the .357 in the direction of the car. "Let's go."

He looked at his gun where it had fallen on the roadway like a heroin addict staring at his last fix. After a couple of seconds, the man shook his head sadly and walked toward me. When he got within two or three feet, he made a lunge for my gun. Probably not the smartest decision he'd ever made. I side-stepped his charge, and as he went by, cracked him across the back of his head. He fell heavily onto his knees, hands clasped to his bleeding cranium.

I said to Aaron, "Have one of those guys take their shirts off. Their buddy here needs it."

He rattled off something in rapid-fire French and one of the men grudgingly removed his shirt while muttering what I took to be some very unkind and unflattering words. I'll say this about the French: they seem to be masters of profanity.

When the shirt was off, Aaron had the man walk it over to his friend who was still kneeling. As he handed the shirt to him they exchanged a few sentences.

I asked Aaron what had been said.

"You mean after the general derisive descriptions of our

character and questions regarding our sexuality?"

"Yeah, after that."

"He asked the man on the ground what they should do, so I'm thinking he's the boss."

I replied, "Which is why I wanted him to come with us. I sort of figured that the boss of this crew would be riding shot-gun."

"You figured right."

"So, did he have anything to say to his friend?"

"Just that he should do whatever we tell them to do, and that they'd be okay once the big boss found out what was going on."

I squatted down beside the man.

"The big boss...who is he?"

He shook his head slowly refusing to tell me. So I punched him in the face and repeated the question.

His colleague made a move like he was going to jump me, so I fired off a round that purposely missed his ear by about an inch, and suggested that it was probably not a good idea. He seemed to agree and walked slowly backward toward the car with his hands raised.

The man on the ground painfully returned to his knees from where he had fallen.

"Monsieur, I cannot tell you who the big boss is. He will kill me and everyone in my family."

"Well, we can't have that...and I'm not really interested in continuing my efforts to beat the information out of you."

I glanced at his phone where it rested in the roadway and jerked my head toward it.

"Call him."

"Monsieur?" he said in confusion.

"Call the big boss on the phone, and then hand it to me when he answers. He and I will have a nice little chat, and then we'll see what happens next."

He started speaking rapidly in French.

Aaron translated, "He's saying that what you ask is impossible because he doesn't know how to reach the big boss."

"Well, then," I said. "Call the biggest boss you can."

He seemed to consider it and then sighed as if in resignation. He gestured toward the phone while looking a question at me. I nodded and he crawled about five feet away picking up the phone just as a car approached from the other direction. Aaron quickly lowered his weapon and moved behind the cover of the wrecked vehicle. I shoved mine behind my back and the car slowed down. The old gentleman behind the wheel gawked at the scene with a worried expression.

Aaron shouted something in French and the old fella waved and went on his way without seeing the guns. To his eyes, it simply looked as if someone had had a wreck with one of passengers sustaining a bloody nose. Two good Samaritans had stopped to offer their assistance, which most likely restored his confidence in mankind. Or something.

When the car was out of sight, I told the man to get into the back seat of the Range Rover and make the call. He complied and once seated stabbed out the numbers on the screen and then held it to his ear.

As soon as the call was answered, he said in English that someone wished to speak to whoever was on the other end of the call and pulled the phone away from his ear handing it to me.

I said, "Who am I speaking to?"

In a heavy Japanese accent the man replied, "Who am *I* speaking to?"

"Jake Moriarity."

"I have no idea who you are. Goodbye."

I spoke before he could terminate the call, "Yes you do. You know exactly who I am."

A few seconds of silence ticked by.

"All right. Let's assume for the moment that you are correct and that I do know who you are. Why should anything you have to say matter to a man like me?"

I chuckled darkly.

"A man like you? Well, let's see...you have taken my friend, Gaspard Ducharme, and I plan to get him back. But in the process I will more than likely cause irreparable harm to your business empire and inflict as much physical and emotional pain on you as it is humanly possible to bear."

Now it was his turn to laugh. It was a laugh completely devoid of humor.

"You seem to overestimate your abilities *and* your importance, Mr. Moriarity. You do not even know who you are dealing with."

I hated egotistical, condescending bastards like this guy.

"I don't care who you are, how much you are worth or even the stature you hold in the global community. To me you are just another thug. You should have figured out by now that the two amateurs you sent this morning, along with the four you sent this afternoon have already been incapacitated. If these are the best you can do, then you might want to reconsider your options."

There was more silence on the line, then, "You bore me, Mr. Moriarity. And the reason you bore me is that there is no substance to your words. There is—"

"FBI."

"Excuse me?"

"I'm with the FBI. Is that enough substance for you? We have been on your trail for several years now. In fact, as I speak a multi-national task force is closing in on your little operation." I paused for a beat. "I can tell from your silence that you knew nothing of our investigation."

Suddenly, I knew who was on the other end of the call. And in knowing this it made me wonder: if this man was not the "big boss," then what the hell had I gotten us into?

CHAPTER 14

I had nothing to lose at this point, so I decided to just go for broke.

"So let me fill you in on what is going to happen to you and your friends...Mr. Momotani."

The man inhaled sharply.

My guess had been right. Hayato Momotani was the Oyabun, or family boss, of the Yakuza, a transnational Japanese crime syndicate continuously operational since the fifteenth century. Momotani and I had actually met briefly—a decidedly non-cordial occasion, by the way—in New York four years earlier when the FBI had shut down one of his operations in the Bronx. My role in the effort, which took over a year to finalize, had been to provide the FBI with the Yakuza's connection to fencing of stolen electronics in Manhattan. Let's just say that I did what I was tasked with doing.

"I should have killed you four years ago, Moriarity," he growled.

"Yes," I replied. "You should have. Because now I'm going to do everything in my power to bring you down."

He laughed again.

"What could you possibly do that would cause me even one second's worry? As I said earlier, you bore me, for there is no substance behind anything you have to say. Gaspard Ducharme is already dead. So walk away while you still have the chance."

And then he disconnected the call.

I glanced over at Aaron who had herded the other three

men back into the car after confiscating their weapons. He backed slowly toward my position keeping the G36 trained on his captives.

I said to our new best friend, "You heard my end of the conversation, so you now know that *I* know that Momotani is one of the principles in your organization. As for who the other actors are, it's only a matter of time before I figure that out. But, first things first: Where did they take Gaspard Ducharme?"

He subconsciously touched the back of his head, pondered my question as if weighing his options, and then shrugged.

"It makes no difference to me. I have money put aside. I can get away—go hide where they cannot find me." He sighed. "Okay. They have taken Monsieur Ducharme to Barcelona."

"Barcelona?" Aaron questioned. "Why there?"

He shrugged again.

"I do not know. It is merely what I have been told."

Barcelona was a big place.

"Where exactly in Barcelona?" I asked.

He stared up at me with a calculating expression.

"If I tell you, you let me and my friends walk away? You don't kill us?"

"Kill you? What kind of person do you think I am?"

"I *know* what kind of person you are, Monsieur Moriarity. You have a reputation, you know."

"Then you know that I don't kill people unless they try to kill me first."

"So you let us go?"

I glanced at Aaron who nodded his head.

I said, "Okay. We'll let you go. Now, where is Gaspard Ducharme?"

"They have taken him to a city called Tarragona. It is about—"

Aaron interrupted, "A hundred kilometers south of Barcelona—site of the old Roman occupation. I did a concert in

Barcelona a few years back and the promoter took us on a tour of the ruins there."

I asked the man, "And do you know the specific location within this city?"

"Yes. There is an estate just south of the city. I have no address, but I give you landmarks."

Aaron mused, "It's got to be at least a seven or eight hour drive from here, wherever the hell *here* is."

That was way too long.

"Did they drive or fly?"

"I believe they hired a plane," the man answered.

"So they could already be there."

He said, "Oui, Monsieur. But they will not kill Ducharme until his partner from Belgium arrives. Do them both together, you know, less chance for a mistake. Cleaner, too."

Aaron rumbled, "Yeah, and we *do* want our killings to be clean."

"Aaron, get the information from this guy—directions, landmarks, whatever you think will be helpful. I'm calling Zack."

CHAPTER 15

Hayato Momotani stared at the phone in his hand as if it were an alien artifact. Jake Moriarity! The man had caused him incalculable grief and should have been killed years before. But, regrettably, he had never given the order and now...Moriarity was here again, troubling his soul and attempting to thwart his carefully laid plans.

He spoke a name into his phone and the number was dialed automatically.

"Yes?" the refined male voice on the other end of the call answered, annoyance evident in his tone.

"We have a problem," Momotani said succinctly.

"*We* have a problem, or *you* have a problem?"

How he hated the man's arrogance. How he longed to have him snuffed out like one would smother an irritating flame.

"Do not use that tone with me, Persian. You sometimes forget who is the real power here."

The Persian chuckled humorlessly.

"I have not forgotten. How could I when you remind me at every opportunity." He paused. "But let's not quarrel. Tell me about this problem."

"It is Moriarity."

There was silence for the space of three or four seconds as The Persian processed the information.

"Jake Moriarity?"

"Yes."

"And how has he become our problem?"

"He is a close friend to Gaspard Ducharme. He has taken out both teams I sent after him as easily as you or I would eliminate a colony of ants."

"Hmm...I have heard of his prowess. They say he is the best in his business. But he is only one man. We have many."

Momotani's tone sharpened.

"Do no underestimate this man, Persian! I have gone up against him before with less than satisfying results. He seems to have an edge—an advantage—that cannot be explained. How else do you explain the ease with which he dispatched my operatives?"

The Persian did not like the hint of panic he heard in his colleague's voice.

"Is he God? Is he the president of a country? Is he even the head of a paramilitary group? No! He is not. He is a man. Just. One. Man!"

"He is FBI, Persian. Do you have any idea of the reach of the American FBI? Do you?"

"From what I have heard, he is merely a consultant."

Momotani sighed.

"What you do not know amazes me. Regardless of your ignorance concerning this man, the simple truth is that he has the ability to cause us great grief. I suggest extreme measures be taken to eliminate him."

The Persian mulled over the suggestion.

"Be more clear on what you are suggesting."

"You *know* what—or should we say *who*—I am suggesting."

"And you are certain that asset is available?"

"Unquestionably."

After a few moments thought, the Persian replied, "All right. Do it. I will tell the others."

The connection was terminated. Momotani should have felt elation. He should have felt confidence that the problem would be solved expeditiously.

He did not.

What he felt instead was a sense of foreboding—a premonition that the situation was about to dissolve into complete and utter chaos.

And that Jake Moriarity would be at the very center of it all.

CHAPTER 16

While Aaron pulled the man out of the back of the SUV and walked him over to the Mercedes, I climbed into the driver's seat of the Range Rover and checked my phone for signal. There seemed to be enough. As was my custom when traveling, I had unlocked my phone and secured an international SIM card so I could use my personal phone instead of having to rely on local service while in Europe. I had just opened my favorites folder and started to tap Zack's number, when I realized that given the time differential it was barely 5:00 a.m. in Los Angeles. I debated whether to go ahead with the call and finally decided that given the gravity of our situation, I had no choice.

I tapped his icon and waited for the connection.

It rang once, twice, three times and had just started on the fourth when Zack's obviously groggy voice answered.

"You *do* know it's oh-dark-thirty over here in LA, right?"

"Sorry about that, buddy, but this couldn't wait."

He became immediately alert.

"Okay. Fill me in."

I gave him an abridged version of the events that had compelled me to place the call and finished up with, "And now we're somewhere around seven to eight hours away from Tarragona by car and I'm not sure we're going to make it on time to be of any use. Nor am I sure if Gaspard's jet is even available. So, what do we do?"

Zack was silent for a few seconds before replying, "Hang tight for a minute and let me make some calls. We'll figure this out, Jake. We've got way too much skin in the game to just sit around and let these people carry out this assassination!"

"Okay, but we're going to have to get moving. We've been fortunate so far that all the action here happened in such a remote area. But I'm feeling very exposed and would be hard pressed to offer anything close to a plausible explanation of what happened here should the local authorities show up."

"I'm on it. Be right back."

And with that, he disconnected the call.

I got out of the car and walked to where Aaron was keeping the three men in the back seat covered, while our new best friend did his best—or his worst, there was really no way to know—to explain how to find where Gaspard was being held in Tarragona.

I said, "Any of this making any sense?"

"Well, that depends on your definition of 'making sense,'" Aaron replied.

"Let's put it like this, then...based on what our friend here is saying, do we have a prayer of finding Gaspard?"

Aaron moved his head from side to side.

"Well, if you believe in prayer, now would be a good time to start praying."

"That bad, huh?"

"Just saying."

My phone started vibrating.

"Zack! Please tell me you have some good news."

"Yes, and no. I tried to get a chopper dispatched out of Nice to pick you up and take you to Tarragona, but the only one available has mechanical issues and is temporarily grounded."

"How temporary?"

"Like, for the rest of the day."

"Okay. You got anything to go with that, or is that it?"

"How long would it take you to get back to Nice?"

I asked Aaron, since he was more familiar with the area.

"Well," he replied while checking his phone's GPS. "Call

it an hour and a half to two hours, depending on traffic."

Our captive offered a brisk agreement and I relayed the information to Zack.

He said, "Okay, here's what you need to do. Head for Nice as quickly as possible. On the way see if Gaspard's jet is available, if not, I will have transport waiting for you. Either way, you could possibly be in Barcelona in three hours or so and I have already called to have a chopper standing by to transport you to Tarragona. That's about the best I can do from here, Jake."

"Thanks, Zack. We'll be on our way in less than five minutes and will keep you updated as we go."

I terminated the call and told the man to get back inside the Mercedes.

He was suddenly terrified.

"Monsieur, you promised you wouldn't kill me."

"I'm not going to kill you! Just get in the damn car and stay there until we're gone. Then you can get out, retrieve your weapons from wherever Aaron tossed them and be on your way."

He smiled and thanked me profusely as if I were an international serial killer who had just spared his life.

What the heck were people saying about me, anyway?

CHAPTER 17

Gaspard Ducharme braced for the landing. He hated landings. Hated flying in general, but especially that weightless moment when the plane seemed to hover eternally above the landing strip as if some invisible force were denying its return to terra firma. And then came the jolt of touchdown and the desperate effort to brake several hundred tons of machine hurtling down the runway at better than 150 mph. Even in his luxury Gulfstream, the terror was just as pronounced. Then again, he mused, as they reached the end of the runway and began the turn back toward the airport's small terminal, it was a profoundly ironic topic to be pondering when he would most likely be dead before the day was through.

As the turboprop came to a halt, the scarred man rose from his seat in the cockpit and moved toward him.

"I trust you had a pleasant flight and will consider flying with us in the future," he said sarcastically and then added, "Oh, forgive me, I forgot...you don't have a future."

The man's associates seemed to think it quite hilarious.

Determined to hang on to his dignity, Gaspard replied, "The service was terrible; the flight turbulent and the landing amateurish."

The man looked at him without expression for a second or two before allowing an evil smile to claw its way past his thin lips.

"Bravery *and* a sense of humor. I like that. Well played, Ducharme."

He barked a few orders to the men who arose immediately and began ushering Gaspard unceremoniously off of the plane and into a waiting SUV.

"Where are we going?" Gaspard asked boldly.

The scarred man sighed and then shrugged, as if he had come to a decision.

"It makes no difference to me whether you know the place of your execution and the circumstances surrounding it. So...we are taking you to a remote estate outside of Tarragona, where we will await the arrival of Monsieur Fournier from Belgium. After we have you both together, we will execute you and take steps to ensure that no one will ever be able to identify your remains. To the world, you and your partner will have simply disappeared."

So, it was a bit worse than Gaspard had feared.

"Would you consider allowing me to speak to my daughter before I die? As you said, it makes no difference one way or another, for I will die anyway. But it would mean a great deal to her if she could speak to me."

"This I cannot allow. Too many complications. Better she remember you as you were, for I assure you...she would not wish to remember you as you are about to become. It will not be pretty."

And with that, he slammed the door and climbed into the front seat.

As the vehicle began moving, Gaspard said, "You are forgetting an important detail."

The scarred man turned his head slightly.

"Oh? And what is that?"

"Jake Moriarity is coming for me."

The man slammed his fist against the dashboard and turned to face him, shouting, "Stop saying that! He is *not* coming! Of this fact you can be assured. And besides, even if he were...what can one man do against all of my men and myself? You need to surrender this fantasy! Your friend cannot save you. No one can save you!"

Even though he knew it would infuriate the man, Gaspard smiled confidently.

"Monsieur Moriarity can...and he will. And you, mon ami, know it. It is the reason your emotions are so out of control."

Piercing Gaspard with a deadly gaze, the man replied, "If you do not be quiet, I will have the driver pull the car over and I will kill you right here!"

Gaspard shook his head.

"No you won't. Your orders will not permit it."

The man flicked his fist backward over the top of the seat faster than Gaspard could react. It caught him on the tip of his nose, bringing with the blinding pain a simultaneous flow of blood.

"I am quite capable of causing you unimaginable pain without actually killing you, Ducharme. Perhaps I should break your jaw. That would shut you up nicely. Is that what you wish?"

Gaspard had never experienced any manner of physical violence against his person. Apart from a brief stint in the military, he had, in fact, stayed as far away from physical conflict as possible throughout his life, believing in his soul that the development of one's intellect and gaining financial power, were far more profitable enterprises. There were always physically resourceful men to be hired for everything else. Sitting there now with hands clamped around his nose in a vain attempt to staunch the flow of blood, he found that he was just as stunned by the fact that he had been struck, as he was by the prodigious pain resulting from the blow. It was an outrage that a lowlife such as the scarred man would do such a thing to a man of his station in life.

He stammered, "That...was...unnecessary."

The man grinned his horrible grin.

"You are correct. And yet, if I'm being truthful, I found the experience to be enjoyable. Exhilarating. And I will not hesitate to escalate the pain should I find it necessary to keep you quiet. Are we clear on this point?"

Gaspard nodded his head slowly but emphatically.

"Good!" the man said. "Now perhaps we can drive the rest of the way in peace."

He spoke to the man seated to Gaspard's right.

"Give Monsieur Ducharme a handkerchief for his nose. We're not animals here."

CHAPTER 18

W e left the four bad guys behind and drove back down D562 toward Nice, breaking virtually every traffic law known to mankind in the process. And as luck would have it, the local constabulary seemed to be on break or otherwise occupied because, thus far at least, we hadn't encountered a single member of law enforcement.

I said, "You should call Philippe and tell him what's happening—see if he can have the jet waiting for us when we arrive."

"Philippe" referred to Philippe Lévesque, Gaspard's pilot with whom we had found an easy camaraderie on our flight over.

"You keep driving like this, we won't be needing transport to anywhere but the afterlife!"

"Just call him!" I shouted while sliding through a tight curve.

Aaron reluctantly surrendered his death grip on the passenger side handhold and dialed Philippe's number. After explaining Gaspard's dire situation, Philippe assured Aaron that he would move heaven and earth if necessary in order to get us to Barcelona on the Ducharme Enterprises corporate G6. However, even with that it would take a good hour for him to reach the terminal and prep for takeoff. Aaron thanked him and disconnected the call.

"So, I can slow down?" I asked.

"'Spect so."

"Doesn't seem right."

"What? Slowing down?"

"Yeah. I mean what if he gets the plane prepped faster than an hour? Don't you think we should be there waiting?"

A sharp corner snuck up on me causing me to nearly lose control of the vehicle.

Aaron shouted, "Dude! You know I hate speed. Back it off a little."

He was right. I really needed to slow down. According to our GPS, driving at normal speed should take no more than forty minutes to get from our current position to Nice. Driving like I was, we'd probably get there in thirty.

I decided to go for twenty-five and stomped on the accelerator, feeling the powerful vehicle surge forward.

Aaron glared at me with thinly veiled disgust.

"You did *not* just do that."

"You'll get over it."

"*If* I live through this, you mean."

"What's that we're always saying to each other about not being safe, but being dangerous?"

He scoffed.

"Only thing dangerous about this is the danger to our longevity!"

I laughed and blew past one of those tiny Fiat sedans.

"Come on. Where's your sense of adventure?"

"My sense of adventure went right out the door when you nearly rolled coming out of that turn back there."

"I did *not* almost roll!"

He stared wide-eyed at me.

"Uh-huh. And who was that back there jerking the wheel around and cussing like a sailor? Your twin brother?"

"Yes. As a matter of fact, it was. I've never seen him...but I know his voice."

We suddenly came to a line of cars stacked up behind a slow-moving farm produce truck.

"Now that's more like it," Aaron said in relief.

I counted the cars.

"Eight cars behind that sucker! This is not good!"

He turned toward me.

"Oh, dear Lord! You're gonna pass them, aren't you?"

"Life is too short to drive slow."

I mean what's the point of having an incredibly fast car if you merely content yourself with accepting traffic tie-ups as though they were something handed down by fate and to be borne with grace and forbearance? I waited for a pair of motorcycles to pass from the other direction and punched the accelerator leaving a fifty-foot strip of rubber behind me as I pulled around the cars and jetted toward the front.

And wouldn't you know it! At that moment, a passenger van appeared from around the corner ahead.

"Good timing, bro! *Real* good timing!" Aaron said sarcastically.

I was already too far into it to turn back, so I kept the pedal down and felt the turbocharger kick in as we went screaming by the other drivers.

"There's plenty of room," I replied with more confidence than I felt.

Cars were honking. Drivers were gesturing. People were yelling, and I had to assume that they weren't wishing us well. I passed the produce truck and pulled in front of it with about ten feet to spare seeing the face of the oncoming van's driver through the windshield, his eyes wide and mouth forming a perfect "O" as he laid on the horn.

Aaron jerked his head around as we went past.

"Can I just go ahead and tell you right now that if you ever do something like that again, I'm gonna have to break something on your body?"

"Point made, point taken."

I slowed down a bit, and by "a bit" I mean that our speed dropped below a hundred.

Aaron said, "So, now that we got that behind us, you given any thought to what we gonna do once we get to wherever it is they're holding Gaspard?"

The simple answer was, "No."

But I wasn't going to tell him that.

"Well, I sort of figured that we'd, you know, just go in there and request that they release our friend so as to avoid having their bodies riddled with bullets, or something."

"That's it?"

I glanced quickly in his direction.

"You got a better plan?"

"That's a plan?" he said incredulously. "Bro, I've heard better plans from kids playing cops and robbers!"

"I didn't say it was a *great* plan."

He laughed, "No you didn't, because that plan blatantly sucks!"

When Aaron was right, he was right.

"Okay. So, let's say that it could use some tweaking."

Out of the corner of my eye I saw him grinning.

"What?"

"Come on now, Jake. We both know that you up to something and that you've got it all figured out, 'cuz that's what you always do. You figure stuff out that nobody else got a clue about."

I shrugged.

"Maybe."

"Ain't no maybe, brother! Just tell me what's cooking. You know you going to eventually."

I didn't really want to tell him what I was thinking, because he wasn't going to like it. But he was right...I had to sooner or later.

"Look, I don't like this, but there's no way around it."

I waited for a few seconds before continuing.

"As soon as we get to Nice, I need you to turn around and head back to the villa."

"What!"

"I've got a bad feeling about this, Aaron. And, let's face it, you're not an operative. You're a highly decorated musician

—"

"Who has helped you on dozens of cases! I'm not a rookie! I was a Marine! I know what's up."

"I know you do," I replied with a sigh. "But, like I said, I've got a bad feeling about this and I don't want to put you in harm's way. If the men who are behind this are anything like Hayato Momotani, they'll have the best operatives money can buy."

"You mean like those six clowns we already took down?"

He had a point.

"Okay, maybe those guys were an exception. Look, all I'm saying is—"

He cut me off, "I know what you're saying, but in case you've forgotten, I was right there beside you when we took down Yves Barreau and several other very serious dudes here and there. If that doesn't qualify as being in 'harm's way' I don't know what does. And we both walked away from every single case."

"Yes, we did. But, come on, Aaron! If your record label knew what you did for a hobby, they'd probably sue your ass from here to Sunday!"

"What I do in my spare time is none of their damn business!"

"I'm not sure they'd agree."

"Don't matter none if they agree or not. It's the way it is. Now, I need you to shut-up about this and just drive the damn car. I'm goin' with you and we ain't talking 'bout this no more."

He was upset, and when Aaron gets upset he lapses into the deep, urban brogue of his childhood.

I turned my head and said, "Okay, but if you get hurt, I'm gonna' kill you!"

He held his hands up in submission. "Fair enough. But...we good?"

I fist-bumped him.

"Semper Fi, bro."

"That's nice, because we've got company," he said, jerking his thumb toward the rear.

I glanced in the rearview mirror and saw a large SUV coming up fast behind us.

CHAPTER 19

As the SUV got closer I could see that it was occupied by at least four passengers.

"Could just be an aggressive driver," I suggested.

"Maybe," Aaron replied with his eyes on the side mirror.

I glanced down at the speedometer and saw that we were going just a little over 160 kph, and the SUV was gaining on us.

I said, "Whoever it is, he's in a hurry."

The driver pulled to within a car length behind us before whipping into the other lane and surging past. As it turned out, there were two young couples in the vehicle. They all smiled, waved and gave us a "thumbs up" as they went roaring by.

Aaron and I returned their waves.

"That's a relief!" I said while watching them pull away.

"Yeah, man. Not really in the mood to be trifled with any more today."

"Trifled? Seriously, dude?"

He grinned and punched me in the shoulder.

"Just tryna' keep up with you, bro." He was silent for a few minutes and then said, "So, what do you think is going on with Gaspard? You really believe he's mixed up with a bunch of jokers like Momo-what's-his-name?"

I chuckled.

"How about we just call him Momo from now on. And, yes, I *do* think he's involved with them, although to what extent I'm not sure."

"But Ducharme doesn't seem like the kind of man who would involve himself with illegal things."

"Listen, when hundreds of millions of dollars are at stake, people often do things that are completely contrary to their natural way of being."

"Even for a straight up honest dude like Gaspard?"

I saw flashing lights up ahead and slowed to the posted speed. It seemed that our jolly friends in the other vehicle had run afoul of the one and only law enforcement representative we had seen all day and were standing by the side of the road looking a bit less chipper than they had a few minutes earlier. I gave them a thumbs-up as we rolled past.

They didn't think it was funny.

Aaron said, "You should go back there and thank them for distracting that officer."

"Right?"

"So, back to my question. Gaspard has more money than he could ever spend. Why would he compromise everything he stands for to get more?"

"Like I said...the possibility of acquiring huge amounts of money makes people do inexplicable and unreasonable things."

"Nah," Aaron shook his head. "Has to be something more than that."

"And what if it isn't? What if he's just greedy?"

"Look, I know Simone and I've gotten to know her dad over the past month. Had some really great talks with him. He's solid, Jake. I just can't find it in me to believe that the man would willingly do anything wrong."

I knew what he was talking about, because I had the same feeling.

"Okay. Let's say we give him the benefit of the doubt and work from the belief that there is more to this than meets the eye."

"Be nice to know, though...wouldn't it?"

"It would," I agreed. "But even if he's up to his eyeballs in something illegal, it doesn't change the fact that we still have to go get him."

It took us about another fifteen minutes to drive to the airport, during which time I thought through our conversation. While neither one of us wanted to believe that there was even the slightest possibility of wrongdoing on Gaspard's part, the simple fact remained that Hayato Momotani was not your average crook. He was a crook of crooks, to put it bluntly, and the leader of one of the most potent and far-reaching underworld enterprises on the planet. And if a man like that was a principal player in whatever operation Gaspard Ducharme had gotten sideways with, then the other players—even if only by association—were every bit as vile. Considering that Momotani wasn't even the "big boss"...Gaspard's integrity and credibility were eroding by the minute.

CHAPTER 20

The man known as The Persian placed a call.

Just one call, for one was his limit.

A voice colored with the tonalities of Southern Ukraine answered.

"Yes, sir?"

"Do you have a team equipped and ready to be activated?"

"We do. What is the target?"

"There is a villa in Villefranche-sur-Mer, just east of Nice. I want you to descend on this villa like the black plague. Leave no one alive."

"It will be as you desire. Send me the coordinates."

"It will be done. Time frame?"

"Within the hour."

With that, the call was terminated.

And *that* was the way you got things done.

Jake Moriarity or not, if you struck at the core of what, or in this case *who* someone loved, priorities changed rapidly.

Immediately.

Momotani may be the Oyabun of the much-vaunted Yakuza, but he did not control even a tenth of the wealth that this man controlled. Money was everything. And it was shocking, even alarming, how few people realized this fact.

The Persian's father had known it. Had, in fact, known and exploited the knowledge—knowledge that he had inherited from his father and his father's father before him. By the time his father passed it along to him, it was a fortune so vast as to be nearly immeasurable—a fortune that had been made through the sale and manipulation of what the Americans called "black gold," or crude oil.

But, as he had been taught when still a very young boy, the oil was merely a way to fund the family's true passion, which was power. Had his father and grandfather been "mad" with that power? To be truly "mad" one must have taken leave of one's senses. And those two men—the only entities he had ever truly worshiped—were anything but mad. They had been brilliant! Dazzling! Magnificent!

The Persian—completely under the spell of the gifted hands of his twin masseuses—allowed himself to drift into realms of fantasy in which he, not the "Oyabun"—was the master of the world as he knew it.

"Is that good for you?" one of the twins asked in a heavy, Korean accent.

Turning his head to the side to regard her beauty, The Persian replied, "Always, my sweet. Always."

The daily massages were a luxury afforded to few men. But, he felt entitled, just as he felt entitled to the vast sums of money he realized from the sale of stolen art. His justification was that he didn't steal it. Therefore, it was fair game.

Life was good. And neither Jake Moriarity nor anyone else had the power to alter that reality in the slightest.

Or so he believed.

CHAPTER 21

We drove up to the entrance of the Business Aviation Terminal in Nice and were met by a uniformed valet who seemed to have been anticipating our arrival. As we were getting out of the car, a second uniformed man appeared sporting the Gaspard Enterprises logo—someone I did not recognize as having been on our previous flight.

"Welcome," he said enthusiastically in barely accented English while vigorously shaking our hands. "I am Étienne, and I will be serving as First Officer on your flight today. The plane is almost ready and our Captain will be along shortly."

Étienne was a twenty-something, slender young man of average height with stylish hair and trendy eyeglasses. There was a nervous energy about him that I found to be off-putting. But then, there are a lot of people who have that effect on me. We shook hands. His grip was cold, clammy and weak.

That *really* bothered me.

He barked a few orders to the valet and then beckoned us to follow him into the terminal. We hurried inside and just as it had been on the occasion of our arrival a few weeks past, we didn't stop or slow down, nor were we questioned by anyone on our way through. But Gaspard had been with us then. Apparently his influence was sufficient that even in his absence we were given elevated and expedited treatment.

"Gotta tell you, bro," I said to Aaron as we went out the doors and onto the tarmac toward the waiting jet. "I could get used to this private jet stuff."

Once through the terminal and crossing the tarmac, Étienne directed us toward the red-carpeted AirStairs where a very pretty, thirty-something flight attendant awaited our arrival. She *had* been with us on our flight over.

"Bonsoir, messieurs, and welcome back. In case you've forgotten, my name is Désirée. If there is anything at all I can do to make our short flight more comfortable for you, please do not hesitate to ask. Now, if you will follow me…" Glancing at Aaron she added, "And as before, please watch your head, Monsieur Perry."

As we entered the lavishly appointed cabin, I was struck once again by the sheer brilliance of design combining form and functionality that was practical without sacrificing luxury. The first thing you noticed was the lush carpeting on the floor, then came the exotic wood veneers followed by Corinthian leather seating surfaces. And then there was Gaspard's stateroom in the back. I'm just going to go ahead and say that it was nicer by far than most hotel suites I've been in. Then again, I suppose it's no less than what one would expect from an aircraft that cost more than many corporations clear in yearly profit.

Once inside, Étienne took our duffel bags and was stowing them in a closet adjacent to the cabin door just as Captain Philippe Lévesque entered. Lévesque was a short, broad fifty-something American ex-pat from Baton Rouge, Louisiana who spoke not a word of French but who fully embraced his heritage by loving expensive wine, great bread and beautiful women.

But not necessarily in that order.

He winked at Désirée and walked toward where Aaron and I were just settling in to our ridiculously comfortable chairs.

"Moriarity!" he bellowed as he shook my hand in a meaty grip. "Good to see you again. Good to see you! You too, Aaron. Been listening to your recordings. I'm not really a jazz guy, but I have to admit...you're pretty good. Pretty good."

One thing you learned immediately about Philippe Levesque was that he repeated almost everything he said at least once, and sometimes twice.

I said, "Are you going to actually fly this bird today, or are you gonna have your First Officer take the wheel like you did on the way over?"

He laughed and leered at Désirée.

"Hell's bells, Moriarity! I'm fifty-two, divorced and so horny I honk! How do you expect a man to keep his attention fixed on flying when a hot little number like that is back here." He leaned in and added conspiratorially, "Besides...the girl is sweet on me...ain't that right, baby doll?"

Désirée walked over, slapped him on the rear and replied, "You're really quite handsome, mon Capitaine...for an older gentleman."

As we all laughed, Philippe grew suddenly serious.

"So is it true? Somebody has kidnapped the boss?"

I said, "I'm afraid it's worse than that. They kidnapped him, all right...but it's not for ransom. They're going to kill him."

Désirée gasped.

"But why kill Monsieur Ducharme? He is the sweetest man I have ever known."

"I'm afraid I'm not at liberty to discuss it. Let's just say that it's complicated."

Lévesque took off his hat and scratched the back of his balding head.

"Well, it should take just under an hour to get to Barcelona once we get this bird in the air. I hope it's in time to do whatever you have in mind to do."

I did too. Of course I wasn't going to tell him that I didn't really have a plan that included anything more than basically storming wherever it was that Gaspard was being held, and doing whatever was necessary to secure his release.

Aaron said, "You just get us there, brother. That's all that matters right now."

Lévesque gave his head a curt nod, turned and hurried toward the cabin.

Désirée caught my gaze.

"Can you do it? Can you rescue Monsieur Ducharme?"

"I believe so or else I wouldn't have come. But we have to first find him, and that may prove to be more difficult than actually rescuing him."

She forced a smile and asked if we would care for a pre-flight beverage. We both declined and she walked away, stopping to say something to the First Officer.

Lévesque hollered from the cockpit, "Wheels up in ten!"

As we strapped in, Aaron said, "Something about that First Officer bothers me."

I glanced toward where he stood conversing with Désirée in the forward cabin.

"Me too. But I can't really explain it. Something's just off."

"You got that right! Dude bears watching."

Étienne touched Désirée on the shoulder, letting his hand linger, which seemed to my eyes to be way more familiarity than she was comfortable with, and then entered the cockpit, shutting the door behind him.

"Well," I said. "It's a short flight. Shouldn't be too hard to keep him under surveillance. Just the same..."

I stood and made my way toward the closet where our duffel bags had been stowed, opening the thin door and checking the contents to make sure that everything was still intact.

It was.

I glanced at Aaron, shrugged, picked up the bags and carried them back to our seats where I sat and slipped one foot through the handles, anchoring it to the floor. "Not saying that I don't trust the boy...but...I don't trust the boy."

"Heard that," he replied while doing the same thing.

Philippe's voice came over the overhead cabin speakers.

"We've finished our pre-flight checks, have been cleared

for takeoff and are about to begin taxiing. Buckle up, gents."

The powerful Rolls Royce jet engines whined and the sleek aircraft eased away from the terminal.

"You think Gaspard's still alive?" Aaron asked.

It was the very question that had been troubling me for the past hour.

"I hate to sound so pragmatic, but either he is...or he isn't. If he is, then we'll bring him home and most likely cause whoever took him to have second thoughts about ever doing anything so rash and foolhardy again. If he isn't...then I plan to kill everyone who had a part in his death."

Aaron grinned.

"You one cold son-of-a-bitch when you want to be, you know that?"

I stared straight ahead.

"Yeah. Sadly, I do."

The plane slowed, made a turn and Lévesque immediately throttled up the engines sending the jet screaming down the runway. In no time at all we were airborne and arcing across the clear, early afternoon sky on our way to a very uncertain future.

But that was okay. In fact, if you want to know the truth, I preferred uncertainty to a sure thing, mainly because I've never encountered a sure thing that was actually "sure."

CHAPTER 22

Cassie, Muriel and Vanessa sat around Gaspard's office at the villa, fidgeting and fighting off boredom and fear of the unknown. No one seemed to know what to say and, therefore, said nothing.

Rémi was posted up in the safe room from where he could keep tabs on every room in the villa, as well as the exterior areas of the estate, through an extensive bank of high definition video monitors.

Muriel stood suddenly.

"I can't just sit here all day waiting for something to happen!"

"But, it's what Jake told us to do," Vanessa replied.

"I know! But what if the threat isn't real? What if no one is coming here because Gaspard's already been taken and—"

"We're here!" Cassie said, interrupting her friend. "And they know we're here. These are not normal people, Muriel. These guys don't just take out their primary target. They keep going until everyone in the family is also dead. And that's a fact!"

Muriel sat back down.

"You're right. And I'm sorry. I just don't do waiting very well."

Cassie grinned slyly.

"Oh, I don't know about that. You waited for Aaron to get with the program for years."

"Well, there is that."

Vanessa said, "It certainly seems like he was worth the

wait."

"He was...is...whatever. And it's not just because he's rich, famous and handsome. There's just a way about him that...heals me...you know?"

"Actually...I don't know," Vanessa replied sadly. "Well, except of course what I've experienced from Jake and you guys. That has been incredibly healing." She was quiet for a few seconds and then continued, "I'd just like to know what it's like to have a guy fall in love with me—*really* fall in love with me and not pretend just so he can have sex with me."

Cassie scooted a couple of spaces over on the large, leather sofa and put her arm around Vanessa's shoulders.

"Muriel and I understand, sweetie."

Vanessa wiped away an unexpected tear.

"I know you do, and it means so much to be able to talk to you guys on a level that ninety-nine percent of women wouldn't be able to understand."

Muriel said, "The hardest part about recovering from sexual abuse—at least for me, anyway—was, well...how hard it has been to shake the sense that there was something in me...something that *I* did that caused it to happen. You know?"

Vanessa and Cassie were both nodding their heads.

Cassie said, "Well, I absolutely know that I caused it."

"You did not!" Muriel fired back.

"No, it's true. You're forgetting that even when I found out what Paul Morgan was doing to me and how he was using me for his sex parties—I let it go on."

"And why did you let it go on?" Muriel asked rhetorically.

"Because I was hooked on the drugs and the sex was the only way to continue scoring the drugs."

"So, there! It wasn't your fault!"

Vanessa said in a tiny, far away voice, "I used to lay in my bed at night, waiting for Collin to come in and start in on me; wishing I was ugly—trying to figure out ways to make myself unattractive, you know? Like, scarring my face or gaining a bunch of weight or not bathing. Anything to cause him to leave me alone."

"Did you feel like you were responsible for the abuse?" Muriel asked.

"Well, sort of. I mean in my mind if I hadn't been, well... pretty...and had the type of body that I had then he never would've done what he did."

"And you were how old when he started?"

"Twelve."

"Well, excuse me for saying, but most twelve year-olds aren't exactly 'built', you know what I mean? So it couldn't have been that he was attracted to your body because you basically didn't have one."

It broke the tension and all three laughed.

"I know," Vanessa said. "But it's still there...you know, what you said, Muriel, about feeling responsible."

Muriel shook her head emphatically.

"It's a lie, Vanessa! And the sooner you acknowledge it as a lie the sooner you will be healed. Counter the lie with the truth!"

"And what is the truth?" Vanessa asked.

"The truth is that you were an innocent, pure twelve year-old girl who was abused sexually and physically—basically tortured—by a monster to satisfy his sick and perverted pleasure. And he did it all with absolutely no remorse."

"It was the same for Muriel and me with Paul Morgan," Cassie added. "She was sixteen and I was eighteen. Muriel came to him because she was living on the streets of Seattle and coming very close to starvation. I came to him because, like I said, he got me hooked on drugs. But eventually, both of us suffered torture along with sexual, spiritual and emotional defilement at his hands."

"It must have been horrible," Vanessa said quietly.

"It was," Muriel replied. "But nothing on the level that you endured, little sister."

Vanessa stared into Cassie's eyes, and then Muriel's.

"And now, it's over; Collin's dead; and I have you guys, Aaron and Jake."

"And don't you forget it!" Cassie said while giving her a squeeze.

"We have, as you say, company!" Rémi hollered from the safe room.

The three girls stood and rushed inside.

Rémi pointed to monitor that showed a large, black sedan parking across the end of the driveway, blocking it completely.

"I'm thinking that you aren't going to be bored anymore, Muriel, "Cassie said.

"Most likely not. What do you think they will do, Rémi?"

He thought for a few seconds before responding.

"They most likely think that there are only helpless females here and that they will not have to deal with Rémi. But they will soon learn better."

Vanessa said, "You're not going to try to take on...?" she paused to count the men on the screen. "Four guys by yourself, are you?"

Without taking his eyes from the screen, Rémi replied, "It is nothing. I have faced much worse situations before and prevailed."

"You have?" they all said in unison.

Rémi laughed.

"But, of course. I was Monsieur Ducharme's personal bodyguard for many years. I have, how do you say...skills?"

Cassie patted his shoulder.

"We trust you, Rémi. But we have skills too."

"Yes. It is what I hear. But you will stay now here in the safe room with the household staff and Rémi will deal with these men."

And with that, he summoned the staff, ushered them inside and then left without another word, shutting the massive door behind him.

"Is he serious?" Vanessa asked.

"Well," Muriel observed. "We are apparently about to find out."

Louie, the groundskeeper said with conviction, "Rémi will protect us. He always protects us. You will see."

Cassie shook her head. "That boy is just full of surprises."

CHAPTER 23

We had been airborne for about fifteen minutes when Étienne emerged from the cockpit. He closed the door softly behind him and glanced quickly at the storage closet before making his way through the cabin toward where Aaron and I were seated on opposite sides of a small dining table Désirée had unfolded between our seats. She had just poured a cup of coffee for Aaron and was in the process of doing the same for me.

Étienne stopped at the table, his face unreadable.

"I hope your needs are being attended to."

Although I couldn't explain why, I was immediately on high alert.

I said, "No complaints so far."

He nodded his head slowly while producing a large caliber pistol he had concealed behind his back.

"Very good. Now, hands where I can see them."

"Étienne!" Désirée shouted, dropping the coffee mug. "What are you doing?"

He quickly stepped forward and backhanded her hard across the face while keeping the gun trained on us.

"Silence! Sit down and do not speak again or I will be forced to scar your pretty face."

Désirée staggered backwards and collapsed into one of the rear seats, sobbing and clutching her cheek.

I had just started to reach for the duffel bag when he cracked the butt of the pistol across the back of my head. I have to tell you, it hurt. In fact, it hurt like bloody hell! Dazed from the blow, I grabbed my head and sat back in the seat.

Aaron growled, "You better hope you maintain control of that gun, little man, because if you take your eyes off of us for even a second, I'm gonna make you regret it."

Étienne smiled cruelly, but kept his distance.

"As we French say, Monsieur, you are 'le cadet de mes soucis'."

"Yeah, well, I won't be 'the least of your worries' if I get my hands on you!"

"Please, Monsieur Perry, do not do anything recklessly or rashly. This will all be over soon."

"Does the term 'rashly' include me turning your face into ravioli?"

I grabbed one of the linen napkins and pressed it against my head to stem the flow of blood.

"So," I said. "Are you going to tell us why you are doing this?"

He seemed to consider my question for a couple of seconds before replying, "I don't see why not. After all, you will be dead by morning, so there's no sense in keeping it a secret. You see, Monsieur Moriarity, the men you are going up against are not only powerful, they are also very smart—smarter than you, actually. They have anticipated your every move thus far. We correctly assumed that the men sent against you would be no match and that you would eventually learn of our plans from them. We also correctly assumed that having learned of those plans you would attempt to use Monsieur Du-charme's jet to fly to Tarragona. We, therefore, arranged for the First Officer to, shall we say, have an occasion to sleep in? I fear he will be sleeping for a long while."

Désirée sobbed, "Why are you doing this, Étienne? I will never speak to you again!"

Étienne turned briefly toward her.

"You are correct, mon ange. In fact, after tonight, you will never speak to *anyone* ever again."

She gazed at him in wide-eyed horror.

He continued, "Now, as to Désirée's question of why am I doing this. My life is, how do you say...going nowhere? They offered to pay me enough money to ensure my comfort for a good long while. And since I am a man without convictions or conscience, it matters little to me whether you live or die. So, I took the money. My orders are to deliver you to our men on the ground in Tarragona. They will then make sure you are eliminated efficiently and quietly." He looked back and forth between Aaron and me. "To be honest, given your reputations, I thought subduing you would require much more effort."

Aaron said, "So, we land in Tarragona; a car meets us, takes us somewhere—I assume to the same place where you are holding Gaspard—and you kill us all at the same time? That about cover it?"

He bowed slightly.

"Congratulations, Monsieur Perry. That is exactly what will happen."

"And how you going to get Captain Lévesque to go along with this nonsense?"

He chuckled wryly.

"Captain Lévesque is, how do you Americans say it...on our payroll? Yes, he is on our payroll."

Désirée gasped and rattled off a long, quite obviously deprecatory sentence in French that caused Étienne to momentarily shift his gaze in her direction. He was standing about two feet to my right with the gun pointed at me, his hand well away from his body.

Big mistake!

I was sitting hunched over the table with my left hand pressing the napkin against my head and pretending to be in more pain than I actually was. Thinking I was out of commission, he never saw it coming.

I whipped my right hand out and caught the barrel of the gun, twisting it upwards and in a counter-clockwise motion. If he would've had both hands on the weapon, or had been left-handed, the maneuver would've been much more difficult. As it was, the pistol was in his right hand and had he tried to hang on to it, his wrist would have been seriously damaged. In the end, he did what any sensible person would do in that situation...he let go. And as soon as he loosened his grip, I put all of my weight behind a left hook that landed somewhere between his jaw and his right ear, sending his trendy glasses flying and causing him to hit the deck in an inglorious tangle of arms and legs.

Aaron quickly drew his pistol from the duffel bag and covered Étienne. It wasn't necessary. He was out and would most likely stay that way for the next several minutes.

Aaron leaned over him.

"I do believe you broke the boy's jaw."

"Good!" I replied while tending to Désirée.

She had a slight welt across her cheek where Étienne had struck her, but seemed otherwise fine. Rising unsteadily, she walked a few steps toward where he lay on his back, and before I could stop her, stomped with no small measure of authority in the general vicinity of his, well, balls. Even passed out cold, his body jerked spasmodically and he curled into a fetal position. She was raring back to kick him again when I caught her and eased her back into the seat.

I said, "I take it that there is history between the two of you?"

Glowering, she replied, "He is an animal! Always pawing at me even when I say no. Filthy pig!"

Aaron gestured toward the forward cabin.

"What are we gonna do about your boy Lévesque?"

"What are we *going* to do, or what do I *want* to do?"

"Let's go with *going*."

I thought for a few seconds.

"As far as Philippe knows, Étienne has everything under control back here."

Aaron was shaking his head and pointing at a video camera just above the cockpit door.

"Yeah...no."

I should have seen that coming.

"Well, so much for the element of surprise."

I walked toward the camera and stared into the lens.

"Philippe? You need to open the door. Do it now!"

His voice came over the speaker system.

"I sense anger in your voice, Jake. And I've been warned that I should stay away from you when you're angry...just, you know, stay completely away from you."

I put on my best scowl, which, if you don't mind me saying so is pretty darned intense.

"Open the damn door, Philippe, or I'm going to start shooting."

"Go ahead," he replied. "It's bulletproof. If you start shooting there's a good chance that a ricochet will tear a hole in the fuselage, at which point you'll all be sucked out into the atmosphere...sucked right out. Not a pretty way to die. Not pretty at all!"

Aaron said, "So, what do you want to do now?"

We exchanged glances. He knew what I was thinking.

CHAPTER 24

Aaron gave his head a slight nod before backing up and planting his size eighteen shoe—with all two hundred and sixty pounds of his weight behind it—right in the middle of the door. It buckled a bit but didn't cave in. So, he backed up and tried again; then he did it again and then three more times. On the seventh try, the door blew inward.

I walked casually into the cockpit with my gun trained on Lévesque's head.

"Bulletproof, maybe…" I said, "…but it's damn sure not Aaron-proof."

Philippe stared straight ahead through the jet's windshield, his face white and sweating.

"Okay. Just take it easy, Jake. You don't understand the situation…don't understand it at all."

"Oh really? And what part about you conspiring with that little prick back there am I not getting?"

"It's not like that!"

Étienne was starting to come around, so Aaron casually walked back and punched him again and then sat in one of the chairs with his gun pointing at him.

I stared Philippe in the eye and said, "Okay, you've got ten seconds to tell me exactly what is going on or I'm going to start doing things to you that you've only imagined in your nightmares."

He laughed.

"You can't hurt me. If you hurt me, who's going to land

the plane?"

Désirée appeared in the doorway.

"I will land it."

He whipped his head around with enough velocity to dislodge a couple of vertebrae.

"You? Don't be ridiculous! You...you're nothing more than a glorified waitress! You couldn't land a prop much less a sophisticated aircraft like this!"

Désirée smiled as she eased her way into the co-pilot's seat where she immediately and expertly seized the controls.

"I have been a pilot for five years, Philippe—something you would have known had you ever been able to see anything about me other than my breasts! I have been studying for my G6 certification for the past year. I have a few more hours to go, but I will have no problem with the landing."

I turned to Philippe.

"Well...it appears that you are, as they say, screwed, glued and tattooed."

As he sat there in utter stupefaction, his mouth hanging open comically, I heard groaning coming from the cabin and turned just in time to see Étienne coming out of unconsciousness.

I waved my gun at Philippe and told him to get out of the cockpit. Not being a brave man, he complied immediately.

I said, "You got this, Désirée?"

"Oui, Monsieur. Do not worry about the plane," she replied confidently, and then added, "Worry about that little *fils de pute* back there if I get my hands on him!"

As I followed Philippe into the cabin, Aaron pulled Étienne to his feet and dragged him toward the back of the plane where he deposited him roughly into a seat and proceeded to zip-tie his wrists to the armrests. I did the same with Philippe and then sat down to have a chat.

As Étienne groaned in pain from his injuries, I said, "Here's the way this is going to go. I'm going to ask you questions and if I don't like the answers you are giving me, Aaron will begin hurting you. Oh, there won't be any blood because, for one thing, neither one of us are particularly fond of seeing it, and for another, I'd hate to get Gaspard's beautiful jet messed up. But, we also hate lying. And if I'm being honest, we probably hate lying more than we hate the sight of blood. Just so we're clear, we will do what we have to do in order to find out what we need to know. Do you understand?

They both nodded hesitantly.

"Good! So, here we go: What is supposed to happen once we land?"

Philippe and Étienne glanced at each other but said nothing.

"Aaron?" I prompted.

He reached out and grabbed Étienne's broken jaw and wrenched it to one side causing him to bellow in pain.

I said, "The question is still on the table...or do you need me to ask it again?"

Philippe replied, "Okay, there's no need for this. I'll tell you what you need to know. The first thing is...I'm a victim here. A victim!"

Étienne shouted through clenched teeth, "That is bullshit! We agreed to pay you one hundred thousand Euro's!" and immediately regretted the outburst as evidenced by the sudden onset of pain.

"How about it, Philippe?" Aaron asked. "You really get paid that much to help them kill us?"

His glance shifted back and forth between the two of us for several seconds before he said, "Okay, yeah. I *did* take the money. But I like you guys and it made me feel terrible to betray you like that. Just terrible!"

There are times that I do things, say things, which I later regret. And I don't know why I do and say those things. But punching Philippe in the eye did not fall into that category.

He screamed, "Ow, hey! Why'd you do that?"

"Because you deserved it and I wanted to. Now, tell us

everything you know about what is waiting for us on the ground, or you will not enjoy what happens next."

With his eye swelling nearly shut, Philippe started talking and continued unabated for a good five minutes, interrupted only by random threats and protestations from Étienne.

When he was through, and I felt confident he had told us everything he knew, I cut the zip-tie from one of his hands so he could hold an icepack to his eye.

Apparently, we were to land at a private airfield on the outskirts of Tarragona where we would be met by a team of operatives. We would then be transported to an estate owned by the criminal conglomerate that had ordered Gaspard's death, and of which he had once been a part. Once there, we would be killed along with Gaspard and Maxim. Étienne was quick to add that neither he nor Philippe knew where the estate was.

I believed him.

I took Aaron into Gaspard's stateroom for some privacy. He said, "So, how are we gonna play this?"

"That's a good question."

"And do you have a good answer?"

"Not really."

"I can see why people pay you so much money."

"Yeah, it's a gift."

"Have you thought about letting our boys in there loose, and then when we land pretending to still be their captives?"

"Actually, I have," I replied. "And if you want to know the truth, that's the way I'm leaning. We come off the plane as if we were still prisoners and then take control of the operatives and force them to take us to the estate. Of course, if a struggle ensues, we run the risk of being shot."

"And what would be the other option?"

"Exit the plane with guns blazing and try to kill everyone they send."

"But?" he prompted.

"If we do that, we *still* run the risk of being shot—"

"And we still won't know where they are holding Gaspard," he said, completing my sentence. "So, we have to go with option number one?"

"Unless you can come up with another idea, it looks that way to me."

Désirée announced over the speaker system, "I am starting the descent and we will be landing in roughly fifteen minutes."

Aaron said, "Doesn't give us much time to solidify our plans."

"You got that right!" I paused and then added, "Let's go explain the situation to the guys."

We walked out of the stateroom and stood over Philippe and Étienne.

"Here is the way you both can survive this situation." I waited for a reaction, and seeing none continued, "After we land, Philippe will stay in the cockpit—which is exactly where they would expect him to be—while Étienne takes us off the plane at gunpoint." His eyes widened and I explained, "The gun will, of course be empty."

"What a shock," he mumbled.

"Aaron and I will have concealed weapons and they will *not* be empty. You will go through the motions of following whatever instructions you have been given regarding the handoff."

"And if I don't?" Étienne asked.

I shrugged nonchalantly.

"One of us will be forced to kill you. Which, while unfortunate for you, I assure you matters little to either one of us."

He gazed at me as if processing the information.

"Okay, Monsieur. I will do as you ask—largely because I am not yet ready to cease living, but also because they have already paid me and I have nothing more to gain."

I grinned.

"I knew you'd see things my way."

CHAPTER 25

The SUV carrying Gaspard Ducharme to a rendezvous with death bounced along the narrow, packed earth driveway moving slowly toward a hillside estate that looked out over Tarragona and the shimmering Mediterranean beyond. Had his situation not been so grim, Gaspard would have been rightly awed by the view, for it was nothing if not spectacular. While it would suffer greatly in comparison to his villa, the estate was, nevertheless impressive. The landscape was dominated by a large, classic Spanish country house that appeared to his trained eye to have had its origins in the Middle Ages. Slightly rundown, it still possessed a unique charm and beauty.

He said sarcastically, "At least my final hours will be spent in a place of beauty."

The scarred man turned his head slightly.

"As I said, we are not animals."

The vehicle navigated around the circular driveway and pulled to a stop in front of the dwelling. Peering through the side window, Gaspard confirmed his initial assessment—the house most likely dated from the thirteenth century. In spite of his virtually hopeless situation, he found himself subconsciously wondering what treasures were to be found within its dry and dusty walls.

The right rear passenger door was jerked open and his seatmate got out ordering him to exit as well. He stood shakily on the driveway wondering how much time he had left to live, a question that was answered quickly.

The scarred man said, "We anticipate your partner's arrival within the hour and..." he paused as an evil grin contorted his features. "The others will be along shortly after that. When all have arrived I see no reason to prolong the inevitable. So enjoy the two hours of life you have left, Ducharme."

As the man turned to enter the house, Gaspard asked, "Do I get a meal?"

"What?" he replied as he stopped walking and returned to where Gaspard stood with his guards.

"It is customary that the condemned man be allowed a last meal and a visit with a chaplain before his execution, is it not?"

The man seemed a bit flummoxed by the question.

He hissed, "This is not some humane government operation where the needs and rights of the prisoner are considered. Here you *have* no rights because to me you are not even a person! Therefore you have no needs. Are we clear?"

Gaspard gave a quick nod of his head.

"Abundantly."

"Good! Then let us go inside." He paused before adding, "If you are lucky I may be able to find some bread and hard cheese to accommodate your...eh, *needs*."

Gaspard followed him through the entryway, which led immediately and ironically into a large, eat-in kitchen with ancient tiled floors and plastered walls stained with the smoke from ten thousand fires. The rough-hewn table dominating the center of the space appeared to have not been used in decades. Glancing toward the ceiling, the numerous cobwebs and empty bird's nests confirmed his suspicion that they were among the first who had crossed the masia's threshold in many long years.

"I love what you've done with the place," Gaspard said facetiously.

Without a word, the scarred man took two steps toward him and chopped him on the left hand side of his neck where it joined his shoulders causing Gaspard to cry out in pain.

"I am sorry to have to do that, Ducharme, but I gave you fair warning when we were still in the car. I do not like the sound of your voice and if you persist in talking, I will be forced to pull out your tongue with pliers. Nod if you understand how serious I am."

With his right hand massaging his neck, Gaspard nodded silently, the pain being of sufficient intensity that he feared he might lose consciousness.

Turning his attention to the two guards, the scarred man said, "Take him below and lock him inside the room."

With curt nods, the two men grabbed Gaspard roughly by the arms and drug him toward a descending stairway, nearly lifting him off the ground. The blow had struck exactly on the point of a nerve root, and it felt as if an unrelenting river of fire was now traversing the length of his left arm. Nausea roiled his stomach and several times his knees threatened to buckle.

They proceeded down a long, dark and musty hallway coming at last to a doorway on the right that one of the guards threw open, while the other one shoved Gaspard unceremoniously inside. His right shin collided with a piece of unforgiving furniture and he went sprawling in the semi-darkness as the guards laughed at his misfortune. Curling into a tight ball he heard the door being slammed and locked, and the Japanese guards moving away making casual conversation about two local girls they hoped to bed after the executions were completed.

On that point he had been untruthful, for he did possess a passing knowledge of Japanese—enough to follow basic conversations. It was how he had known of the scarred man's concern that Jake Moriarity was coming after him. In spite of his bravado, he seemed terrified of Jake.

Not only had he never experienced such intensity of pain before in his lifetime, he had never even considered that it was possible. In addition to the river of fire in his arm, he now had the white-hot lance of pain in his shin. It was all too much for a soft man such as himself. He turned his head to one side and vomited, which only made the pain all the more severe.

"Mon Dieu," he muttered over and over in hopeless supplication before surrendering to the oblivion of blessed unconsciousness.

CHAPTER 26

aron and I buckled Étienne and Philippe into their seats before doing the same for ourselves. As we were making our final approach to the airfield, there was a fleeting moment when it occurred to me that allowing someone who had yet to receive their Gulfstream certification to be in control of my destiny was no doubt a profoundly stupid thing to be doing. But, before the thought could develop any further, we were on the ground. To her immense credit, Désirée had done a rough, but commendable job of bringing the jet in for the landing.

As she taxied toward the small terminal, I cut the zip ties from Philippe's feet and took him into the cockpit.

Once I got him seated, I whispered in his ear, "If you do anything that does not meet with my approval, I will deal quite severely with you. Do you understand?"

Philippe turned large and frightened eyes—well, *eye,* for the left one was swollen completely shut—in my direction.

"Perfectly! You don't need to worry about me."

Through the jet's windshield I could just make out a black sedan flanked by four men awaiting our arrival.

We were still too far away for anyone to be able to see inside of the cockpit, so I patted Philippe's shoulder and then grabbed his throat.

"I know what you're thinking, Philippe. But these guys can't beat us. People may die tonight, but I guarantee you, it will not be us. You're done! You've made your choices and now it's time to reap the consequences. Now, Désirée is going to go into the cabin and play her role as flight attendant and you are going to take the plane the rest of the way. Get it?"

He choked, "Okay, okay. I get it. Please...let go."

I released my grip and followed Désirée to into the cabin where Aaron was bringing a limping Étienne, wearing his bent glasses, down the aisle at gunpoint.

Locking eyes with him I said, "In the unfortunate instance of you growing a pair and alerting our friends out there that something is amiss...you will be the first to die. Understand?"

By the look in his eyes I could tell that it was *exactly* what he had been thinking.

He smiled humorlessly and, speaking carefully to favor his injured jaw, replied, "You have nothing to worry about from me, Monsieur. I love my life and wish above all to keep it. Besides, as I said...they have already paid me."

The plane came to a complete stop, Aaron and I concealed our weapons and Désirée opened the cabin door releasing the AirStairs.

We exited the plane with our hands raised and Étienne played his role well by prodding me in the back with the barrel of his pistol. Except for two or three people I could see behind various counters inside the terminal about two hundred feet away, the small airfield seemed to be nearly deserted.

The four men, looking quite fierce and appropriately burly, were fanned out in a loose half circle. Three had their weapons drawn but held casually, trusting that Étienne had us firmly in his control. The fourth man, obviously the leader, stood with his arms folded across his chest, a smirk on his less than handsome face. I detest smirks and decided I would knock that one off his face in short order.

When we got to within six or seven feet I hollered, "Now!"

As Aaron and I drew our weapons several things happened simultaneously: Étienne dropped his empty gun and sprinted back inside the airplane; the smirking boss-man turned and ran for the car; his three armed colleagues started to bring their weapons up into firing position but were about a second too slow, which didn't stop one from attempting to shoot us anyway. So I shot him in the knee. It pays to be a good shot, especially in tense situations. After he fell to the ground, the other two threw down their weapons and raised their hands.

Boss-man had just climbed into the car and was trying to start it when Aaron put two rounds through the front windshield missing his head by mere inches. He froze as if experiencing a moment of indecision and fixed his eyes on Aaron who was advancing slowly on his position.

Aaron hollered, "I missed those two shots on purpose. Now get out of the car or the next one goes through your forehead!"

I looked toward the terminal. The people inside *had* to have heard the gunshots, but it appeared that no one had moved even slightly from their original positions. I found that very strange. Could they have been paid off? Told that no matter what they saw or heard to just mind their own business?

The man inside the car did as ordered and came out with his hands raised. Aaron herded him over to where I had his colleagues on the ground and was in the process of securing their hands behind their backs. After Aaron ordered him onto the ground I zip-tied his hands as well before checking on the man I had been forced to shoot. The bullet had taken him square in the kneecap, and while the injury was without question one of the most painful one can endure, there was very little bleeding.

I heard a commotion coming from the direction of the plane and turned to see Désirée ushering Étienne and Philippe down the stairs using one of our backup guns as encouragement. I couldn't help but smile when I saw Étienne with one of his hands pressed against a rapidly swelling lump on the side of his head. I looked questioningly at Désirée getting a shrug and a smile in answer.

Staring at the men on the ground, I said, "Do any of you speak English?"

They all stared straight ahead silently while Aaron retrieved their weapons.

"Okay, then here's what I'm going to do. Starting with the man on my left, my associate is going to begin shooting your balls off until—"

"No, Monsieur!" the man in question said loudly and I could see by their wild eyes that all of them spoke English.

"That's better. What is your name?"

"Julien, Monsieur."

"Okay, Julien." I gestured toward Boss-man. "And who is this?"

"He is Jean. We are under his authority."

Jean tried to look contemptuous, but couldn't pull it off and wound up looking petulant instead.

"Okay, Jean, since I'm not really in the mood to waste time, you're going to stand up and take us to wherever you are holding Gaspard Ducharme."

The smirk crawled its way back onto his swarthy face.

"And if I don't?"

Aaron knelt in front of him, whipped his right hand out and did one of those nerve lock things on his neck. The man's jaw dropped open in a silent scream, which he held until Aaron released the hold.

As Jean caught his breath, I remarked casually, "That's level one out of approximately fifty levels of pain and debilitation. So, in answer to your question...that's what will happen to you if you don't tell us what we need to know."

He began, "You don't know who you're de—" before Aaron grabbed him again, this time ratcheting it up to at least a twenty.

With his eyes bulging and tongue protruding from his mouth, Jean made strangling noises and jerked spasmodically. When Aaron let go after about ten seconds the man collapsed onto his side breathing heavily as his companions looked on in terror. And when I turned to them and asked, "Okay, who's next?" they began speaking rapidly and eagerly in a mixture of French and English.

Within about sixty seconds all of them, including the man with the wounded knee, had volunteered to provide detailed directions to the villa where we, along with Gaspard and his partner from Belgium, were scheduled to be executed before the sun rose on the morrow.

Yes, I just said, "On the morrow."

I have no explanation.

CHAPTER 27

I asked Étienne, "Who is in charge at the villa?"

He simply shrugged and shook his head slowly.

"Philippe?"

"Look, all I know is that I was supposed to fly you boys here and turn you over to, well, these fellas. Étienne brokered the deal. I didn't talk to anyone else. Say, can I have some water or something, I'm not feeling so good."

"Maybe. That depends on how well you continue to co-operate."

Julien cleared his throat.

"Monsieur? I can answer your question. The man in charge is only known as 'The Scarred Man.' No one knows his true name. He is very bad, Monsieur. Very, very bad."

"Duly noted. How many men are with him?"

"Not counting us, there are three more."

I glanced at Aaron.

"Two against four. I like the odds."

"Me too," He replied. "Although it'd level the playing field a bit were we to let a couple of these jokers go."

The men on the ground stared at us as if we were mad. Well, perhaps we were.

Jean, the Boss-man, said, "The Scarred Man will have no problem dealing with the two of you on his own. You are making a terrible mistake."

Aaron roared, "The only mistake was when you people took our friend! And trust me, we're not gonna let that pass without consequence."

I added, "He's right. Gaspard Ducharme is family, and we take care of our family."

Jean was chuckling.

"I know who you are, Moriarity. And your reputation doesn't scare me."

"Really? Is that why you're on the ground trussed up like a market pig and I'm standing with a gun on you?"

He stared balefully.

"If you did not have that gun..."

"What?" I said. "What would we see?"

I don't know why I did what I did next. I think it was because I just didn't like the guy's smirk.

"Cut him loose, Aaron."

Aaron pulled the man roughly to his feet and cut the zip-ties. It was then I first noticed that he was nearly as tall as Aaron, and just as muscular.

I handed Aaron my weapon and said to the man, "Okay, big guy, let's see what you've got."

Without a word he charged me.

Now, I must tell you that I do not possess sophisticated martial arts techniques. I am a street fighter. I have picked up a little of this and a little of that along the way and have managed to win more than I've lost, which is good, because I absolutely *hate* to lose! Street fighters present a daunting challenge to someone trained in martial arts.

The striking-based martial arts, such as Tae Kwon Do, Kung Fu, Karate, etc., are largely based on the assumption that the conflict will be waged on one's feet, with precious few strategies on how to deal with getting thrown to the ground. And since we're on the topic, getting thrown onto a sidewalk or pavement is a vastly different experience from being thrown to the mat in a dojo or MMA gym. Being slammed onto a hard, unforgiving surface like a city street can jack you up beyond belief. Conversely, someone trained in one of the grappling based disciplines such as Judo, Russian Sambo or even the Brazilian Jiu Jitsu that is so popular with the MMA crowd, will be similarly challenged when forced to defend against a skilled striker.

The common denominator in all martial arts disciplines is that word "discipline." There are rules that must be followed and you cannot progress through the belts without following the rules.

It took me about three seconds to tell that Jean was a karate guy. A very good karate guy. But I was a better street fighter. So, after letting him throw a few strikes and kicks so I could get a feel for his rhythm and assess his defenses, I waited for an opportune moment and exercised a little trick Aaron had taught me. It's called a "vertical suplex", and is a very efficient tool if one is seeking to take all the fight out of one's opponent.

I spotted a weakness in his defense and waited until he was exposed. Then I moved in quickly, got my left arm around his head, grabbed him by the crotch and basically lifted him upside down. From there it was just a simple matter of falling backwards and letting gravity drive the entire weight of the man's body into the ground with his head taking all the impact. The result wasn't pretty. There's a reason the Japanese call this move the "brain crusher."

He was out cold and struggling to breathe. So I knelt and gently maneuvered him onto his right side in a classic recovery position. It was the least I could do. I mean I'm not a thug.

Since it didn't appear that Jean was going anywhere for a while, I stood and beckoned for Aaron to follow me, trusting Désirée to keep things under control.

As we walked toward the car he chuckled.

"You just showing off! You know that, right?"

"It's not showing off if there is a point to be made! I needed him—*and* his associates—to know that their best guy was no match."

"I'm thinking they got the message. So what are we gonna do with them?"

We stopped and stood by the rear of the sedan.

"Wonder how big the trunk is?"

"One way to find out," Aaron replied as he opened the driver's door and triggered the trunk release.

I examined the large compartment.

"Damn! You could probably fit four of those guys in there if you had to."

"'Bout that. So, what are you thinking?"

"Well, we obviously can't put the wounded guy in there. That'd be heartless."

"It would."

"So, how about we keep him and the other one, Julien, up front with us so they can give directions and we shove Philippe, Étienne and the other two in here?"

Aaron grinned and said, "They not gonna like that one bit."

"Don't expect they will." I paused for a second and then continued, "You know, it's probably going to get a little crazy from this point forward."

"Be disappointed if it didn't. Why you saying that?"

"Just giving you another chance to come to your senses and stay back."

He laughed, "If I had any 'sense' I probably never would've become your friend."

"But just think of how sad and meaningless your life would have been."

"I know. I would've had to content myself with touring, concert performances, five-star hotels and recording—boring shit like that."

"Basically, a living hell."

"Basically."

CHAPTER 28

Much to his vexation and annoyance, as soon as Jean came to, we gagged and then unceremoniously tossed him into the trunk along with Étienne, Philippe and the other thug. They tried to scream and did a bit of thrashing about, but after about ten minutes gave up and accepted their fate. After checking on the wounded guy's knee, we settled him into the back seat, applied a tourniquet and put Julien, whose hands and feet were still zip-tied, next to him. My effortless dismantling of their boss had obviously produced the desired effect, as they seemed genuinely terrified of me, flinching involuntarily whenever I came close to either of them.

After loading our tactical bags into the front seats, I left Aaron to watch over our little posse and walked over to the plane to have a chat with the lovely Désirée.

Stopping in front of her I said, "That was very impressive. *You* are very impressive."

She actually blushed.

"Merci, Monsieur. I am just happy to be helpful."

"You were far more than helpful, Désirée. We could not have done this without you and I will make sure Gaspard hears of your service and compensates you appropriately."

"It would be welcome, but not necessary, Monsieur."

"Jake. The name is, Jake."

She giggled girlishly.

"Oui...Jake. And for the record, it is *you* who are impressive. The way you just took over and saved all of our lives. I will never forget you."

Okay. So that just happened.

I may not have had a serious relationship for twenty years, but I'm not stupid! I can still tell when a woman is flirting with me. And Désirée was definitely flirting. And I was enjoying it. And why not? She was, in a word, "Hot!" And I was...well, what was I?

She said, "I could give you my phone number, if you'd like. That way when all of this is settled you could, perhaps, call me?"

And then a little voice in my head inquired, "But what about Gabi?"

I hated that voice!

"Gabi" was Gabriella Marcus, my lady friend from Vegas.

I liked her.

I liked her a lot.

And she liked me.

Even though we weren't officially a "thing", she definitely had my attention. Okay, she had more than my attention. My budding relationship with Gabi had already caused me to begin unlocking areas of my heart that had been closed off for years.

That said, why should I feel guilty about spending some time with Désirée? It's what single men and women do when they find each other attractive and are experiencing a particular level of chemistry. I mean, right? What could be the harm? It would be just for coffee, or drinks, or dinner, or...

"I would definitely like that," I replied, basically telling the voice to buzz off. "How about I give you my cell number and you can text me yours. That way we'll both be covered."

Did I mention that she had blue eyes? Those eyes now flashed with pleasure at the suggestion, and she smiled that oh-so-fetching smile of hers.

When the transfer of information was completed she asked, "Would it be okay if I gave you a hug, Jake?"

Oh, a hug, a kiss...anything you'd like.

Of course, that's not what I said.

"I think I'd like that."

So she did.

And I did…like it, that is.

I said, "You going to be okay here by yourself while we go find Gaspard?"

"Staying on the jet is like staying in a luxury hotel suite. I think I will be okay."

"And how about having the weapon? You okay with that?"

She pulled the pistol from her shoulder bag.

"My father always had guns and he taught me to shoot very well. So, yes."

I gave her a tight smile and said, "Okay, then. I'll be off."

"À bientôt, Jake."

That phrase I knew.

"Yes, I'll see you soon, Désirée."

CHAPTER 29

Aaron hadn't said a word since I returned to the car. Not unusual given his pensive nature. But I suspected this was more about my overt display of interest in Désirée, than the esoteric benefits of silent contemplation.

I started the car and said, "Something on your mind?"

"Well," he began and then paused. "That was just very unexpected."

"What?" I replied pulling away from the plane and waving at Désirée.

"You know what, bruh! That little conflagration of chemistry over there between you and the lovely Désirée."

"Oh, that."

"Yeah, *that!* What the hell was 'that' exactly?"

I wish I knew.

"You want the truth?"

"'Be nice."

"Okay...I don't know what 'that' was. Right now I'd just have to say that there appears to be a mutual interest."

From the back seat Julien said, "If you are talking about the young lady with the large pistol, she is one of the most beautiful—"

"Shut up!" Aaron and I said together.

I saw him grin in the rearview mirror.

"No problem. I will shut up now."

Aaron began a conversation with Julien in French that lasted for several minutes, during which time I mainly concentrated on how badly my head hurt and how lucky I had been that Étienne had clubbed me where he had. If the butt of the gun had connected about an inch lower, I would have been in serious trouble. As it was, I merely had a lump and slight bleeding, which, fortunately, had already stopped. Feeling around with my fingers I figured I'd need at least three, maybe four stiches to close the wound properly.

Aaron said, "All right. Our boy Julien here says that Gaspard is being held in a hillside villa about fifteen minutes from here."

"And how about the approach? Any way to sneak in?"

"No. First of all, the driveway is dirt so a dust cloud follows us wherever we go. Secondly, it's long and straight, meaning that you could stand at the villa's entrance and see a car coming from a long ways off."

"Perfect! Did he say what was on each side of the driveway?"

"Yeah. It's tree-lined with heavy brush and an old olive orchard beyond that."

The way my head was feeling, I didn't really relish the idea of having to do battle in order to free Gaspard, but in my business you did what you had to do in order to get the job done. And if stone-cold killers held my friend captive, then a stone-cold killer I would become to see him freed.

Julien rattled something off in French.

Aaron interpreted, "Julien says that we're only a couple of miles away. How do you want to play this?"

I thought about it for a few seconds.

"I don't like it, but ditching the car and going in on foot is our only real option if we wish to remain unseen."

"Agreed. And what about our friends here? Can't exactly have them tagging along."

I glanced in the rearview mirror to check for anyone following us. It was clear, so I hit the brakes bringing the car to a stop off to the side of the roadway.

I found Julien's eyes in the rearview mirror.

"What is your friend's name?"

"He is Serge."

I turned toward Aaron.

"Serge obviously needs medical attention, and the boys in the trunk can't stay in there indefinitely."

"I know," Aaron replied patiently. "But I'm not sure we can find the place without them."

There was that.

"Okay," I said. "We take Serge with us. I mean his best shot at medical attention is to stay with us."

Julien mumbled something from the back that neither one of us could understand, so I asked him to repeat it.

"I was just suggesting, Monsieur, that you drive us to a hospital. Serge is in terrible pain and in need of immediate medical attention."

"That's out of the question!"

"But you shot him, Monsieur. Surely you have some compassion."

"Hazards of war, my friend."

Someone in the trunk started kicking and causing a general ruckus.

I said to Aaron, "Want to go and see what that's all about?"

He got out and I triggered the trunk release.

After a few seconds I heard him holler, "Jake, you might want to come and check this out."

I got out of the car and joined him. Looking into the trunk I saw Étienne and Philippe both passed out, whether from lack of oxygen or some form of mischief from their trunk-mates, I couldn't tell.

I said, "Are they breathing?"

Aaron reached in, removed the gags and checked for a pulse on each man. "Barely. And they got some weird white stuff around their mouths."

I pulled the gag from Jean's mouth and asked him what had happened.

"Je ne sais pas! When the car stopped I saw they lost consciousness. That is why I start kicking the lid."

"And you didn't do anything to cause them to pass out?"

"Mais non, Monsieur! What could I do? I am gagged; thanks to you, my head feels as if it will explode; and my hands and feet are tied. If anyone is responsible it is *you* for forcing four men into such a small, airless space!"

Aaron said, "Things just got complicated."

CHAPTER 30

I said, "So we've got one guy with a gunshot wound and now these two have mysteriously lost consciousness."

"So, what are we gonna do?" Aaron asked.

A big part of situational success is being able to adapt quickly and readily to changing circumstances, something I had always been able to do. But for some reason, I found myself temporarily stymied by the situation with which I was now confronted.

In short, I was stumped!

The clock was ticking.

We had to get to where they were holding Gaspard or he was a dead man. And if we didn't get medical attention for three of our captives, it seemed highly likely that they would die as well.

I suppose a different sort of man would have simply dumped all six men at the side of the road and wished them, as the French say, "*Bonne chance.*"

But I was not that sort of man.

I opened the rear passenger door.

"How far from here to a hospital, Julien?"

He considered my question for a few seconds.

"It is not far. Maybe five kilometers? Six?"

I pulled Aaron away from the car.

"I know what you said, but we have no choice but to find that villa on our own. Can we do it?"

He glanced at the sky, which was turning dusky.

"If we get after it before dark, I think so. What you got in mind?"

"Since we have to go in on foot anyway, how about if we get as close as we can to the driveway, take our gear out of the car, cut Julien free and have him drive these guys to the hospital?"

"But what if they don't go to the hospital? What if they decide to try and warn the guys who have Gaspard?"

"We have their cell phones and money. And even if they find a phone, it'll be too late. We'll already be on site and creating havoc."

"And what if they decide to come back and try to help out their friends?"

"With what? They have no weapons, and Julien will be the only one whose hands and feet are free. Don't forget, one of them is severely wounded and two more barely breathing."

Aaron started to reply when a car approached from the other direction, slowing down a bit as it got closer. Aaron waved and smiled, holding his cell phone up and miming taking a picture. The car's lone occupant grinned, returned the wave and sped off.

He said, "This is one of the lamest plans you've ever had, and you've had a few."

"Okay, then...suggest something else."

"Well," he replied after a few seconds silence. "We go ahead and send Julien to the hospital but only with Étienne, Philippe and Serge. We take Jean and the other guy with us, gag and tie them to a tree, or something, so they won't be a factor."

I didn't like it, but what else were we going to do?

"Okay. That'll work."

When we got back to the car, Philippe and Étienne were semi-conscious but unresponsive.

Aaron said, "Why didn't the other two pass out?"

I asked Jean if he or his friend had felt light headed and he assured me that they had not.

"Okay, so here's what's going to happen: Julien is going

to drive Serge, Étienne and Philippe to the hospital, but you two are coming with us as soon as we get close to the villa's driveway."

The smirk was back, making me wish I hadn't taken the gag off.

"It is of no importance. The Scarred Man will deal with you shortly. You will see."

I slammed the trunk without replacing the gags since at this point it no longer mattered.

After we got back into the car and started moving, Aaron explained the plan to Julien who received the news quite agreeably as did Serge, whose pain must've been unbearable.

But, like I said, hazards of war.

CHAPTER 31

I saw an overgrown path up ahead on the left-hand side of the roadway, about a hundred yards past the spot Julien had pointed out as being the entrance to the villa, and slowed down in order to check it out more closely.

I gestured toward the path.

"Does that look wide enough to pull in and out of?"

Aaron replied, "One way to find out."

Easing the car off the road and through the narrow opening between two large eucalyptus trees, I drove fifty feet or so down a deeply rutted pathway. Even though it had quite obviously been intended for foot traffic and the occasional wagon, it was just wide enough to accommodate the large sedan. Given the path's steep decline from the roadway, there was no way anyone passing by could see anything unless they were specifically looking for it and even then, with sunset approaching—not to mention the presence of heavy under-growth—it would be next to impossible.

I brought the car to a stop and we got out to deal with our passengers. Starting with Jean, we pulled him and his hygienically challenged companion out of the trunk, sat them down and roped them back-to-back on opposite sides of a tree. We then cut Julien free and put him in the driver's seat. Philippe and Étienne were still barely conscious and unable to move under their own power, so we maneuvered Philippe into the front passenger seat and placed Étienne into the back next to Serge.

As we were strapping Philippe and Étienne into their seats, I said, "Julien, when you get to the hospital you will tell them that you found these three by the side of the road and brought them in. You do not know them, and they do not know you. Understand?"

"Oui, Monsieur."

"Serge, you understand?"

He nodded his head weakly.

I turned back to Julien.

"After you deliver these men to the hospital, I don't care what you do. You've been very cooperative and I have no wish to harm you, but if I see either you or Serge again..."

Julien replied, "Oui, Monsieur. I understand completely."

"Good! As for these two," I jerked my thumb toward Jean and his partner. "After we rescue Gaspard, I am quite sure he will have some business to conclude with them. Now get going!"

As we watched him slowly and carefully navigate backing down the constricted pathway, Aaron said, "I still don't like this idea."

"Yeah, me neither."

We watched until Julien finally reached the road and then drove away as if the devil himself were on his tail.

Kneeling down by Jean, I caught and held his gaze.

"I know what you're thinking: As soon as we're out of sight, you and your foul-smelling friend here are going to somehow be able to free yourselves and come after us. I assure you that there is not the slightest possibility of that happening, so save your energy. Also, my associate has very keen hearing and if we hear so much as a peep from either one of you...he will come back and shoot you. Understood?"

They just scowled and mumbled inarticulately around their gags, so we picked up our tactical bags and set off toward the villa.

The sun had been down for about ten minutes but there

was just enough twilight to make our way through the dense vines and olive trees that had once provided a living for the villa's original owners. Even focused as I was on the task at hand, I could imagine how beautiful it must have once been —acres and acres of vineyards interspersed with olive groves and winding lanes through the middle of it all. A balmy, teasing breeze infused the atmosphere with the heady scent of eucalyptus making me think of hours spent on the veranda of Gaspard's villa, smoking great cigars and sipping rare cognac while engaging in familial chatter with Aaron and the girls. It all seemed so far away now.

We had been walking for about five minutes and pulled up under the cover of a large olive tree to get our bearings and come up with an assault strategy.

Aaron whispered, "If I remember correctly, this scarred dude only has three other men with him to guard Gaspard."

"Right. But don't forget that Gaspard's partner is being brought in from Belgium and we don't know how many men were sent to fetch him."

"So we need to get in and get this done before they show up."

"Exactly!" I said. "Our responsibility is to Gaspard, we can worry about dealing with his partner if the opportunity to do so is there."

"If you were this scarred man, how would you utilize your resources?"

"Well," I said, pondering the question. "If he is anything like his minion we've got tied to the tree back there, he is almost certainly overconfident. And overconfidence makes you sloppy. It doesn't matter what he has or hasn't heard about me. In his mind, I'm just one guy going up against what I'm guessing is his "A" team. And, don't forget, at this point he doesn't know that we took out Jean and his posse."

"Right. So he will probably only have two guys working the perimeter and the other one inside with him to watch Gaspard."

"That's the way I'd do it," I said while ramming a thirty round clip into the HK416. "Our first priority is to take out the perimeter guys. This 416 has great range and the Nightforce scope is a definite advantage, but I want to get as close as possible before I start firing."

Aaron picked up the G36 and stared down at it.

"What?" I asked.

"Oh, you know...I've just never had to shoot anyone, and every time I go out with you I wonder if this will be the time."

Being that Aaron is a "civilian", I have always tried my best to protect him from ever having to experience taking someone's life. But if it came right down to it, I had no doubt that he'd do whatever was necessary. Now when it came to non-lethal cracking of bones and busting of heads, that was another matter entirely and one he pursued with near fanatical relish.

"Don't worry about it," I said. "We'll be in and out so fast they will barely have time to register that we've been and gone let alone put up a fight."

"You sound awful damn confident for a man that up until five minutes ago didn't have a viable plan."

My cellphone vibrated in my pocket.

It was Zack.

"Yeah, Zack. What's up? We're just about to go hot on the villa where they're keeping Gaspard."

He was silent for a few seconds, which put me immediately on high alert.

"Jake," he said, his voice dripping with weariness. "It's a little more complicated now."

"Why? What's going on?"

He sighed deeply.

"They apparently hit Ducharme's villa, Jake...and...well, the girls are gone."

CHAPTER 32

I've heard people describe being so overwrought that their heart stops beating. Well, my heart stopped beating.

"When? How?"

Aaron's eyes were huge, appealing for a clue as to what was happening. I held my hand up as if holding him back.

"We're not certain," Zack replied. "Our team got there about ten minutes ago and found the place torn apart. Lots of blood. It...it doesn't look good."

That made me think.

"Are you sure they're not in the safe room?"

What he said next was beautiful.

"Safe room?"

"Yeah. It's behind the bookcase in Gaspard's office. Hang on."

I lowered the phone and looked at Aaron.

"Call Muriel. Right now!"

Aaron dug his phone out of a pocket in his tactical vest and speed-dialed Muriel while I waited for something to happen.

"Baby. Where are you?"

He looked up at me and winked.

"Safe room? No...stay there. I'll tell you what's up in a minute."

I said, "Zack...they're in the safe room."

"Damn!" he replied. "I never even thought about that. Okay. Great. I'll tell the team and have them—"

"Let me tell the girls that it's your guys out there so they don't get shot."

"Who, the girls?"

"No! Your guys."

He laughed, breaking the tension.

"Of course. Sometimes I forget who I'm dealing with here. Okay. We'll work it out on this end. As far as Gaspard is concerned...go get him Jake."

"Roger that, bro."

I hung up and had Aaron relay the info to Muriel who, in turn, gave him a condensed version of the events that had transpired barely twenty minutes before our call.

After hanging up with her, he said, "An assault team hit the villa, all right. But our girls and Rémi hit back harder!"

"How hard?"

"Hard enough that every operator that had been sent in was either killed or severely wounded."

I didn't like the sound of that.

"Did the girls..."

"Have to shoot anyone? No. That was all Rémi. Apparently the boy can be quite lethal when pressed into service."

I breathed a sigh of relief.

"I'm glad he was there. So, the girls are okay?"

"Yeah. After taking care of business, Rémi hustled them back into the safe room and they've been waiting there for backup."

"Impressive. So, we can get on with it."

Aaron said, "You can see what they tryna' do."

"Oldest tactic in the book—take the people we love and hold them hostage until we back off. At which point, they would most likely kill them anyway and then come after us."

"They don't know us very well."

"No...no, they don't."

He looked at me for a few seconds without speaking before saying, "So, let's do this."

CHAPTER 33

After a meticulous check and recheck of our equipment to ensure that we were indeed prepared to do what we were intent on doing, we began moving methodically toward the old villa. About three steps into the journey I realized that outside of a very vague description by Julien, we had no idea of the layout of the grounds, the building or even the specifics of the opposition we would be facing.

I pulled up under the cover of another olive tree with Aaron stopping beside me.

I said, "I need you to stay here while I go check the layout of the villa. See if you can get eyes on the lookouts and let me know if it seems like I've been compromised."

"Got it!"

I began moving in a counterclockwise direction around the right-hand side of the house. I knew I should be careful about making any undue noise, but time wasn't on my side, so I moved quickly. When I had covered about fifty yards Aaron's voice came over my earcomm.

"Got movement. In front of your position about ten o'clock."

"Roger that."

It seemed highly unlikely that I could have been discovered that quickly. Just in case, I stayed put until Aaron gave me the all clear.

"Dude was just tossing a cup of coffee over the balcony railing. No other movement that I can see. You're good to go."

"On it."

Fortunately, I had a clear pathway between two rows of olive trees and was almost entirely shielded from view by the undergrowth in-between, so I sort of threw caution to the wind and started running as fast as my twenty-five plus pounds of tactical gear would allow. It wasn't pretty—more of a controlled stumble than anything else. But it got me to where I needed to be. I crouched behind a dilapidated pump house that just happened to be positioned with a clear line of sight toward the front of the villa and paused to slow my breathing and to listen. Somewhere a horse neighed and dogs barked in response; off to my right I heard children's laughter as the breeze carried the tantalizing aroma of barbequed beef to my nostrils; somewhere a cricket began sawing away at his nocturnal mating song.

Just another night in the neighborhood.

I couldn't see many details. In fact, about all I could see was that the house was old, and that it was large. There were two stories with the lower level being built partially into the hillside and the upper level having a balcony that circled the entire top floor. With the lack of windows facing the front entrance, my assumption was that most of the effort had gone into maximizing the view from the side of the house that overlooked the valley. That meant that there was only one direction from which to assault the bottom floor—the one with all the windows.

Perfect!

A pair of feral cats suddenly appeared, hissing and letting me know that I was trespassing on their turf. I tried to shoo them away quickly and quietly, which, as you've no doubt learned from your own dealings with felines, is next to impossible. Since they were obviously not giving up their domain, I was forced to move on to my next vantage point. Luckily, I was able to find cover behind a low-lying rock wall about a hundred feet away. From there I could see around the opposite end of the house, which provided me with a view of the layout of the property on the other side.

Through the night scope, I could just make out a level area that looked to contain a large, cement deck and pool, although whether it had water in it, I couldn't be sure. Beyond that, I could see structures that seemed to have once housed livestock of some sort. Stalls for horses and cattle; coops for chickens; pens for pigs.

Like that.

Up the hill from that was another structure that had probably once been a barn, but now stood as just one more victim of the ravages of time.

Aaron's voice came over the earcomm.

"You might want to look sharp. Got a dude coming your way across the yard. Could be just going to the car, but all the same..."

I acknowledge his alert, crouched behind a low, stone wall and swung the scope around toward the front entrance. The man carried an automatic weapon slung around his neck and was headed quite purposefully toward my position. When he was less than thirty feet away he veered off to my left and popped the trunk on a late model Mercedes. As he leaned in and rummaged around as if searching for something, I thought about taking him out right there. But, as I said before, I don't like killing people indiscriminately. I didn't really want to do what I was thinking of doing, but I felt like I was running out of time. So, I got up, hopped the wall and ran toward him. He was so surprised that by the time he turned around to see who or what was making all the noise, I was right on top of him. Before he could even cry out, I belted him right between the eyes with the butt of the 416. His eyes rolled up in his head and he was out cold. He fell backwards into the trunk as I knelt down and checked the villa for any signs that I had been spotted.

I whispered, "How's it looking?"

Aaron came back, "Nothing's moving that I can see, but then, I can't see everything."

"That's real helpful."

"I'm here for you, bro."

I emptied the man's pockets and relieved him of the rifle, two knives, car keys and cell phone. After cutting two strips of cloth from the man's shirt for a gag, I zip-tied his hands and ankles together and closed the trunk lid as quietly as possible.

I said, "I can't see any sense delaying the inevitable. I'm going in."

"What should I do?" Aaron replied.

"There's an old pump house about fifty yards down the path with a couple of territorial feral cats you'll have to chase off, but it'll give you good cover and a wide open vantage point. Make your way there and let me know when you're in position."

"Will do."

The last thing on earth I wanted to do at that moment was to initiate a face-off with the guys holding Gaspard. Three against one was never good odds under the most ideal circumstances, let alone when one was going in blind and ignorant of the battlefield. But I had no choice.

Aaron said, "I'm there. And you were right about those damn cats. Good thing I'm suited up 'cuz I had to fight one of them off!"

"And I'm assuming you prevailed?"

"For now."

"All right. I'm going in."

"I got your back."

He was going to have to have more than that in order for me to survive. But you don't go into my line of work if you are prone to worrying about your safety.

I had just started to move when I heard the telltale click of a weapon being taken off safety. Turning very slowly I saw the barrel of a .44 Magnum pointed at my head from about five feet away. If you want to know the truth, it is an unsettling sight...almost as unsettling as the face of the man holding the weapon—a face that was profoundly scarred.

CHAPTER 34

Mr. Moriarity, I presume. We meet at last," he said calmly with a heavy, Japanese accent.

It bothered me that he had managed to sneak up on me. It bothered me a great deal.

"And you are...?"

"Oh," he said dismissively, "people refer to me by various names depending on their level of either contempt or admiration. It matters not to me. Mainly I am called, The Scarred Man."

"I can see why. Can I stand, or do you prefer me to crouch in this very uncomfortable position?"

He smiled wryly and lowered his weapon.

"Stand. Please. There is no need for further pretense." As I stood he continued, "I had not intended to interrupt your very bold assault, but you left me no choice."

"Excuse me for a second." Cupping my ear I said, "Aaron, do you have our friend in your sights?"

"Roger that."

I smiled.

"My backup has you under a scope, if that makes any difference in the outcome of this conversation."

He turned and waved in the direction of the pump house.

"None whatsoever. In fact, please invite your friend to join us."

I shook my head in confusion.

"You'd better explain to me what's happening here."

He holstered the pistol and stepped forward with his hand outstretched in greeting.

"Permit me to introduce myself formally. I am Field Agent Daiki Chida with the ELAC, the European Looted Art Commission."

"Yeah, I know what it stands for. Want to tell me how you're involved?"

"I have been working on this operation for two years now and we are closer than we have ever been. As you can imagine, I cannot in good conscience allow you to—how do you Americans say it—mess it up?"

As I shook his hand, Aaron walked up behind Agent Chida, his weapon at the ready.

"You can relax, Aaron. This is Agent Chida with the ELAC."

They shook hands.

"So I heard."

Chida said, "Has anyone ever told you that you bear a striking resemblance to that jazz pianist?"

Aaron smiled, "Oh, maybe once or twice."

I asked, "Closer than you've ever been to what?"

His facial expression hardened.

"Closer to bringing to justice the men who control the largest cache of Holocaust art, precious stones and artifacts in the entire world!"

"Is Hayato Momotani one of them?"

He seemed surprised by my knowledge.

"Yes. He is number two."

Aaron said, "And who's number one?"

"We don't know. He only goes by The Persian. Our assumption is that he's highly positioned in the Saudi Sheikdom. Perhaps even at the very top given the amount of authority he has over men such as Momotani."

I cleared my throat.

"Not to be mundane, but where is Gaspard?"

He gestured toward the house.

"He is inside the villa, under the control of my two remaining men. And, for the record, I appreciate you not killing my man a few minutes ago."

"Is he working *for* you or with you?"

"It's complicated. My cover, meticulously constructed over a period of many years, is that I am an enforcer; an assassin; a man who can take care of things that are in need of being taken care of, if that makes sense."

"Perfect," Aaron replied. "So, is Gaspard something that needed taking care of?"

"It was all part of the ruse. As you are no doubt aware, Gaspard Ducharme is one of the most highly respected art brokers in all of Europe. ELAC approached him several years ago about working with them to expose this 'cartel', as you call them. At first he was unwilling, citing concerns for his family's well being among others. But a little over two years ago he agreed and began a relationship with the cartel, working hand-in-hand with them in fencing untold millions of dollars worth of art."

"But something went sideways," I suggested.

"Yes. They somehow learned of his duplicity and contacted me to take care of their...problem."

Aaron asked, "And may we assume that you've taken care of other *problems* for them?"

"As far as they are concerned I have executed many men *and* women on their behalf. What they do not know is that all of these people are either in protective custody or in prison serving sentences for their crimes."

I said, "May we also assume that Gaspard doesn't know that you're one of the good guys?"

He grinned.

"That is a safe assumption. He is terrified of me."

I returned the grin.

"I can see why."

He leveled the gun at us.

"And now, my friends, we must continue the ruse for a

little longer—until Monsieur Ducharme's partner arrives. It is only then that we may spring the trap I have so carefully laid."

I understood the reasoning, but if you want to know the truth...it didn't make me feel any better about having a gun held on me.

"When is he scheduled to arrive?"

Agent Chida checked his watch.

"Approximately thirty minutes from now."

He rattled off a series of commands in Japanese into a radio Velcro'd to his shoulder.

"To maintain appearances, you should probably drop your weapons and raise your hands."

We did as he requested, and without warning he stepped forward and hit me with a very nicely placed left hook that caught me square on the jaw. I am ashamed to say that I hit the ground faster than a halfback diving for a lost fumble! I'll give him one thing—the man can punch. I lay there seeing actual stars swimming around in the periphery of my vision, vaguely aware that others had joined Agent Chida, or whoever the hell he was, and rough hands were jerking me to my feet and securing my wrists behind me. Out of the corner of my one good eye, I saw Aaron starting to resist, only to be subdued by a fierce and knowing look from our friendly captor.

Chida said, hopefully for the benefit of his men, "Take these two downstairs and put them with Monsieur Ducharme. I will attend to poor Willie who they unceremoniously locked in the trunk of the Mercedes."

I allowed myself to be shoved forward, amused by the attempts made by the bad guy assigned Aaron to get him moving. First, he tried shoving him, but given that Aaron had about seventy pounds and eight inches on the man, that didn't work out so well. Plainly said, Aaron just doesn't like being shoved. The poor guy tried again. Same result.

Finally Chida said, "Sir, if you would be so kind as to join us in the house, I would consider it a personal favor."

Aaron grinned and winked at the frustrated bad guy.

"It would be my honor. Now, see? That right there is how you do it."

And with that, we all walked toward the house.

CHAPTER 35

Except for a well-used table and four mismatched chairs in the kitchen, the top floor of the villa seemed devoid of furnishings. Chida's associates led us down a steep set of stairs that terminated in a long, dank hallway with several doorways set along each wall. When we reached the end, my bad guy unlocked a door and shoved me through the opening with more force than was necessary. Aaron's bad guy tried to do the same and only succeeded in making himself look like a fool.

Once we were inside they slammed and locked the door with Aaron's guy muttering under his breath in Japanese.

Gaspard Ducharme looked at us in wide-eyed wonder from across the room.

"Jake. Monsieur Perry. What are you doing here?"

I shambled over to where he sat on an overstuffed love-seat that had seen better days.

"A question I have been asking myself repeatedly over the past few minutes."

"Well?" he prompted.

Aaron and I both laughed.

"We're here to rescue you."

Gaspard glanced at our restraints and smiled ruefully.

"And may I assume that things have not exactly worked out as you first imagined?"

"It's a bit more complicated than that," I replied as Aaron and I found places to sit. "Let's just say that there is more going on here than meets the eye."

He seemed to consider my statement.

"I see. And would you care to enlighten me?"

"Well, it seems that ELAC has not left you here alone."

He seemed shocked by the mention of the organization.

"So, you know about my arrangement with them?"

"They have an agent working undercover for the cartel and he told us about the relationship you've had with them for the past couple of years."

"I apologize for not telling you before, but I was sworn to secrecy. Even Simone does not know." He paused and then said, "You said agent. But, who could it be?"

"The Scarred Man."

His eyes widened in disbelief.

"Oh, bonne mére! This is impossible! This man is a monster! He nearly broke my nose! He is responsible for the deaths of dozens—"

"His name is Daiki Chida. All of the people he has purportedly executed are either in protective custody or in prison. It was all an elaborately crafted and well-executed ruse."

Gaspard seemed unconvinced.

"If this is true..." he paused to spit blood onto the floor. "Then he plays his role quite well."

"Yes. Yes, he does," I agreed while being acutely aware of my throbbing jaw.

"Do you have any proof of his claims?" Gaspard asked.

"No. But the things he said make sense."

"And you are willing to take him at his word?"

Aaron replied, "Look, Gaspard, either the man is a world-class actor and lying through his teeth, or he's telling the truth. It doesn't matter either way to us. We're here to rescue you."

He sputtered, "But your hands are tied and you have no weapons."

"Not gonna be a problem, is it Jake?"

I tested the zip-tie securing my wrists behind me.

"Well, maybe a small problem. But overall, Aaron is right, Gaspard. We are not only on the premises, but in the same room with you."

He indicated his own hands that had been bound with nylon rope.

"And, how do you propose to do this with no hands and no weapons?"

"Well, I'm counting on Chida to be who he says he is, but if he isn't, then we'll go to plan B."

Aaron chuckled.

"There was a plan A?"

"Well, sorta."

Gaspard said, "What did the Scarred Man tell you?"

I moved around in a futile attempt to find a more comfortable position.

"According to Chida, your partner will be here in less than thirty minutes. As soon as he arrives, the trap against the cartel will be sprung."

"What does that mean?"

"I don't know, Gaspard," I replied, suddenly feeling very nervous.

I looked across the room at Aaron with his hands bound behind his back like mine. Did I really trust Chida? Was he really who he claimed to be, or had I just been taken in by a world-class con man?

I suddenly feared the latter.

CHAPTER 36

I stood and made my way over to Aaron, turning so my back was facing him.

"I'm not saying that I've changed my mind about Chida, but just the same..."

"Want me to dig out the emergency blade?"

"Might be prudent."

The tactical trousers I was wearing had a concealed pouch inside the waistband at the small of my back where one could conceal low profile things like credit cards, cash, or in this case a razor-sharp blade constructed out of flexible polymers designed to look like a credit card. There was enough material surrounding the place of concealment that it couldn't be discovered vis-à-vis a cursory pat down. The trousers would have to be removed and gone over meticulously. Even then, discovery was difficult. Because he knew exactly where the knife was concealed, Aaron was able to find the Velcro flap and within seconds had the knife free.

It was a very clever design. You may have even seen a consumer version advertised. The blade of the knife was tucked into the body of the "credit card" and freed by simply turning a small locking screw with your thumbnail. You could then slide the blade forward, fold the angled sides of the card around it to form a handle and presto-change-o, you had a functioning knife.

It wasn't an easy thing to accomplish with one's hands tied behind their back, but Aaron's fingers are nothing if not deft.

"All right," he said. "Hold still. I don't want to add any more scars to your hands."

I spread my hands apart as far as they would go in order to expose the zip-tie and in thirty seconds or so I was free. I took the knife from Aaron and was able to cut through his restraint in one motion and then performed the same operation on Gaspard.

Aaron angled his chin toward the little knife, saying, "That right there is a wonder of technology."

Gaspard rubbed his wrists in an effort to restore circulation.

"Apparently, trust only goes so far, eh Monsieur?"

I replied, "Let's just say that I'm a man who believes in, as we Americans say, 'covering all my bases.'"

"Oui, I understand. But, what do we do now that we are free?"

I sat back down in the chair and motioned for Gaspard and Aaron to do the same.

"There are multiple issues, the most pressing being to disrupt their plans to execute you and your partner. Our lack of weaponry notwithstanding, I feel that we are well on our way to accomplishing that."

Gaspard nodded his head in agreement and asked, "What else?"

"We are dealing with an alliance of men who are not only phenomenally powerful, but also consummately ruthless."

"Without question. It is, in large part, what has made them so wealthy."

Aaron said, "I think what Jake is getting around to is that it won't be enough to simply remove you and your partner from their control."

Gaspard's eyes brightened in understanding.

"But of course...we must strike the head of the snake."

"Which," I said, "in this case means The Persian."

"Yes." After a pause, he continued, "I wish I could help

you, Monsieur. But I have never met these men. I only know them by numbers."

"Can you explain?"

He paused to collect his thoughts and then began, "Two years ago when I agreed to help ELAC shut down this cartel, I let it be known throughout my circles that I was looking for certain, very specific pieces to satisfy the demands of some of my upper echelon clients. For five or six weeks nothing happened and I just went about my normal business. Then a very mysterious man who refused to give his name contacted me. He basically said that he could provide me with pieces not available through normal channels if the price was right and if I proved to be trustworthy.

"I asked for a meeting to discuss it further and he immediately terminated the call. Due to his number being blocked I had no way to call him back. So, I told ELAC about the call and they assured me that he would contact me again. Two days later, he did. This time I played it cool, as you say, and told him that as long as the provenance of the pieces could be verified a meeting would not be necessary. He told me that it would take a few weeks for his people to check me out thoroughly, but a man of my reputation and experience was just the sort of partner his association was seeking.

"Another two weeks passed before further contact. This time it was a different man. When I asked for his name, he only said, 'You may call me number four.' When I asked him to explain, he suggested that people who ask too many questions often miss out on great riches."

I stopped him.

"So, just to clarify...you believe that there are four principles involved in the cartel and that the leader is this Persian guy?"

"That is correct. He is called number one."

Aaron said, "If the Persian is number one, I'm guessing that Momo is number two."

Gaspard frowned.

"Momo?"

"Hayato Momotani," I replied. "The Oyabun, or world leader of the Yakuza."

"Yes, I am certain that is the way it is. As for the other two, I only know them by their accents. I am quite certain that number four is from Russia, or some Slavic nation, and that number three is German."

"So, one man is Persian—which would most likely make him Iranian—one Japanese, a German and a Russian. Interesting spread."

"I have only ever dealt with the German and the Russian, which is another reason I do not trust Chida! But, be that as it may, in my conversations and correspondence with those two I have heard each of them refer to the Persian as number one. Today is the first time I heard anything about this Momotani...number two."

I said, "How were the transactions set up?"

"As with nearly all transactions on this level, it is all electronic. Art provenance is verified; price agreed upon; delivery options discussed and bank routing numbers shared. That is all. No names and no faces, gentlemen...just money. That is all that matters. It is now, has ever been and always shall be, all about the money. He who believes otherwise is either profoundly ignorant or inexpressibly foolish!"

Aaron chuckled.

"Isn't that a bit cynical?"

Gaspard smiled wearily, replying, "Perhaps, Monsieur Perry. But in this world—the world where presidents and heads of state are raised up and then brought low; where decisions are made that affect global economies; where the course of history is literally and subjectively determined in boardrooms—money is the most important thing there is. Nothing is its equal. Even with my fortune, which is relatively small by global standards, I am afforded rights and privileges, not on the basis of my character, wisdom or intelligence, but on the basis of that fortune. It is pathetic and I am sick of men like them...pathetic little men with their large mountains of cash. Oh, they think so highly of themselves! Bastards! They walk vaingloriously through their world trampling people under-foot and ruining lives the way a careless oaf stumbles through a colony of ants leaving devastation in their wake."

I said, "Very eloquent. All the more reason to get to the top and take out the whole organization."

"I agree, Monsieur. What would you have me do?"

I suddenly heard the sound of multiple pairs of feet tramping down the hall.

"I'm not sure yet, but it'd probably be a good idea to come up with something pretty quickly."

CHAPTER 37

I heard a key being inserted into the door lock and whispered, "Put your hands behind you as if they're still restrained and sit down."

When the door opened we were all sitting and pretending to be in the middle of a conversation. The two bad guys who had escorted us entered carrying weapons followed by Willie—the man I had cold-cocked. Willie was giving me the stink eye and none of them appeared to be in a particularly good mood. Willie walked around his two cohorts and stood there glaring at me looking mean and tough. At least I'm pretty sure that's what he was going for, and had it not been for his broken nose, swollen eyes and dried blood crusted around his moustache he probably would've pulled it off. As it was, he merely looked pathetic.

No one spoke, and since I didn't have all night to wait around for something to happen, I decided to, well, stimulate the situation a little.

"I don't think I've ever seen a nose broken that badly, Aaron. Have you?"

Aaron glanced at Willie and winced.

"Damn! That must hurt like a son of a bitch. You think it hurts, Jake?"

"I don't know. Why don't we ask Willie? Hey Willie, does your nose hurt?"

He still didn't say anything so I suggested that Aaron repeat the question in French.

Willie finally exploded, "Enough! I can't wait for you

two to be dead!"

I said, "Why Willie, where are your manners? That's a horrible thing to say to someone. Don't you think it's horrible, Aaron?"

"Boy's about to hurt my feelings."

Willie pulled his weapon and pointed it at my head. In that moment it occurred to me that perhaps I had pushed him too far. Cassie has been cautioning me about that for years, but I just can't help myself. You see the thing is...unless you push someone you never get to see what they're really made of.

Willie walked a few steps toward me.

"Up! Get up!"

"Where are we going?"

He leaned forward slightly, an evil little smile on his swollen face.

"*You* are going to die, and after that," he turned and gestured toward the other two. "*We* are going to go to dinner—a very nice dinner courtesy of the men who hired us to make you go away. Now get on your feet!"

We all stood slowly making sure no one could see our hands. Amazingly, no one checked to see if we were still restrained in spite of the fact that I could see the plastic zip-ties on the floor in front of where Aaron had been sitting.

I faced Willie.

"Now what?"

He stuck the gun in my face and had just started to say something nasty when I took it away from him—my second takeaway of the day. It's not hard if you know what to do and have a combination of technique, speed and a certain level of fearlessness.

Not that I'm suggesting that you try it.

He stared at me; his eyes wide in shock as I put my arm around his throat and stuck the barrel of the gun in his right ear.

His two companions didn't seem to know what to do so I yelled, "Drop your weapons or Willie dies."

They looked at each other. Looked at Willie. Looked at Aaron. Looked at the door behind them as if considering running away.

I pulled the gun from Willie's ear and trained it on Tweedledum and Tweedledee.

"Okay, if you won't drop your weapons to save Willie, how about you drop them to save yourselves. And, by the way...I don't miss."

Apparently they weren't half as tough as they believed because after another few seconds of hesitation they both threw their guns on the floor and bolted from the room.

As Aaron retrieved the guns I said, "Gaspard, may I assume from your impressive armory back at the villa that you know how to handle a firearm?"

"Oui, Monsieur. I am a passably good marksman."

"Good!" I shoved Willie onto the love seat and handed one of the guns to Gaspard. "Where is Chida?"

Willie shook his head in confusion.

"Chida? I know of no such person."

"The Scarred Man?"

"Ah, okay. His name is Chida?" He shrugged. "Regardless of what his name is, I do not know where he is. I assume he is somewhere killing Monsieur Ducharme's partner."

And then he laughed. I leaned forward and backhanded him on the end of his nose. He wailed like he was being disemboweled and fell over on the loveseat clutching his nose and writhing in pain.

Aaron said, "Boy shouldn't have laughed."

"Damn straight! See if you can find something we can use to tie him up."

Aaron grinned and pulled a handful of zip-ties from a pocket in his trousers.

"You mean like these?"

I just shook my head, amazed at the collective ineptitude.

"I can't believe these guys!"

Aaron secured Willie's hands and feet and cut a strip of cloth from his shirt to use as a gag, making sure he could still breathe given the ruined state of his nose.

Gaspard asked, "What do we do now? I am worried about poor Maxim."

"First we have to find out where he is being kept."

Aaron finished securing Willie and made him as comfortable as possible on the love seat, which, given his condition, wasn't very comfortable at all.

He said, "I'm assuming that they found the tactical bags and all our toys."

"That's a fair assumption." I ejected the magazine from Willie's pistol and found it full. "How are you two fixed for ammo? "Aaron and Gaspard checked their respective weapons and found them to be full. "Okay. That means that we have forty-five rounds between us. We'll have to make them count."

Aaron asked, "What are you thinking?"

I glanced at the largest window.

"I'm thinking that we should go pay Chida a visit."

"And are you also thinking that he's dirty?"

"Look...either he is or he isn't, and there isn't a thing I can do about it. So I'm going to do what I have to do in order to make sure Maxim is safe and I'm confident that somewhere along the way we'll find out everything we need to know about agent Chida."

"Heard that."

CHAPTER 38

I said to Aaron, "Keep an eye on the door while I check out the window."

The window in question was framed by a heavy drape and looked out onto a large, flat expanse of patio that featured the pool I had seen earlier. It was indeed empty. Sadly for us, the window was plate glass and, therefore, impossible to open so I abandoned that idea and looked for another way out.

There was none.

"Well, damn!" I said. "Unless we want to bust out that huge window, we're going to have to go back the way we came."

Aaron stuck his head briefly out the door and was met with an immediate burst of gunfire from the opposite end of the hall.

He ducked quickly back inside.

"I guess that answers the question of whether or not they're still here. Got any other ideas?"

I gestured toward the window.

"Given that the fight is apparently already on, I think our best bet is to just go ahead and take out that bad boy."

Gaspard picked up a heavy, iron lampstand.

"Allow me, Monsieur."

It took two swings, but the glass finally yielded under the blows and fell in huge sheets, one of which almost pierced Gaspard's foot.

"You okay?" I asked.

"Oui, Monsieur. I may be old, but I am quick."

I took the lampstand from him and knocked the remaining shards loose from their lodging.

Aaron said, "Pretty sure they heard that."

I stepped through the opening while Aaron kept the doorway covered. Motioning for Gaspard to wait, I listened for any signs of Chida and his boys converging on the patio. And then I realized that if they had Maxim that meant that one of them would be assigned to him, leaving just two to cover both the hallway and all other areas of the house. I was starting to like the odds.

"Come on."

They joined me and I explained the situation as I saw it.

Aaron said, "So, how about if Gaspard and I find Maxim and you go neutralize the other bad guys?"

"Sounds good, but I'm betting that Chida will be with Maxim...so be careful. Gaspard, do you have any knowledge of the layout?"

"I only know that this level is only bedrooms, so I am thinking that he won't be down here. My guess is they will have him either upstairs, or maybe in the building that looks like a barn."

"Okay. I'm going to take out whoever is left here in the main house. You two head for the livestock stalls. If any of the bad guys are there, do *not* engage them until I arrive. Is that clear?"

They both nodded.

"Give me a few seconds to create a diversion and then take off."

Aaron bumped knuckles with me.

"Be careful, bro."

"Always."

I cautiously went back through the window, across the room and stood by the doorway. Glancing at Willie, who looked as if he expected me to kill him at any moment, I picked up a cushion from one of the chairs, tossed it into the hall and waited for the expected gunfire. There was nothing. I decided to risk a peek, so I stuck my head around the corner. Still nothing. Either the guy was being very cagy, or he had been summoned to another area of the house after we broke the window. That had to be it.

I've never been overly cautious. I don't know why, but it's a fact. So, I decided to just bolt into the hall and take whatever came my way.

It was clear.

Fortunately.

I mean I don't have a death wish...at least I don't believe I do.

I moved slowly down the long narrow confines, alert for any threats that might present themselves from behind the closed doors. I made it to the staircase. Now I had a problem. It's one thing to walk down a long hallway. It's another thing entirely to be walking up a staircase facing live fire. I stopped and had a little discussion with myself and my conscience, in the middle of which I could swear I heard Cassie's voice—along with Muriel and Vanessa—telling me that it was a pointless gamble and that I should think more of them than accomplishing what, at the end of the day, was in reality a very arbitrary mission.

Yeah, I told the voices to go away and drew in a deep breath of air before charging up the stairs screaming like a madman.

As it turned out, I was the only one there.

CHAPTER 39

I stood at the top of the stairs and surveyed the immediate area. It looked deserted, but I had to be sure.

After systematically clearing the other rooms on the floor I ended up in the large kitchen whereupon my stomach reminded me that it had been a long time since lunch. Wishing I still had my earcomm, I moved to the outside door and did my best to see through the gloom that filled the space between the main house and the barn. It was impossible! Retracing my steps, I wound up at the front entrance where I opened the door slowly and stepped onto the front landing. I started thinking that since these guys were demonstrably inept, there was a possibility they hadn't taken the time to check Aaron's original position. And if that were true, his tactical bag would still be there.

Drawing another big breath, I dashed across the front drive fully expecting to be lit up by incoming fire. Instead there was just silence. Harsh, deafening silence. I leapt the low wall without breaking stride and charged headlong toward the pump house.

The bag was there.

The cats were sitting on it.

I shooed them away with difficulty and inventoried the contents. There were six flashbangs, each capable of delivering a burst of light and sound in excess of 170db; a backup Sig Sauer P229 pistol and, most importantly, the Standard DP-12 tactical 12-gauge shotgun with four extra mags. I immediately swapped Willie's Savage Arms 9mm for the 12-gauge and the Sig, loading up with as many magazines as I could carry along with two of the flashbangs.

By this time, I had a fairly high degree of certainty that Chida had concentrated his remaining resources in the barn, so I stood and ran along the tree line with impunity. Given my tactical training, it was a stupid thing to do!

But it worked.

Across the patio I could just make out Aaron and Gaspard where they crouched in the shadow of the livestock stalls, which presented an immediate challenge: how do I reach them without exposing myself to the highly motivated men in the barn who were no doubt just waiting for someone to do something reckless?

Once again, my impatience got the best of me. I stood and raced across the patio as a line of lead stitched its way toward my back. Fortunately, I was just a little faster than the shooter's reactions. And in my line of work, "just a little faster" is all it takes.

As I dove behind Aaron, he said wryly, "So much for sneaking up on them."

"Stealth is highly overrated."

"Do tell. What we gonna do next, march boldly in rank and file and hope they drop dead from sheer terror?"

"You're hilarious, you know that?"

Aaron noticed my enhanced firepower.

"I see you found my bag. You bring me anything?"

I handed over the P229 and extra mag's.

"If your guy's nine was of a similar quality to Willie's, you might find this useful."

"Yeah, man," he replied, drawing out the *yeah*. "Now that's what I'm talking about right there. Just the same, I'm holding on to his little POS."

Gaspard frowned.

"POS?"

"Piece of shit."

"You Americans and your colloquialisms."

"Just tryna keep it real, brother."

I edged in front of Aaron and peeked around the corner of the stall only to be rewarded by a burst of fire from the barn that sent chips of wood flying, one of which barely missed my left eye.

I said, "Apparently they have night vision."

"Yeah," Aaron replied gesturing toward the 12-gauge. "We should trade. You take the Sig and give me the DP. That way you can lay down covering fire while I try to get around behind them."

"Okay, but even if you manage to do that, what makes you think that one of the bad guys won't be guarding the back?"

"Remember...there are only three of them."

"How do you know that?" Gaspard asked. "Someone had to bring Maxim."

Do you ever have moments when you feel just plain stupid? I had totally forgotten about how Maxim had arrived on the property. There had to have been at least two guys who accompanied him. Maybe more. That seriously complicated our situation.

I said, "Okay, so maybe doing an end run isn't as smart as I thought it was a few minutes ago."

"You got that right!" Aaron agreed.

"However, these guys have verified conclusively that they aren't exactly tactical masterminds."

"No, they are not. So?"

"So, I'm thinking that while Chida might be a very successful assassin, he doesn't know jack about deployment."

Aaron considered this for a few seconds.

"You thinking he's keeping everyone together over there except for the dude with the night scope?"

"It's a distinct possibility."

"And is it fair to assume that in your mind there's only one way to find out?"

"That would be a fair assumption."

Aaron blew out a long breath of air, "So we're back to what we were planning a few minutes ago?"

"Seems like it."

Gaspard said, "Messieurs, I want to help rescue my friend. Just tell me what to do. I am not a coward."

"I know, Gaspard," I replied. "But this is highly specialized stuff we're dealing with here. Bravery counts for a lot, but it can't replace training."

"But what about Monsieur Perry? He is a jazz pianist. What training does he have?"

Aaron said, "For one thing, I'm a former Marine. Besides that, I've been on dozens of cases with Jake. I know what I'm doing."

Gaspard smiled.

"And I, Monsieur, am a former member of the Armée de Terre. I too have training. So, please...allow me to help. Give me one of the pistols and extra ammo. I can cover you from here while at the same time staying out of harm's way."

Aaron turned his head slowly to look at me.

"He's got a point, Jake. And as much as I don't like leaving him here, where else could he go that would be safer than staying here with that Sig in his hands?"

I took the .357 from Aaron and tossed it to Gaspard.

"Show me that you know what you're doing."

He caught it and smiled.

"You seem to forget whose arsenal you raided to get this pistol and all of the other tactical gear you brought with you."

He then expertly and smoothly flowed through a series of actions that only a trained tactician would know how to perform.

That was two times in the space of five minutes! I guess Forrest Gump was right. Stupid, most definitely, *is* as stupid does.

Aaron raised his eyebrows, "Works for me."

CHAPTER 40

Aaron and I left Gaspard in place while we skirted the livestock stables and moved toward the opposite end of the barn. Once there, we took a minute to catch our breath and prepare for the ragtag plan of attack we had formulated. It wasn't much, but we had to do something.

I said, "You ready?"

Aaron nodded his ascent.

On a prearranged signal, we broke cover and raced toward the structure while Gaspard poured a constant stream of fire toward where we had seen the shooter. Once we were in position, Gaspard stopped firing and a deadly calm settled over the area prompting me to wonder what the neighbors must be thinking.

We leaned with our backs against the outer wall of the old structure and heard voices raised in argument coming from inside.

"Can you make out what they're saying?" I whispered.

Aaron put his ear against the wall.

"I hear Chida. He seems to be arguing with two other men...sounds like they have French accents. They're saying something about...how if he would've listened to them there wouldn't be people shooting at them."

"That doesn't exactly sound like trained operatives, which I find very puzzling. I mean wouldn't you expect a cartel as substantial as this one to be able to hire the best?"

Aaron was silent for a few seconds.

"Yeah, but on the other hand...maybe Chida *is* really who he says he is and he hired a bunch of jokers just to give the appearance of compliance."

"Now that's something I hadn't considered."

"And?" he prompted.

"It's definitely a possibility. But if he really *is* one of the good guys, then we can't exactly go in there with guns blazing and run the risk of him being injured or killed in the shoot-out!"

Aaron mused, "I suppose we could just ask them all to surrender, seeing's how we have them surrounded."

"We could, although the likelihood of them being amenable to that suggestion is way down on the list of probabilities."

"True, true."

"Can you tell how far away they are?"

He put his ear to the wall again.

"They sound fairly close."

"Anything happening?"

He listened for a minute.

"Uh-oh. Chida just threatened to shoot one guy where he stands."

"Can you tell how many men there are besides Chida?"

"Hang on." He listened intently for a few seconds. "I'm hearing three distinct voices not counting Chida."

"Makes sense. If one guy is up front trading fire with Gaspard and two guys brought Maxim, that leaves Chida and one of our friends from the house."

Aaron said, "Hang on. Sounds like there's a scuffle."

"Well, now's as good a time as any to do this!"

I stood and ran around the end of the barn, kicking in the first door I saw. It was so old that the poor thing flew off its hinges and caught a guy in the back of the head before he could even turn around. I quickly took in the situation and saw Chida actively engaged in a fight with two men who seemed intent on doing him great bodily harm. While Aaron held a gun on the man that had been flattened by the flying door, I fired two rounds into the ceiling and pointed the shotgun at the other three who immediately stopped fighting. Chida's two assailants were, well, beat to shit while he looked as if he had just been out for a run.

CHAPTER 41

Chida smiled and walked slowly toward me.

"Good timing, my friend."

"Yeah, it sounded as if things were going sideways."

He rubbed his raw knuckles.

"Nothing that I couldn't ultimately manage, but thanks just the same."

I ordered the two men onto the ground and asked, "What about the guy up front—the one with the rifle?"

Chida said, "He was told to not leave his post regardless of what he heard transpiring in here. Give me two minutes."

With that he walked quickly into the semi-darkness toward the front of the barn.

"Aaron, why don't you make our guests a little more uncomfortable and get them trussed up?"

"Be my pleasure."

I covered the three men as he grouped them together in the center of the room, sat them down and zip-tied all of their hands together so that no one could stand unless the other two stood with him.

I said, "Where is Maxim Fournier?"

Before any of them could answer, I heard groaning coming from behind a stack of wood pallets. When I went to investigate I saw a small man lying on the ground. He had been hogtied with his feet pulled up behind him and tied to his hands. The knots looked as if they were cruelly tight. He appeared to be in his fifties with thinning brown hair and a fine featured face that had been beaten so badly his features were misshapen. The damage included at least two of his front teeth knocked out; his nose horribly broken along with his jaw; severe swelling behind his left ear; both eyes swollen shut and a copious amount of blood staining all of his clothing. Someone had really done a number on him. I wondered if that hadn't been what started the argument.

Kneeling down I cut his bonds loose and whispered, "Maxim, I am Jake Moriarity—a friend of Gaspard's. We're going to take you out of here and get you some medical attention. It's over. You're going to be okay now."

His breathing seemed to be severely restricted, but he managed to mutter, "Merci, merci," through split lips.

Chida came back with the other man walking in front of him at gunpoint.

He said, "Gaspard should be joining us at any moment. Perhaps you can do with this one as you did with the others?"

"Not a problem," Aaron replied. "Always room for one more."

It was the man who had escorted Aaron to the holding room. I have no idea why he thought it was a good idea, but he suddenly lunged toward Aaron intending, no doubt, to surprise him and possibly land a lucky punch, or something...maybe take some revenge for Aaron having embarrassed him earlier. But Aaron caught him in mid-lunge, picked him up and somehow flipped him in the air slamming him on his back onto the hard-packed earth. All the air was forced out of him in a loud, "Whoosh!" and the poor guy lay there jerking spasmodically trying to force air back into his deflated lungs. If you've ever had the wind knocked out of you, you know what I'm talking about.

While Aaron tied his guy to the others I pointed toward Maxim.

"He's in bad shape. We've got to get him to a hospital."

Chida agreed as Gaspard entered, his gun at the ready. Seeing the four men bound together on the floor and me talking to Chida, he lowered his weapon.

I pointed toward the pallets.

"Maxim is behind there. Someone nearly beat him to death."

Gaspard hurried over to his friend and knelt beside him, speaking rapidly and passionately in French.

I said, "So, how are you going to play this with your bosses?"

Chida grinned and replied, "They trust me completely and have no reason to suspect that anything is wrong. As far as they are concerned, Gaspard Ducharme and Maxim Fournier are no more."

"But what about Julien and the others? Isn't' there a possibility that they will try to contact—"

"I am the one who hired all of them. They know nothing of what has transpired here, nor shall they. They have no reason to call anyone even if they could."

"But we sent Julien to the hospital with them. Won't he —"

"Julien works for me."

"Right, but so do all the others."

"No, my friend, you do not understand. Julien works for *me*. He is one of us. Besides, Philippe, Étienne and the others have no idea how to contact anyone except me, and Julien will make sure they do not make it back to Gaspard's jet."

I smiled and nodded.

"Very impressive. So, what now? My responsibility was to rescue Gaspard, so technically I'm done. But if you could use some help, well..."

Gaspard stood quickly and shouted, "Bonne mere! He has stopped breathing! Maxim has stopped breathing!"

CHAPTER 42

I hurried over and knelt by Maxim's motionless form feeling for a pulse. It was there, but only just. Given the difficulty he was having with his breathing, I suspected that his airway was clogged.

I flipped him over onto his back.

"Chida, I need my tactical bag."

He rushed over to a makeshift table, pulled my bag from underneath and tossed it to me. Extracting a small medical kit I sorted through it until I found the alcohol swabs, X-acto knife, a plastic straw and a couple of fentanyl "lollipops" for pain control. Swabbing the area directly below the Adam's apple, I cut through the cricoid cartilage and inserted a straw into the airway. After a couple of pumps on his chest he started breathing again. Opening his mouth, I tore the protective coating off the fentanyl and shoved it between his cheek and gums.

Swabbing the blood from around the wound, I taped the straw in place surrounding it with heavy gauze.

"He should be stabilized now and that fentanyl will kick in shortly. But we need to get him medical attention ASAP."

Aaron said, "What about our friends here and the dude in the house?"

"We'll come back for them later."

The four men on the ground all started protesting loudly and simultaneously causing Chida to put a boot to the jaw of the man closest to him.

"It is you who caused this man's injury! Be thankful I do

not kill you all!"

The blow rendered the man unconscious, which seemed to make the others reconsider their protestations.

Aaron and I picked Maxim up carefully and carried him through the barn and across the patio with Chida and Gaspard clearing the way in front of us so we didn't lose our footing. There was a stairway at the side of the house that led to the perimeter balcony, but besides being ridiculously narrow, age and lack of proper maintenance had left it unstable. Under the best of circumstances it would have been a challenge for either Aaron or I to ascend. But tasked with carrying a severely injured man, it was nearly impossible.

Given that we had no other options, I waved Aaron off and shouldered Maxim in a classic fireman's carry, feeling the staircase shudder with every step.

"I know this hurts, Maxim, but I have to do it. I am sorry."

It seemed to take an eternity, but I eventually cleared the final step and made my way across the balcony and onto the front drive where I saw a Range Rover that hadn't been there before. It would make transporting Maxim much simpler.

Chida opened the hatch, cleared a few things out of the way and lowered one of the rear seats to provide an area where Maxim could recline. Between Aaron and I we managed to get him into the vehicle with a minimum amount of further trauma.

I rolled up a coat and eased it under Maxim's head.

"Gaspard, go with Chida to the hospital. Aaron and I will be right behind you. Daiki, do you have the keys for the Mercedes?"

He reached into the pocket of his coat and tossed me the keys, saying, "It is not far."

Aaron said, "Maybe Julien and the gang are still there."

"Probably are," I agreed. "We'll deal with that when we get there. Let's roll!"

Chida took off like a driver in the *Grand Prix de Monaco* and I had to hustle to keep up. Once we were off the dusty driveway and on the main road, I called Cassie so I could bring the girls up to speed while we drove.

"Uncle!" she said breathlessly as she answered my call.

I put the call on speaker so Aaron could hear.

"How you doing, little girl?"

"First of all, are you okay?"

"We're fine."

"We're both fine," Aaron added.

"Then I'm doing good. What about Gaspard?"

"We have him *and* his partner and we're on the way to the hospital."

"Why? Are you or Aaron hurt?"

"No. But Maxim, Gaspard's partner, is in pretty bad shape. It seems someone tried to beat him to death and nearly succeeded." I paused and then asked, "How about you? I hear you had some excitement."

"We did. These guys—I assume they were from the same group who kidnapped Gaspard—surprised us while we were just sitting around talking. Fortunately, Rémi never took his eyes off of that bank of video monitors and was able to see them when their car first arrived."

"But…you didn't have to shoot anyone?"

"No, thank God! Rémi, though. Wow! He was amazing."

"Yeah, that's what Muriel told Aaron."

"He had the three of us go into the safe room with the household staff and seal it behind us. Then he just sort of sat back and waited for the bad guys to show up. After that it almost wasn't fair."

Aaron said, "That good, huh?"

"Seriously! He told us that he was Gaspard's personal bodyguard for years, but from what we saw, he's more like a high level commando, or something! We watched the whole thing on the monitors. It was like watching a James Bond movie. It was almost as if he had the whole thing choreographed ahead of time, you know, and lured them one by one into certain areas of the house and then ambushed them."

Aaron grinned widely.

"Boy's just full of surprises."

Cassie said, "So, what happens now? I assume these guys won't just go away even though you managed to rescue Gaspard."

"No, they won't," I answered. "It's kind of a complicated story, but there's a lot to be done. My plan as of now is to wrap things up here and have Gaspard's jet take us back to Nice—hopefully later tonight."

She sighed.

"It's been a long day, hasn't it?"

"Yes...yes it has. So, I'll call you as soon as we have some sort of schedule."

"Okay."

"By the way...did you hear from Michael?"

"I did. I told him things were a bit tense here and if he could delay his arrival it would probably be for the best."

"And?" Aaron prompted.

"Nothing doing! He wants to be with me regardless of what's happening."

"He's a keeper."

"I agree completely."

I said, "Okay, little girl. I love you."

"Love you more."

Aaron said, "What about me?"

She laughed.

"Oh, shut it, Aaron! You know I love you."

"Man just likes to hear it."

"Goodbye, Aaron."

"Bye, sis."

As I terminated the call we came around a corner and I

could see a sign up ahead in Catalan that read: *Hospital Universitari Joan XXIII de Tarragona Urgències* 1 km.

Aaron cleared his throat.

"Question."

"Yes?"

"So now that we know Gaspard's, well, secret, and are relatively certain that Chida is for real...you got any ideas on how we go about shutting down this cartel?"

"You mean besides my hope that Chida and the ELAC will take the lead and we will simply be there to provide support?"

"Uh-huh."

"None whatsoever!"

"That's what I was afraid of."

"Yeah...I know."

He sighed, "Might be wise to come up with a contingency plan."

"Such as?"

"Well...if what Chida says is true, and the cartel in fact believes that Gaspard and Maxim are dead, then his cover is still intact and at some point he will have to report in."

"I like it. Maybe he asks for a meeting, you know, to...to...what?"

Aaron picked it up.

"To..." he thought for a few seconds and then snapped his fingers. "To tell them something he got out of Gaspard and Maxim before they died that he only feels comfortable delivering face to face."

I said, "That just might work."

"Be worth a shot."

CHAPTER 43

The hospital came into view—a multi-floored, white building with more windows than I had ever seen. There was also a bas-relief sculpture on the top floor that, while no doubt having deep meaning for the locals, was of no artistic interest to me given the urgency of the moment.

Chida pulled around into the emergency entrance, while Aaron and I parked the Mercedes in the closest spot we could find, which, as it turned out, was about two blocks away. After locking the car and tossing the shotgun and tactical bags into the trunk, we concealed our weapons and jogged down the sidewalk toward the entrance. Once inside we followed the signs in Catalan for *'Urgències'* and eventually came to a waiting room filled with sick and injured people of all shapes, sizes and age groups. Across the room I spotted Chida and Gaspard engaged in an intense conversation with a severe, forty-something woman in a formal business suit.

Actually, they were *attempting* to speak to her, which was proving to be quite difficult. You see, in Catalonia, the region of Spain covering approximately twelve thousand square miles in the upper westernmost corner of the country (and home to nearly eight million souls), the "indigenous people", i.e. the Catalans, are fiercely independent. It is, therefore, a near dead certainty that you will encounter individuals—such as this triage administrator—who patently refuse to soil their tongue on such an inferior language as Castellano, or Castilian Spanish.

As we walked up, Gaspard turned toward us with an exasperated expression on his face.

He said, "This...this...*person* will not speak with me in Spanish."

Aaron stepped forward and said pleasantly, "Bon dia."

The woman smiled and began speaking in rapid-fire Catalan, which, to be honest, sounded to my ears like, "La-la-la-la-la-la-la-la-la," and so forth. Once again Aaron had surprised and impressed me.

After several minutes of conversation he turned back toward us and explained, "She says that they are happy to treat our friend, but that they will require payment in advance in order to do so."

Gaspard replied, "But, what about my EU health card?"

Aaron relayed the question.

"She says that Spain does not honor it, and that you will still have to pay in cash and recoup the expenses from your travel insurance."

Gaspard swore in French and stomped around gesticulating.

"These stupid Spaniards! What is the point of the EU if they act in such an irresponsible manner?" After a few more curses—during which time the administrator stood there, completely stoic—he relented. "All right! It will be no problem. Please tell her."

Aaron relayed Gaspard's request and then listened to her reply.

"Okay, so, she says that payment is not only required in full, but in cash."

Gaspard grabbed his head and walked a few paces away sputtering in French.

"But...this is ridiculous! Inhumane. My friend is dying! Have they no heart?"

Aaron raised his eyebrows.

"Apparently 'heart' is way down the list from policies and practices. So, what are we gonna do?"

Gaspard snapped his fingers.

"The jet! I have a reserve of Euro's on the jet."

I dug my cell phone out, found Désirée's number and called.

She answered, "Monsieur Jake. Please tell me that Monsieur Gaspard is all right."

"He's fine, but we have a situation."

"Okay. Please explain."

"Do you know where Gaspard keeps his reserve cash?"

"Oui, Monsieur. But—"

"It's a long story, but I need to come and get it and we need to have the plane prepped to fly back to Nice tonight. Can you do that?"

She hesitated only slightly and then replied with some authority, "Everything will be ready when you need it, Monsieur."

"Okay. I will be there in about twenty minutes."

I disconnected the call without waiting for her reply.

"Désirée will have the cash ready for me as soon as I can get there. How much will we need?"

"All of it!" Gaspard replied without hesitation.

"But we need to fly back to Nice tonight. How about fees for prepping the plane, fuel, etc.?"

He frowned.

"Ah, yes. But of course. Tell her to hold back five thousand Euro's and to give you the rest."

Aaron brought the administrator up to speed on what was happening, and she agreed to begin treatment.

After he finished with her, I pulled him aside.

"Can you manage things here while I go get the money?"

"Of course. Get going."

I slapped his meaty back and jogged through the entrance and down the sidewalk while working my way mentally through the events that had just transpired. Everything seemed to be in order and I should have been pleased, but I wasn't. Something was off. But, what?

I had just maneuvered out of the parking area and was heading for the airport when my phone buzzed signaling an incoming text.

It was Gabi.

CHAPTER 44

*H*i, Jake! It's probably a bad time to talk...nothing unusual there with you, LOL! Anyway, it's been a while and I was just thinking of you. Hope you are well. Maybe I'll hear from you sometime this century.

After the woman who apparently lives in my phone finished reading the text to me, I was finally forced to admit that I liked Gabi.

I liked her a lot! And it didn't matter that she was three years older than me.

Gabi was actually the first woman that had managed to stir more than a cursory interest in the fairer sex since the death of my wife, Abby nearly twenty years ago. Everyone kept telling me that it was time to move on. Had, in fact, been telling me the same thing for years now. I suppose I was beginning to listen.

I engaged the voice to text feature and said, *Gabi, good to hear from you. I'm right in the middle of something and can't talk. It's seriously life and death. But I promise...I'll call soon.*

The oh-so-friendly voice read my text back to me and asked if I would like to I send it, to which I replied in the affirmative.

Gabi's reply back was swift.

Wow! You texted back. I'm not sure I can adequately respond due to feeling so faint. LOL! Okay, I understand. Sorta wishing you had a normal job. Then again, I probably wouldn't like you as much as I do. (She inserted a smiley-face emoticon) *Be well, Jake. Las Vegas misses you. I miss you!* (This time she inserted a heart-eyed emoticon)

As I listened to her text being read, it occurred to me that one of the things that had enhanced my effectivity over the years had been my ability to abstain from romantic entanglements—entanglements that compromised literally every facet of one's decision making process while at the same time delivering little more than dubious emotional satisfaction.

Cynical? No, practical.

Or at least that's what I told myself during those all too regular long and lonely nights when I couldn't sleep and desperately longed for someone I could just hold on to.

That's what I missed the most about my Abby. The way we could just hold each other during the hard times, knowing that what we had was so special that nothing could ever beat us.

That is until the pancreatic cancer diagnosis.

The cancer beat us...beat us all the way down and took her life. And I have never been the same. It also beat out any sense of, as the evangelicals are fond of saying, "relationship" with God. Actually, that wasn't completely true. I *had* a relationship with God. He was there and I was here and as nearly as I could ascertain we didn't much like each other. Aaron, on the other hand, has a very robust faith, which, to be honest, I don't begrudge him in the slightest. Basically, you do what you need to do to get through the day, the weeks...the years. And if faith did that for him, so be it. Fact is...I envy him.

The airport came into view and I turned my thoughts back to the issue at hand. I pulled up to the terminal, parked and trotted toward the entrance colliding with Désirée in the process. She had been coming out to greet me and wound up in my arms as I held on to keep her from falling.

She stood and smoothed her clothes and patted her hair.

"Well, I can't say that I hadn't hoped to be in your arms at some point, but that wasn't exactly what I had in mind."

It was awkward.

"Yes, well..." I muttered, attempting to extricate myself from the situation. "I...so, do you have the cash?"

She smiled.

"I do. It is on the plane. If you will please follow me." She turned and started to go, but stopped and linked her arm through mine. "Perhaps if I hold onto you we can avoid another collision."

I laughed nervously.

"Do I appear to be that helpless?"

"All men are helpless, Monsieur. Didn't you know that?"

We walked the rest of the way in silence and once onboard the plane she became all business.

"Okay," she said, while opening what appeared to be a substantially armored briefcase. "Here is Monsieur Ducharme's cash reserve in the sum of fifty thousand Euro's. I counted it."

"Thank you! Gaspard said to keep five thousand back for expenses required to get the plane ready to fly and for me to bring the rest."

"Of course. We will be ready to go whenever you return." She paused and then added, "And am I to assume that I will be needed to serve as pilot?"

I hadn't thought of that.

"Yes, now that you mention it, that would be a fair assumption. Are you okay with that?"

"Oui, Monsieur. I will look forward to the challenge."

"Okay. Well, I should be going."

I started to leave, but she placed a hand lightly on my arm.

"Jake...I feel like I made you uncomfortable earlier. Please forgive me. It's just...well, I feel an attraction toward you. Perhaps it has to do with the events of today and the intense emotions they stirred up." She giggled girlishly. "Listen to me...babbling on like a...a...écolière...umm, a schoolgirl."

"No, it's all right. Life and death situations can have strange effects on people."

She suddenly leaned in and kissed me full on the lips.

Stepping back she looked me in the eye.

"I would never have been able to live with myself if I hadn't done that. I hope it was okay."

And was it? Was it okay? And if it was, then why was I wondering how Gabi would feel if she knew another woman had just kissed me? And what did it matter what she would think?

Apparently it mattered more than I was prepared to admit.

"Look, Désirée, I'd be lying if I said that it wasn't enjoyable, even though my efforts to return the kiss were clumsy at best."

She dropped her eyes shyly.

"Perhaps you just need a little more practice?"

"While I'm sure that's true, this probably isn't the time or place." After a brief pause I said, "I will see you later, Désirée."

"Au revoir, Jake."

I turned and hurried down the AirStairs, my mind filled with possibilities for the future. I couldn't remember the last time I had actually looked forward to the future, instead of simply resigning myself to the fact that it was coming whether I liked it or not.

It felt nice.

CHAPTER 45

Back in Las Vegas, Gabriella Marcus stared at her cell phone as if willing something more to appear other than her home screen and the face of her cat, Felix. She judged, and rightly so, that it was the way her encounters with Jake Moriarity always left her feeling—the "waiting and wanting for more" thing. But, he was who he was and she liked him for it.

With one last hopeful glance at the phone, she tossed it lightly onto the sofa table on her way to the kitchen where she had been preparing an early lunch.

Why had she texted him? Why indeed! It was the same reason that had been driving her for several months now. She loved him. Was, in fact, *in* love with him, a disturbing reality if one were to effectively play the dating game. She had learned long ago that in relationships the one to whom it meant the least was the one who held all the power. And at this point, anyway, whatever relationship they had definitely mattered far, far less to Jake than it did to her.

Catching a partially distorted reflection of herself in the glass of the pantry door, she stopped for a review. "Dusky" had been how one former lover had described her looks. With her olive complexion and dark hair she could see why. At forty-six she knew that her years of being "stunning" were most likely long past. She could still turn heads when she walked into a room....but could she turn Jake's?

She fought the urge to pick up her phone and check just one more time to see if Jake had sent a new text—a battle that was lost as she hurried through the kitchen and back into the living room to fetch damn thing.

Nothing!

Just as she had feared.

But what did she expect, anyway? It wasn't like he was just down the street and could pop in to her condo for afternoon tea. He was in France, doing God only knew what with some little French floozy! No, that wasn't like him. Look how long it had taken her to even get him to return a glance at the gym.

She laughed at the memory.

It had been a Saturday about eight months before when she had finally managed to get his attention at the gym where they both worked out. She had worn something eye-catching that morning—something her very straight-laced mother would have deemed "scandalous." It was nothing of the sort, but it did show off a girl's charms.

She had been just about to start the second set on a machine designed to tighten the glutes that she had dubbed the "butt blaster" when she sensed a presence. When she turned around, Jake had been standing there smiling.

"So," he had said a bit stiffly. "You been working out long?"

Him just showing up out of nowhere like that had caught her completely off-guard, and she answered a bit breathlessly, "Long enough. Why do you ask?"

"Oh, I don't know," he had said quietly. "I guess it's because you really have great form."

Did that mean he had been watching?

"Really? You think so?"

"Sure. I mean most women who join this club aren't usually interested in actually working out. They're mainly here to be seen. But you're different. You seem to be genuinely interested in the exercise."

"Oh, I am. It's why I drag myself out of bed this early

every morning, six days a week. The war against entropy, you know. It's a fight to the finish, and I'm going to win."

"Well, good for you, ah…I'm sorry, I don't know your name."

"Oh, it's Gabriella—Gabriella Marcus, but my friends call me Gabi."

He had shaken her hand in a grip that was at once both firm and gentle.

"Jake Moriarity. Pleased to meet you…Gabi."

She pondered letting him know that he had been on her radar. But would that be creepy, like she'd been stalking him or something?

"I've seen you around, Jake. In fact, didn't you use to work out over at T.J.'s?"

"As a matter of fact, I did. Were you a member there?"

Oops! Nowhere to hide now.

"Not exactly. I came in a few times on a guest pass from one of my friends."

He seemed to grow suddenly suspicious.

"So, how did you know I used to work out there?"

"I saw you, of course."

"Wait a second, you saw me a couple of times and re-membered?"

She remembered blushing profoundly.

"Okay. You're on to me. Listen, my girlfriend told me to be on the lookout for you—she had a mad crush on you for a while. Besides…you're not exactly easy to forget, Jake."

He laughed. She really loved the sound of that laugh.

"I hope that's a compliment."

"Oh, trust me, it is."

"Well, what a nice thing to say. Thank you."

She could sense that he was about to walk away and de-cided to go for broke.

"I was beginning to think you'd never talk to me."

"Excuse me?"

"It's true. I was beginning to wonder if you were ever

going to come over and talk to me."

"You wanted me to talk to you?"

"Of course, why wouldn't I? You seem like a really nice guy, and, trust me, nice guys are in very short supply."

She remembered him standing there in a sort of silent contemplation for the longest time. So long, in fact, that it had made her uncomfortable.

Finally, he said, "So, listen, I have to go out of town today, Gabi, but I'd like to continue our conversation when I get back, if that's all right with you."

"I'd like that, Jake. I'd like that a lot."

"All right, then, I'll see you soon."

She remembered standing there not knowing what to do, and then surprised herself by suddenly standing on tiptoes and giving him a quick kiss on the cheek.

"You be careful, Mr. Moriarity. And I will see you when you get back."

"Oh, you can count on it."

And with that, he was gone.

The dates and coffee meet-ups had been few and far between, but when they were together...ah, yes...when they were together, there was a definite something—something unmistakable.

Shoving her phone into the front pocket of her jeans, Gabriella walked lightly back into the kitchen.

Suddenly, she was crying.

Must be a full moon...or something.

CHAPTER 46

I'll be honest with you: I don't like carrying around huge sums of money. It makes me very nervous. I once had to carry thirty thousand dollars cash around the streets of Portland, Oregon for close to three hours. My friend, who had unbelievably requested that I perform the ridiculous act, had gotten the cash from a huge stash he kept in safety deposit boxes at his bank—like five hundred thousand huge! The money was for a mutual friend who needed a quick loan to do something or other that I can't quite recall. But after getting the money, my buddy remembered a doctor's appointment he simply *had* to keep.

He didn't even have a briefcase!

The cash was crammed into a large, white bag that basically said, "Hey! Here's lots of money. Come and rob me!"

So I took the cash out of the bag and stuffed it into various pockets and, well, wherever else I could stuff it.

Let's just say that I'm fairly certain that the end recipient would've been shocked and appalled had they known where some of that money had been.

I must've walked five miles going up and down the streets of downtown Portland while I was waiting for him. Every second person I saw looked like a potential mugger!

It was awful!

I had driven about a mile from the airport when it suddenly occurred to me that if Désirée knew of Gaspard's cash reserve on the plane, someone else had to know about it as well. Which made me question my decision to leave her behind.

I pulled off to the side of the road and called her.

She answered breathlessly on the third ring.

"Jake? Are you okay? Is there anything wrong?"

"I'm fine. Listen, I was just thinking that if *you* knew about the money on the plane...who else knew about it?"

She was very measured in her response.

"I see your concern...let me think: Philippe knew, and I am sure that Alex, the late First Officer knew. Étienne...I don't know." Her voice was suddenly filled with concern. "Do you think there is a problem?"

"With everything that has gone on today, nothing would surprise me. I'm thinking that I should come back and get you."

"Do you really think that is necessary?"

"I don't know that it is and I don't know that it isn't. I'd just feel better if you were with us. I mean we know for sure that Philippe and Étienne are working for the bad guys, so it's not much of a stretch to think that they informed their handler of the existence of the cash. Fifty thousand Euro's is not an inconsequential amount of money and if someone knows it's there, I can't see them just leaving it behind."

She was silent for a couple of seconds before saying, "No, I think you should continue to the hospital. I am on the plane with the cabin door locked. In order to get inside someone would have to blow a hole in the fuselage. Even then, if they tried to come inside I would shoot them."

"Well, I still don't like it."

She laughed softly, "I will be perfectly safe here. Now go...go and see to it that Monsieur Ducharme is okay."

I reluctantly terminated the call and pulled back into traffic.

Well, "pulled back into traffic" may be a little too polite.

Probably, "I jetted into traffic like a maniac" would be a more apt description. If having all the cash with me had lent a sense of urgency to my pace, knowing that Désirée may be at risk, increased it tenfold. So I may have broken a few traffic laws getting back to the hospital.

Okay...more than a few.

But, I made it back without incident and handed the money off to Gaspard who then paid the pesky, pecuniary administrator sufficient funds to ensure that Maxim received everything he needed in the form of treatment.

I left Aaron and Gaspard, who were discussing the treatment protocol with the doctor in residence, and took Chida with me to track down Julien and the others.

As it turned out, the man I had been forced to shoot was in the best shape of the three. It seemed that Étienne and Philippe *were*, in fact, suffering from poisoning, but it wasn't from carbon monoxide. And while the hospital staff weren't prepared to say for sure, early speculation was running three to one that the poison was something called methyl bromide, a sophisticated neurotoxin produced naturally and in great quantities by certain marine animals. As to how they could have come into contact with such a toxic substance, no one knew for sure. It could have been concealed in food, inhaled through an aerosol or even absorbed through the skin.

And how had it been introduced to them?

It was a question that assaulted my imagination. I thought through the timeline, and the only place they had all been together had been on the plane. *I* didn't give it to them and Aaron *certainly* didn't give it to them.

Which left Désirée.

There was no other explanation.

Well, that sucked!

The bottom line was that they were in pretty rough shape and likely to stay that way for quite some time. However, on the off chance that they made a miraculous recovery, we left Julien behind to keep an eye on things.

By the time we got back to the ER lobby, Aaron and Gaspard were ready to go.

I said, "Are you sure you feel okay about leaving Maxim

behind, Gaspard?"

"Oui, Monsieur. I have made arrangements for his wife and eldest son to fly here to be with him. The Gestapo-like tactics of the administrator notwithstanding, I feel that he is in good hands."

"So, what now?" Aaron asked.

I replied, "We fly back to Nice and then regroup at the villa to sort out a plan of attack."

"To take down the cartel?"

"Absolutely!"

Chida said, "I can help you with that. I know the organization from the inside out."

"Everything but The Persian's real name," I said.

"I may not know his name," he replied with a smile. "But I know how to find him."

"How's that?"

"One of our friends you left tied up in the orchard...he knows."

"Then we should look in on him on our way to the airport."

"I agree. But when we get there, I will go see him by myself and find out everything we need to know."

"Why by yourself?" Gaspard asked suspiciously.

Chida's eyes grew cold.

"Because...what I am prepared to do to him if he will not talk is something a civilized person such as yourself should not have to witness."

Gaspard glanced at me and then nodded his head sharply.

"It will be as Jake says."

There were really no other viable options.

"Daiki is right. The men already fear him, so information may be gotten simply on that basis without the need for, shall we say, enhanced interrogation techniques."

CHAPTER 47

Turns out that I was right.

About the men fearing Chida, that is. If you want to know the truth, they were terrified of the man.

We drove back to the orchard where Aaron and I had left the men tied up and turned onto the old, rutted lane where I parked the car far enough in as to be invisible from the road.

While Aaron and Gaspard stayed with the car, Chida and I exited and walked a few feet away.

He looked into my eyes for a few seconds before saying, "I know you are a hard man, Moriarity, and used to conducting interrogations. So, if you wish to accompany me I would welcome your presence."

"Okay. But I'll just be there for backup. It's your show."

"Very good. Now, if you will show me where the men are tied up we can get started."

I agreed and began walking toward the tree, which was about a hundred feet from where we stood.

When the tree came into view it was obvious that the two men had been busy trying to escape and had managed to maneuver themselves around the trunk of the tree and were now on opposite sides from where I had left them. Had it not been for low branches, I am sure they could have eventually stood. As it was they were both in a crouch with their feet beneath them. But with nowhere to go, they were mercilessly stuck, unable to go up or down. It must have been quite painful.

They heard us coming and turned angry, frightened and somewhat expectant eyes in our direction.

Chida walked directly to the one called Jean whose eyes brightened at the sight of seeing his boss.

"Hello, Jean," he said while pulling the gag loose from his mouth.

Jean shifted his gaze in my direction.

"Why is that man still living? Get us out of here! My legs, they are..."

"Yes. I am sure you are in no small amount of pain."

"Please cut us loose so we can—"

"Not just yet."

Jean narrowed his gaze and stared at Chida.

"What do you mean, not just yet?"

Chida squatted down a couple of feet from the tree.

"I mean that you and I are going to have a conversation. If I like what I hear then I will consider cutting you loose. If I do not like what I hear..." he pulled a nasty looking, long-bladed knife from his boot. "Then I will begin cutting things loose from your body that you value." He suddenly moved in close, grabbing Jean by the hair and putting the knifepoint against the corner of his left eye. "Starting with your eyes."

The man on the other side of the tree suddenly began screaming incoherently through the gag around his mouth and jerking to free himself.

Chida stood and moved around to stand in front of him.

"Bonsoir, Paul. And how are you tonight?"

The man he called Paul strained against his bonds while keeping worried eyes trained on Chida.

Chida said, "Do you have anything to say to me, Paul, apart from begging for your life, for I assure you that is what you should be doing."

The man said something that I couldn't quite under-stand and Chida leaned in until his mouth was only a couple of inches from his ear.

"I need you to calm down and listen to me very carefully, Paul. I know that you are a reasonable man. I too am a reasonable man and I abhor violence without cause. But I need you to understand that I will have absolutely no problem turning your body into a bloody horror to get the information I require. Do you understand? Nod your head if you do."

Paul nodded violently.

Chida continued in a calm and reasonable voice.

"Good. Now, I am going to remove your gag so that the three of us can have a nice conversation."

He had started to remove the gag when he suddenly moved around to the other side of the tree and returned the knife to Jean's eye.

"I decided that I don't really wish to talk to Paul. I wish to talk to you, my friend."

By then I could see that both men's legs were trembling from being frozen in place for so long and that their efforts to escape had resulted in rubbing their wrists raw and bleeding.

Jean stared at Chida for a few seconds before saying, "I don't understand. What do you want from me? I thought we were colleagues."

Chida grinned. There was no mirth behind that grin.

"Colleagues...ah, yes. That is exactly what I wished you to believe."

By his expression, I could see that Jean now knew that he was in serious trouble.

"So that is how it is now?"

Chida exploded, "It is how it has always been, you fool!"

"I see," Jean said, his voice quivering. "Okay...what do you want?"

Chida removed the knife.

"The Persian. Where does he live?"

Paul began jerking again and trying to speak through his gag.

Chida ignored him.

Jean, shifted his eyes in my direction and then back to Chida.

"You and Moriarity are working together?"

"That is of no concern of yours. Now, where is The Persian?"

Jean gazed into Chida's lifeless eyes.

"And if I refuse to tell you...then what? You kill me?"

"No, Jean. I will not kill you. It will be as I said. I will begin removing parts of your body. Oh, you *will* tell me eventually. They always do. It's only a matter of how much you value your, shall we say...parts."

Jean stiffened.

"I am not afraid. I can endure pain!"

Chida chuckled humorlessly.

"No...you can't. No one can. It is a myth. I will do things to you that hell itself hasn't conceived. It will be horrible! Inhuman. And in the end you will live, but as a grotesque, misshapen monstrosity from whom children will run screaming to their mothers." He leaned in. "And *that*, my friend, is the truth..." After a brief pause, he added, "...as you, more than most, know it to be."

Jean's whole body suddenly began trembling.

"But, we were friends. Why would you do this to me?"

Chida hissed, "We were never friends! I used you to accomplish a greater good." He suddenly shouted. "Now where is The Persian?"

On the other side of the tree, Paul was going ballistic. Chida moved around and tore away his gag leaving one corner of his mouth torn and bleeding.

Paul started babbling in rapid-fire French, information pouring forth like water over a dam's spillway.

Jean started to protest, but Chida simply reached behind him and scored a cut to his face that began somewhere around his right eyebrow and ended at his jawline. As Jean screamed in pain, Paul apparently told Chida everything he needed to know.

After four or five more minutes, Chida stood and motioned for me to follow him a little ways away.

"I must confess that my command of French is limited, but from what I was able to understand, it would appear that Paul actually has more information on The Persian's whereabouts than Jean."

"Enough for us to go on?"

"Far more than that, my friend," he replied with a smile. "I believe that in Paul's terror he told me—whether purposely or inadvertently—not only the city, but the building from which The Persian runs his empire."

"Really? And where might that be?"

He paused for a few beats.

"Would you believe...Los Angeles?"

Well, I didn't see that one coming.

"LA? You're kidding!"

"If Paul is to be believed—and, trust me...I will make sure his story is believable before we leave—LA is where the spawn of Satan resides."

The British have a term for the way I was feeling: "Gobsmacked." It means to be utterly astonished or astounded.

I said, "And where is his headquarters?"

Chida's grin widened.

"He owns a real estate development company in West Hollywood."

"Paul told you all of that?"

"Yes. In about two minutes. He was...how should I put it...motivated? Yes, that's it. He was motivated."

I glanced over his shoulder at the two miserable men who could be heard exchanging insults.

"And what are you going to do with them?"

He turned and stared at the two.

"I'm going to leave them right where they are and call my colleagues to come and fetch them."

He suddenly raised his knife and walked toward Paul. I wasn't sure what he had in mind in the way of insuring that Paul was telling us the truth and to be quite honest, I didn't want to know. So I walked back toward the car, my mind reel-

ing with the revelation Chida had just shared with me.
I had a lot to do in a very short amount of time.

CHAPTER 48

Chida wrapped up his interrogation with Paul and Jean without the need for further bloodshed, and we were now driving toward the airport, once again treating the traffic laws as mere suggestions.

I am forced to admit that it was becoming habitual.

We rolled up to the entrance, parked the car and hurried through the terminal toward the waiting jet. Since I had called Désirée on our way, she had the stairs down and the plane prepped for immediate departure.

We hustled onboard, stowed our weapons, and took our seats.

I must tell you that were it not for the fact that I needed Désirée to fly the Gulfstream, I would've had her back in the stateroom asking some serious questions about Philippe and Étienne's poisoning. But, for now at least, she was useful. Especially since she didn't know of my suspicions.

Aaron got my attention.

"You okay, bruh?"

I debated telling him. In the end, I decided he needed to know.

Leaning in so that no one could overhear our conversation, I said, "I need to tell you something, but at this point it's purely speculative."

"Okay, shoot."

"I think Désirée might be responsible for what happened to Philippe and Étienne."

His eyes widened in surprise.

"Do tell?"

"Well, think about it. How else could they have been administered the poison? The doc said it was either administered in food, by direct contact with the skin, or by means of aerosol."

He screwed his face up in concentration.

"You do make a good point. But, you're not sure?"

"No. But, that is what I hope to find out before we get back to Nice."

"Do you think she's a threat to us?"

Did I? It was a fair question.

"I think she's definitely a threat to somebody, but whether or not it's to us, I can't say."

Désirée's voice came over the intercom.

"Please ensure that your seatbelts are buckled tightly. We have been cleared for takeoff."

The G6 made a long, slow turn and I suddenly felt the powerful engines come to life sending us screaming down the runway, lifting off steeply into the clear night sky.

Gaspard and Chida unbuckled their seatbelts and joined us in the front cabin around the table.

Gaspard said, "Monsieur, what do you intend to do once we are back at the villa?"

It was a question I had been pondering ever since Chida had elicited the information from Paul regarding The Persian's whereabouts.

"The short answer is that we go to Los Angeles and make The Persian and his band of thieves eternally remorseful over their decision to do you harm."

Aaron prompted, "And the long answer?"

I blew out a long breath.

"Well...that's a bit more difficult. There will obviously be logistical challenges to overcome as well as resistance and contention from their end. I mean going after Hayato Momotani by himself is daunting given his vast resources. Add The Persian and the other two, and you could argue that one would have to be straight up crazy to attempt what we are considering."

Chida grinned dryly.

"I actually like our odds."

"You want to explain that?" Aaron growled.

"Think about it. If you were those men, would you be concerned about us coming after you?"

I said, "Us specifically, or any perceived low-level threat?"

"I have been in their 'employ' long enough to have gotten a sense of how they view the world in general, and their place in it in particular. They are arrogant, condescending, and supremely confident in their insulation from any external threat."

"I sense that there's a 'but' coming."

"You are correct. They are well protected from external menace, *but* completely unprepared for a threat arising from within. In fact, given my knowledge of how they think—how they operate—I can safely say that they would find the possibility to be incomprehensible."

"And what is the basis for this confidence?"

He answered, "Within the cartel, there are widely circulated stories of the terrible fate met by those who, shall we say, tried to gain advantage through subversive means."

Aaron asked, "How do you know that those stories are true?"

Chida grew suddenly sober.

"Because I am the one who originated most of them."

I was beginning to see his point.

"So, you're saying that your insider status, coupled with their, how did you put it—supreme confidence that internal threats just aren't possible—puts them at considerable risk. That about cover it?"

"That is it exactly. They will never see us coming because as far as they know I am still a loyal employee and enforcer. I have worked very hard to cement that fact in their minds and anyone who could tell them any differently is unable to communicate with them at present."

I was beginning to like our odds as well.

"Okay," I said. "Here's what we'll do. As soon as we arrive back at the villa, we will eat, bring the girls up to speed on what is going on, discuss our options and retire for the night. As they say, rest is a weapon, and it has been a long day. Oh, and when it comes to resources, my friends, please remember that the FBI is behind everything we do. That is not an insignificant asset."

I figured we had been airborne for most of an hour when Désirée's voice came over the intercom, "We are beginning our initial descent. Please return to your seats and buckle your lap restraints. We will be on the ground in approximately twelve minutes."

Gaspard and Aaron returned to their seats, but Chida remained behind, his expression grave.

"Mr. Moriarity, I know that you are no stranger to violence and have extensive tactical experience, but these people are very bad. They have embraced a level of evil and cruelty the likes of which I have never seen. Even with the FBI — and me working from inside—this won't be, as you Americans say, a walk in the park. It will be very difficult. Very dangerous."

I had no doubt that what he said was true.

"Thank you, Daiki. I fully understand, and yet it has to be done. If not us, who? If not now, when?"

He smiled.

"Very well, my friend. It will be an honor to work alongside you."

I sat down by Aaron who was staring out the window.

He said, "So, what you gonna do about the fair Désirée?"

"Do? I'm not going to 'do' anything right now."

"But, if she's a threat, she sorta has our lives in her hands, seems to me."

"Right," I replied. "Still...I can't exactly go up there and take over the plane, now can I?"

"Guess not. But, are you at least gonna keep an eye on her?"

"Look, I'm not stating categorically that she's a threat... just that I'm suspicious."

He nodded, and then turned toward me, his expression troubled.

"Now...I need to tell *you* something." He paused, and then said, "I'm thinking that it may be a good idea for me to sit this one out, bro."

"I don't disagree. I've been saying that all along."

"Yeah, I know. I've been thinking a lot about what you were saying in the car—you know, about who I am and the responsibility I have to the label, fans, etc. And, well...it's just that this thing is moving toward a level of, I guess, danger that has blown my comfort zone to hell and gone."

"Completely understandable."

"I mean, I'm not a coward—"

"You don't have to justify your decision, Aaron. I'm the one who told you to stay out."

He sighed.

"I know, Jake. But it just doesn't feel right. I mean I've always been there for you. Feels to me like I'm abandoning you."

I turned to face him.

"You're *not* abandoning me. You are exercising tremendous wisdom."

He stared at me without speaking for a few seconds.

"For real?"

"For real."

"So, we're good with this?"

I threw my hands up in exasperation.

"Of course we're good! Besides, I need you to stay close to the girls. You know, give them some protection in case things go sideways."

"Protection? I don't know if I'd be protecting them or they'd be protecting me!"

"Well, there is that."

He formed a fist and we bumped knuckles.

"Thanks for understanding, bro."

And I did understand.

Still, it was weird to think about moving forward without him. If you want to know the truth, the whole thing was feeling weird. The things that had been fluttering at the edge of my consciousness, kind of like threads from a tapestry, were still there. Taken together, the threads would have tremendous meaning. But singly, they made no sense whatsoever. And that was a problem because there was something I was missing. I knew it just as surely as I knew my own face.

The plane touched down and I felt the brakes engage bringing tons of racing metal to a gradual and complete stop.

At the end of the runway.

I glanced out the window and saw nothing that remotely resembled the airport in Nice. In fact...I saw nothing at all.

The door to the cockpit opened and Désirée came out smiling.

And pointing a gun at us.

I must be losing my edge, because I never saw that coming.

CHAPTER 49

Messieurs," Désirée said sweetly. "Please place your hands behind your heads and lock your fingers together. It would cause me great sadness to have to shoot you, so please cooperate."

I locked my fingers together and caught her eye.

"Well played, young lady. Well played indeed. You had me completely taken in."

She formed her lovely lips into a fetching pout.

"It wasn't all an act, Jake. I *do* find you quite attractive and am sure that had the circumstances been different we would have had a wonderful time. But, as they say, c´est la vie."

Gaspard growled, "What is the meaning of this?"

Chida answered, "Isn't it obvious? She is working for the cartel."

"Which means," I mused, "that she has no doubt alerted them as to your true status, Daiki."

Gaspard pleaded, "Désirée! Please tell me that this isn't true."

"Sadly, I cannot. It is quite true. I am in the cartel's employ."

"But you have worked for me—"

"For about as long as you have been doing business with the cartel?" I interjected.

His eyes widened.

"Mon Dieu!"

I ventured a guess.

"So, did you meet The Persian in Los Angeles?"

Her eyes widened.

"Very good, Monsieur. You *are* as good as they say you are."

"And *you* are nothing more than a cheap whore!" Gaspard shouted, his face red, no doubt from anger and embarrassment at having been taken in by such a charming charlatan.

"Monsieur Ducharme," she said, clucking her tongue. "Such unbecoming language for a man of your stature."

"What happens next?" I asked.

"My associates should be arriving momentarily, at which time they will take you off my hands, finish the job we paid Chida-san here to do and I can go have a good, stiff drink and a hot bath. It has been a long day."

Chida made a sudden move to rush her and with virtually no perceptible movement on her part she shot, sending him headlong onto the cabin floor where he lay so still that I thought for sure he was dead.

She leaned over him and prodded him with the pistol.

"You can get up now. I could have killed you easily, but I merely shot you in the shoulder. The bullet didn't hit the bone or any major arteries."

He rolled painfully onto his right side and sat up, his left shoulder bleeding badly.

I thought about going for my gun, but since it was tucked into the waistband at the small of my back there was no way I could retrieve it before she shot me as well. And as had just been demonstrated, she was a very good shot.

Aaron had the same problem, and Gaspard was unarmed.

Désirée squatted down and expertly removed Chida's weapon before telling Gaspard to help him up. It was a very clever move in that it required Aaron and I to remain seated. Now she had two guns trained on us.

"Anyone else care for a little extracurricular activity?"

she taunted.

Aaron said, "Probably a dumb question, but are you really okay with just standing by knowing that all of us are going to be killed?"

"Monsieur Perry, as much as I have loved your music throughout my life, I love money even more. So to answer your question...yes. I really am okay with it."

He shook his head. "That's cold."

"No...that's practical. There's a difference."

I'd been fooled before, but nothing like this. I felt like an idiot. I don't like feeling like an idiot.

If you want to know the truth, I hate it!

CHAPTER 50

Even though he had slept for most of the nine-hour flight back to Los Angeles, the man known as The Persian was still tired. Weary, actually. Things had gone terribly wrong and he couldn't understand why. But he would get to the truth.

He always got to the truth.

He sat in the back of his custom, heavily armored Mercedes Benz G63 AMG, his primary bodyguard, Antoine, seated next to him and Liam, his secondary, in the front passenger seat. Piloting the massive car through the nightmare known as LA traffic was his longtime driver, Charles.

He felt the cellphone vibrating in the pocket of his finely tailored Alexander Amosu suit.

He didn't have to check the caller ID, for it could be only one person.

"Yes?" he said calmly.

"The asset has engaged."

"Very good. And when can we expect for this, eh, irritation to be relieved?"

"Within the hour."

Without another word, he terminated the call and returned the phone to its place.

"Shall we continue on, sir?" the driver asked circumspectly.

"Yes, only...drive toward the ocean. I *do* so love the ocean."

"As you wish, sir," the driver answered quietly. "Any

place in particular?"

The Persian surveyed the passing landscape, seeing it as his own.

"Santa Monica, Charles."

"Very good, sir."

The great man leaned back against the luxurious comfort of the limousine's seat, happy in the knowledge that in spite of the pitiable efforts of those few who had dared to align themselves against him, he was still the master of all he surveyed.

They would suffer.

Then they would disappear as if they had never been born.

It was his way—the only way to appropriately deal with threats whether great or small. Not equal force, but the same force. Always the same force—overwhelming force.

"Charles," he said quietly.

"Yes, sir?"

"I have changed my mind."

"Yes?"

"Drive to Laguna Beach. I want to check on the art piece I loved at that one gallery."

"Very good, sir. We should be able to be there in approximately...thirty minutes."

The Persian smiled and closed his eyes.

"Make it twenty."

"Very good sir."

CHAPTER 51

Headlights swept across the side of the plane, stabbing sequentially through the oval windows and strobing briefly across Désirée's face. But it was long enough for me to see something that hadn't been there before. Her eyes connected with mine as if in silent communication. What was she trying to tell me? Backing slowly toward the front of the cabin she hit the switch that lowered the AirStairs, never taking her eyes from mine in the process. She definitely *was* up to something, but given my overall state of confusion and the mistrust I now had for her, I had no idea what it was.

The plane rocked with the weight of people climbing the stairs and Désirée stepped back from the cabin door as two large men entered. The man in the lead—a forty-something, swarthy man of disproportionate girth to height ratio —stopped at the head of the aisle staring intently in my direction.

"So, this is the great Jake Moriarity," he said in a thick, Spanish accent. "You must not be as tough as your reputation says you are if a..." He glanced at Désirée, "...little bimbo can take you down."

I stayed silent, still trying to read whatever I saw in Désirée's eyes.

She said, "They are all here, Monsieur. As promised."

What was she doing?

He turned his stony gaze in her direction, looking her over like a predator eyeing a potential kill.

"You have done well, Désirée. I will look forward to...debriefing with you later on."

I scoffed, "You sound fairly confident for someone who will be dead soon."

His eyes widened comically.

"Me? Dead? You seem to be confused, Señor. It is *you* who are going to die."

"Don't count on it."

He grinned confidently.

"They told me you would be...how did they say it...tough. Yes. That is it. Tough. Well, it is of no importance. You see, I am well armed and, sadly for you...you are not."

I shifted my eyes quickly toward Désirée and then back...and suddenly I knew. I knew why she hadn't disarmed us.

"Well, time will tell," I replied meekly.

He turned to the man behind him and said something I couldn't make out.

Désirée widened her eyes when his back was turned. It was all I needed. I still didn't know exactly what was happening, but something was definitely going down and she wanted me to be ready.

The man turned back around and seemed to notice for the first time that Chida was injured.

He jerked his head toward Désirée.

"What is the meaning of this?"

"He tried to attack me and I did not wish to be attacked. So, I shot him. He is not hurt badly. No bones were broken and the bullet passed through."

The man frowned.

"How can you be sure?"

"Because I am a *very* good shot, Monsieur. It is one of the reasons the cartel contracted me for this operation. Is there a problem?"

Chida said, "Yes! There is a problem! I have been shot and am bleeding. It is a large problem, you stupid little bitch!"

The fat man's frown deepened.

"This was not supposed to happen!"

I suddenly saw things very clearly. Chida was, in fact, *not* a double agent, but a cartel loyalist. But, if that was true...then what in bloody hell was Désirée?

In response to the fat man, Désirée jerked her head in Chida's direction and said, "Tell that to him."

The fat man seemed unsure of how to proceed.

"Okay...we will discuss this later. All of you. Get up!"

Years before, Aaron and I had developed a secret sign that we used when the occasion demanded. Imperceptible to anyone looking on, it meant, "Get ready, 'cuz something's going down."

I used it.

The man said, "Mr. Chida...you first."

Chida stood with difficulty; his eyes fixed angrily on Désirée and moved toward the front of the cabin.

As he passed by her, he growled, "You will regret this! Oh, how you will regret this!"

The fat man took him by his uninjured arm and guided him gently toward his colleague standing behind him, who then handed him off to someone else I couldn't see.

"Put him in the car. Okay...now you, Monsieur Ducharme."

Completely clueless to what was transpiring under the surface, Gaspard stood and walked stiffly toward Désirée, frowning and muttering under his breath in what I imagined to be very unflattering French.

When he was within arm's reach, the man grabbed him and shoved him roughly toward the stairs where he was caught by the second man and ushered off of the plane.

The man backed toward the stairs.

"Désirée, wait until I am in position before bringing them off."

"Oui, Monsieur. I can handle it in here with no problem."

After he had disappeared through the doorway she

moved closer and whispered, "I have to speak quickly. I am so sorry for this. But it was the only way."

"The only way to what?" Aaron asked.

"The only way to get Chida *and* this man at the same time. He is filth! Even worse than Chida."

I said, "So, am I to believe that Chida is not the double agent he represented himself to be?"

She took a deep breath.

"He is *exactly* who he is rumored to be. All those things he is alleged to have done? It is all true! He was setting you up, Jake."

The man hollered from outside the plane, "Okay. Bring them down."

"One moment, Monsieur. I am securing their hands." To us she said, "Keep your weapons concealed behind you in your waistband. They won't check because they believe I've already frisked you. I'm going to zip-tie your hands, but loosely so you can access the guns when it's time."

As she secured our hands I asked, "Is your name really Désirée?"

She smiled, "Actually it is. I guess I should tell you that I am the one working with the ELAC."

Aaron frowned.

"But, Chida works with the ELAC."

"No. He doesn't. He only pretends to so he can carry out the cartel's dirty work with impunity."

Aaron's brow wrinkled in confusion as he said, "Wait...so...Chida really works for the cartel, but...pretends to work for ELAC who placed him as an undercover operator in the organization he already works for, and you are working with ELAC as an undercover in the cartel. Damn, girl! That's complicated."

"It is, I admit."

I said, "Did you poison Étienne and Philippe?"

She nodded.

"Oui. I had to in order to get them out of the way. It was

not a lethal dose."

"How did you do it?"

"I sprayed some of my 'new perfume' for them to smell when we were all in the cabin."

"Is everything all right?" the fat man hollered from outside the plane.

"One moment, Monsieur. The big one gave me a little trouble, but he is secured now."

Aaron asked, "But how did you avoid breathing it yourself?"

"I sprayed it on their wrists and had them sniff. That way it was absorbed through the skin as well as their lungs."

"So, what's the play?" I asked as she finished securing my hands.

"We need to let them take you to wherever it is they plan to perform the executions."

"And what if they frisk us?"

She shrugged.

"Then I will have to advance to plan B and shoot them."

"All of them?" Aaron asked.

She racked the slide on her pistol.

"I am a very fast and very accurate shot, Monsieur Perry."

Aaron nodded his head and said, "I think Chida would agree."

"Okay. Just follow my lead and try to be convincing." She backed toward the cabin door and hollered, "Okay, Monsieur. We are coming."

CHAPTER 52

Désirée stepped aside and as I got to the cabin door I peered out, pausing before taking the first step. There were two vehicles, both Mercedes sedans. I could see two additional men besides the ones who had entered the plane, all of whom were standing outside the cars about twenty feet away. Chida was slumped in the front seat of the sedan nearest the plane and Gaspard was in the back of the second, his face a despondent tableau of fear and worry.

I turned to Désirée as if arguing.

"Shove me down the stairs."

Playing her roll perfectly she shoved me forward and said loudly, "Just walk, Monsieur. This will all be over soon."

I started slowly down the stairs with Aaron right behind me. When we reached the ground Désirée moved around the stairs and hit a switch retracting them into the fuselage.

"What are you doing?" the man in charge said loudly.

"I'm closing up the plane, Monsieur. You didn't think I would just leave it here, did you?"

"But, you are not coming with us."

"My orders are to accompany you and witness the executions with my own eyes and then report back."

The man sputtered in frustration for a couple of seconds.

"But why was I not told of this?"

"I'm afraid I do not know." She gestured with her pistol toward the waiting cars. "Now, shall we?"

He said, "It will be a tight fit."

"Not if you leave one of your men here to guard the plane."

I had to admire the girl. She was good.

Even in the low light I could see the flush on the man's swarthy face. After staring fiercely at her for nearly a full minute by my reckoning, he turned and jerked his head toward the plane without speaking. One of the men who had been standing by the nearest Mercedes jogged quickly over to Désirée. She appeared to be showing him how to extend the AirStairs and passing along a few brief additional instructions before walking up behind me and giving me a hard shove toward the cars.

I turned on her.

"If you do that again, you will regret it, little girl!"

She smiled sweetly and backhanded me across the face, taking care not to damage my jaw any more than it already was.

"Just hearing your voice makes me want to shoot you where you stand, Monsieur Moriarity. You would do well to do as you are told and hold your tongue."

I stood my ground for a few seconds and then turned grudgingly toward the cars.

As I walked by the man in charge I said, "What are you looking at, pork chop?"

He smiled confidently.

"In spite of my orders, I believe I will shoot you first—maybe in the knee, or in the shoulder, or in the belly? Yes! I will shoot you in the belly so you can suffer while you watch us kill your friends. Now get into the car!"

As Désirée guided me toward the cars she said, "I will put Monsieur Moriarity into the car with Chida and ride in the back so I can keep an eye on him. He is not to be trusted."

The man nodded curtly and took Aaron by the arm and tried to pull him toward the second car. Aaron didn't budge an inch. The man tried again.

Aaron leaned down.

"Say please."

The man's eyes widened.

"What did you say?"

"I said to say please. If you say please I will go quietly. If not, this is going to be the start of a very long night for you."

The guy looked like he was going to have a coronary on the spot. After fuming for a couple of minutes he finally just gestured in the direction of the car without saying anything.

Aaron smiled victoriously.

"Good enough for me."

Désirée put me into the back of the car and climbed into the other side with one of the cartel's men in the driver's seat. Chida was alert enough to sit up straight as we entered, turning to glare viciously at her.

"You shot me!" he hissed. "You will pay for this, you little bitch!"

Without saying a word, she shot her gun hand forward and cracked him on the bridge of the nose.

He bent over in pain, his nose bleeding profusely.

She said, "Chida-san, that is the second time you have used that very unflattering word to describe me. If you do it again, I fear I will lose all restraint and shoot you. Are we clear?"

With his right hand cupped over his nose, he shifted his eyes in her direction and then slumped against the door without speaking.

I could see the driver's eyes in the rearview mirror. I think at that moment even with Chida's reputation he was every bit as afraid of Désirée as he was of Chida. Especially since she was seated directly behind him.

She leaned forward until her chin was close to his ear.

"Do you have a problem with this, Monsieur?"

The driver shook his head slowly and shrugged as if to say, *"Hey, I'm just a hired hand who does what he is told."*

"Good."

She leaned back and caught my attention. Shifting her

eyes downward toward her right hand she indicated that I should look. There was a tiny blade that she had concealed in her sleeve. Without the driver noticing, she passed it off to me and shifted her eyes almost imperceptibly toward my bound hands.

"What are we waiting for?" she inquired of the driver.

"My boss. He is having a difficult time putting the large one into the car."

I ducked my head and looked through the rear passenger window. It was true, but only because Aaron was making it difficult. He turned and peered over the top of the car's roof, found my eyes and smiled like Alice's Cheshire cat. When he was finally seated, the other car started up and moved out quickly with our driver following close behind.

I asked, "Am I allowed to know where we are going?"

Désirée replied, "To your death, Monsieur Moriarity."

She said it with such simple conviction that for a second, I found myself believing her.

CHAPTER 53

From the little I could see through the car's windows, the airfield was abandoned and located somewhere in a rural area. At least that was my initial impression given that the hangers were dark; the terminal was dark; the outlying buildings were dark and the tower was dark. The only light source in any direction appeared to be coming from the car's headlights.

In front of us the other car picked up speed sending a thick cloud of dust billowing up in its wake, making it even more challenging than it already was to discern our location.

The sedan crossed a deep pothole in the dirt road and Chida's head bounced off of the window causing him to cry out and swear at the driver.

"If that happens again, you are a dead man!"

Désirée countered, "I don't think you are in any position to be making threats, Chida-san."

He turned and glared menacingly.

"You won't always have a gun pointed at me. And when that time comes, I will very much enjoy spoiling your beauty."

Moving almost faster than I could follow, Désirée cracked him on the side of his shaved head with the butt of her gun. The blow didn't knock him out, but it opened a one-inch gash that began to bleed immediately and copiously.

"Now you will have another scar to add to your collection."

Chida reached up with his right hand and explored the wound while staring at her in shock and disbelief.

"What are you doing? Don't you know who I am?"

"Ouis. I know exactly who and what you are. You are filth. You are evil. You are cruelty personified. I detest the very skin that hangs from your bones, and I take great pleasure in returning to you a small amount of the pain you have given to others. Now, perhaps you should stop talking and concentrate on not insulting me any further. As you can see, I am not in the mood to be trifled with."

It was clear that Daiki Chida was unused to hearing *anyone* talk to him in such a manner, let alone a woman. He didn't seem to know what to do or how to even respond. After staring at her for a few more seconds he turned slowly back toward the front and sat in stony silence staring through the windshield, a handkerchief pressed alternately against his head and his broken nose.

Désirée said, "Hopefully we can avoid the need for further unpleasantness."

Whereas before I had found her attractive, I now found her to be utterly fascinating, and was already looking forward to learning more about the real Désirée when all of this was over.

As for when that would be, I had no clue.

I don't like not having a clue.

If you want to know the truth, it bothers me. It bothers me quite a lot.

I endeavored to tally the things about which I did not have a clue. It was a long list and, seemingly, growing longer by the second. By now I had fully expected to be back at the villa with my girls, have plans formulated to deal with The Persian, and, having consumed a substantial amount of food and drink, be headed for a decent night's sleep in my very comfortable bed. As it was, I didn't know where we were, where we were going, what was supposed to happen once we got to wherever that was, or even what the current situation had to do with my other situation, which was to, ultimately, bring down the cartel.

It was very confusing.

We suddenly arrived at the end of the dirt road and followed the other car through a tight left turn that put us onto pavement; albeit not much smoother than the ribbed surface we had just been on. At least there wasn't the constant billowing cloud of dust from the other car, which gave me an opportunity to see a bit more of the passing landscape in the glow of the headlights. It looked similar to the countryside Aaron and I had driven through this morning. Was that only this morning?

Désirée was right; it *had* been a long day.

I could feel the car picking up speed and glanced at the speedometer. We were really moving! Doing a quick calculation I figured that we were edging close to one hundred mph, which was a bit disconcerting given the extreme darkness of our surroundings. But the guy seemed to be a good driver and paced the lead car like a NASCAR pro.

Désirée touched my leg and inclined her head subtly toward my back. I took it to mean that it was time to cut through the zip-tie and free my hands. It wasn't as easy as one might imagine. First of all, have you ever tried to sit with your hands tied behind you? Without going into details, let me just tell you that it's difficult! The bottom line is that after a sufficient length of time, your hands go numb. Attempting to wield a sharp blade when you can't see what you're doing is challenging enough, but trying to do it with numb fingers while at the same time not attracting attention, or inadvertently giving oneself a serious wound, is next to impossible.

I somehow made it work and experienced a nearly orgasmic sense of relief when the bonds at last fell away. And I'm not overstating. Not one bit! Shifting the knife to my left hand, I pulled the gun from my waistband keeping my hands behind me to maintain the appearance of being bound. I wasn't sure what Désirée had planned, but she was obviously a high level operator, and I was certain I'd have no problem following her lead when the time came.

I glanced sideways to look at her profile. Of all the surprises that had come along today, she had been both the biggest and the most pleasant.

CHAPTER 54

I suddenly felt the sedan slowing. Ducking my head, I could see through the front windshield that the car ahead of us was turning onto a narrow lane. We followed it closely through the turn, and raced along another deeply rutted and ribbed packed earth surface, clouds of dust obscuring everything but what was directly in front of us. After a few minutes the dim outline of a large, nondescript modern building was illuminated in the lead car's headlights. We gradually came to a stop and as the dust settled I craned my neck to check out our surroundings. Based on its size, the building appeared to be a warehouse of some sort, an observational assumption reinforced by the presence of orchards stretching off in every direction.

Désirée leaned forward, pointed her gun at Chida and spoke quickly, "Chida-san, if you speak without my permission or make any other attempt to communicate, I will shoot you in the head without the slightest hesitation. Nod if you understand."

He turned his bleeding head slightly toward her and nodded.

"Good."

She placed the nose of the pistol against the driver's right ear.

"I am sure you are wondering what is happening, and you will find out soon enough. For now, slowly remove the keys from the ignition and pass them, along with your weapon back to Monsieur Moriarity. Trust me...this is all part of the plan. You are not in trouble nor will you *be* in any trouble by complying."

I could see the driver's eyes in the rearview mirror. There was a brief moment where he considered doing something brave, but it passed quickly, and the items were handed back through the space between the seats.

"Now, Chida-san, put your hands behind your head and lock your fingers. I know it will hurt, but it is of no consequence to me."

After a second's hesitation, he did as instructed.

"Now, Monsieur Moriarity is going to zip-tie your hands to the headrest."

I complied, pulling with far more force than was necessary on his left arm.

"You lied to me, you piece of shit! I don't like being lied to. And I promise you that when all of this is over, you and me are going to have a not-so-pleasant conversation. I figure I owe you for that punch to my jaw."

He growled, "You will never survive what is coming, Moriarity! So your threats are empty."

I gave his arm one last jerk, and was rewarded with a muted cry of pain.

"We'll see about that, won't we?"

The right rear door of the other car flew open and the chassis rocked back and forth as the fat man exited. With his weapon at the ready, he opened the door for Aaron, who came out slowly with his hands still secured behind him. He turned toward me and blinked twice. It meant that he was okay. To anyone looking on, it merely appeared that he was trying to clear the dust from his eyes.

The man said something and Aaron started backing slowly toward the front of the car where he stood facing the headlights and squinting his eyes against the glare. The man then barked an order to the driver who immediately climbed out, opened the left rear passenger door and pulled Gaspard out of the back seat and roughly to his feet. Once he was standing, he shoved him in the direction of the front of the car where he joined Aaron.

The fat man turned and waved toward us.

Désirée said, "Jake, when I take you out of the car, keep your hands behind you until I give you the signal."

"Roger that. Then what?"

She turned toward me and smiled.

"Oh, I think you will figure out what to do."

As she was getting out of the car I leaned forward and spoke quietly but intensely to Chida.

"Don't forget...you and me have some things to discuss when this is over!"

"You have no idea what you have gotten yourself into, Moriarity. No idea at all."

I chuckled.

"I have been listening to people say that to me my whole life, Chida. And guess what...I'm still here. And I intend to be here for a good while longer."

After opening my door as widely as it would go Désirée stood in front of it to provide cover should I inadvertently slip and reveal our subterfuge.

Once I was standing she turned toward the fat man and shouted, "There has been a change of plans."

He raised his eyebrows dramatically.

"A change? But why was I not told of this?"

"Because I just made the change on the drive over here."

Squinting suspiciously, he replied, "But you lack authority to make any changes."

Two things happened simultaneously: she pointed her gun at the fat man, and I drew down on the driver. The shock of what they were seeing froze them in place.

"All right," I said evenly to the driver. "Nice and easy like, I want you to toss your weapon toward me."

The man darted his eyes toward the other driver in our car, who sat staring straight ahead with both hands on the wheel shaking his head helplessly.

"He's not going to be any help to you and neither is Chida who, tragically, suffered further injury on the drive over."

With his gun still pointed at us, the fat man hollered, "We won't be surrendering our weapons. You will have to shoot us first."

Désirée shrugged her pretty shoulders, said, "Okay," and shot the gun out of the driver's hand so quickly that no one even had a chance to react until it was over. The man howled in pain and fell to the ground clutching his wounded hand.

The fat man now had absolutely no place to hide.

"Still want me to shoot you?" Désirée asked.

Aaron whistled. The man glanced in his direction stunned to see him free from his bonds and pointing another gun at his head.

Aaron smiled and waved.

Snapping his head back to the front, he pierced Désirée with an evil glare and began to defame her character in color-ful Spanish. Or so I supposed.

I'd had enough.

"Okay, it's been a really long day and my head hurts, my jaw hurts and frankly I'm tired of hearing your voice. So drop your weapon, or Aaron is going to shoot you in the back of the head."

The man suddenly spun in Aaron's direction, a move Aaron had obviously been anticipating. As the man was still making his turn, Aaron dropped to the ground and proceeded to kick the man's legs out from under him. He hit the ground with a loud "Whump!" and lay there too stunned to move as Aaron confiscated his weapon.

Désirée leaned toward me.

"He's very good for a piano player."

"Yeah, he is. But don't let him know it. His ego is hard enough to deal with as it is."

CHAPTER 55

While Aaron and I bound and then confined the driver and the fat man to the car containing Chida and the other driver, Désirée excused herself to make a call to the ELAC.

I saw Gaspard standing a few feet away shaking his head.

"What's the matter, Gaspard?"

He gestured to take in the whole scene.

"This! This is the matter. I am so confused, I don't know who to believe anymore."

"It is definitely a little hard to follow. But let me try. Chida was working undercover for the cartel *at* ELAC while pretending to work undercover for ELAC *at* the cartel. Désirée was working for you but she was really an undercover operative of the ELAC while *pretending* to work for the cartel."

He gave his head a sharp shake.

"La vache! J'y crois pas!"

Aaron translated, "It's roughly the equivalent of, 'My God! I can't believe it.'"

I replied, laughing, "It's very complicated."

"Just tell me one thing, Monsieur," Gaspard said.

"I will try."

"Is Désirée the sweet girl I thought she was all along?"

She was leaning against the lead car with the phone to one ear and gesturing with her free hand.

"Yes. Definitely sweet...in a completely lethal sort of way."

Gaspard nodded his head slowly, thoughtfully for a few

seconds before shrugging his shoulders.

"Je peux vivre avec, eh...it is how you say, 'I can live with that.'"

Désirée terminated her call and walked over to join us.

"My colleagues from ELAC and a team from INTERPOL will be here within fifteen to twenty minutes to take custody of our bad guys."

She took two steps toward Gaspard and pulled him into a very warm and sincere hug.

"I am so sorry, Monsieur Ducharme, but this was the only way to clear out these two evil men. Please forgive me."

He brightened immediately.

"But of course, ma chérie. It is of no consequence. I am just relieved that this part is over."

"Chida and the fat man will go to jail for a very long time," she said. "That is, after they tell us everything we need to know about the cartel and its members."

"Speaking of which," Aaron interjected. "Do you think Chida was telling the truth about The Persian being in LA?"

"Without question," she replied.

"How can you be so sure?"

Désirée winked at him.

"Because I have seen him there. When Jake asked me on the plane if Los Angeles was where I had met The Persian, I wasn't lying when I said yes."

Aaron said, "What was the occasion, if you don't mind me asking?"

"Not at all," she replied casually. "Over time, ELAC's investigation uncovered that there were four principal actors in the cartel. Digging a little deeper, we learned that one individual was unquestionably more powerful than the other three, but we had no way of knowing who it was. Then we received a completely unexpected call from an art broker in Los Angeles who served the same role in the States that..." she gestured toward Gaspard, "Monsieur Ducharme served here. An individual claiming to have a significant number of unframed art masterpieces from the estate of a wealthy, recently deceased Jewish couple had approached him wondering if he, or any of his clients, might be interested in a private showing.

"Of course he said yes and contacted the ELAC immediately. They appointed me to play the role of an affluent, interested client from an art collective in Marseilles. So I flew to Los Angeles, met Bernard—the art broker—and accompanied him to a prearranged location where a small sampling of the art would be available for preview."

"Is that where you met The Persian?" I asked.

"No, that was actually quite difficult to arrange. The man we met at first is the one who had set up the meeting. An underling. I looked over the two pieces he brought to the meeting and while I can't go into details because of confidentiality agreements, I can tell you that they were genuine and most definitely on our list of stolen masterpieces from World War II."

"And how did you manage to meet the big man himself?"

She laughed.

"I threw a tantrum."

Aaron raised his eyebrows and said, "You're not serious!"

"Completely! We French women are notorious for our tantrums. So, I became furious with the man. I told him that the paintings were nothing more than forgeries—high-end forgeries, but forgeries nonetheless. Then I turned my anger on Bernard, railing at him for making me fly all the way from France for nothing."

I said, "And I assume it had the desired effect?"

"Only after I demanded to meet the man who would dare to perpetrate such an elaborate hoax. Who would do such a thing! Has he no respect for the great artists these obvious fakes are defaming?"

"And..." I prompted.

"He became just as incensed as me; babbling on about

how there was no possible way they could be forgeries. When I asked him how I could be sure, he offered to let me meet the man who could confirm the provenance. I accepted the concession, and he left promising to set up a meeting within the next twenty-four hours."

Gaspard asked, "May we assume he followed through?"

"Yes. The Persian himself called Bernard not four hours later and wanted to know if he vouched for me. Of course Bernard assured him that I was legitimate, even going so far as to provide all of my fake references and contacts back at the equally fake art collective. He inquired relative to how many pieces I was interested in acquiring. Bernard told him that I was looking for five or six for sure, but if I found a few more to be interesting, I would take them as well. Money was not an object."

Aaron said, "Can you bottom line me? All this subterfuge is starting to give me a headache!"

Laughing, Désirée continued, "Okay. I will, 'cut to the chase' as you Americans say. We met The Persian at his offices in West Hollywood where he runs a totally legitimate company—import/export as you might imagine. Very impressive. *He* is very impressive in a sinister sort of way."

"So you bought the paintings?" Aaron asked.

"No. I left promising to do just that, but before we could complete the final purchase, The Persian got nervous and terminated the transaction."

I said, "And you never saw him after that?"

"No. He vanished. And we haven't been able to get a location on him since."

"But you know the location of his corporate headquarters in LA?"

She smiled coyly. "Oui."

CHAPTER 56

I took Désirée by the elbow and led her a few steps away from the others.

"I suppose you're going to be pretty busy wrapping things up here, huh?"

"No, not at all. As far as this is concerned, my job—which was to expose Chida and bring down that fat *connard* with the wandering hands—is finished."

"I see. So, if one were to request your assistance in pinpointing The Persian's location, do you think you'd be interested?"

She raised one eyebrow and said with a surprised smile, "Are you asking for my help?"

I laughed.

"Yes, I'm asking for your help."

Désirée suddenly sobered.

"Look, I know we've been a bit flirty, and that's okay. I enjoy flirting as much as the next girl. But this thing with The Persian is serious."

"Yes, it is. Deadly serious."

Her gaze found and held my eyes.

"I guess what I'm saying is that if I agree to accompany you, we can't have any distractions."

Without warning, Gabi's lovely face interposed itself on my consciousness. I found myself suddenly missing that face.

I then shocked myself by saying, "I find you to be a most fascinating person, Désirée. But, just so we're clear, I am involved with someone back in the States."

Out of the corner of my eye, I saw Aaron's head whip toward me.

"So I have neither the desire nor the freedom to carry on any further flirtation with you."

"I knew it!"

"Oh? And how's that?"

She smiled knowingly.

"A girl just knows when a man's heart is filled up with another woman."

I couldn't believe it. I mean *I* didn't even realize how I felt about Gabi until that moment.

"Am I that transparent?"

"Completely!" she replied with a laugh.

Just then Aaron approached.

"What's going on?"

I said, "Désirée is not only a high level tactical operator, but she is also a psychic."

"That so?"

"Apparently."

"That because she figured out your heart is not your own?" Aaron said with a broad grin.

I stared at him.

"Is there anyone who doesn't know about this?"

"Just you, sugar. Glad you finally figured stuff out."

Désirée said, "In my experience, messieurs, men are most often the last to know."

"So, now that we've got my love life all figured out, could we get back to business?"

Aaron replied, "I don't know, man. I'm enjoying this right here a lot!"

Désirée came to my rescue.

"Actually, we were just discussing the possibility of me accompanying Jake to L.A."

I said, "Since Désirée not only knows where The Persian's headquarters are in Los Angeles, but has actually been there in person, I thought it might be helpful to have her go with me."

"Go with you?"

"Yeah, you know, to help me out."

"Help you out?"

Désirée and I exchanged glances.

"Yeah."

He broke into a wide smile.

"Makes me kinda wish I hadn't been so rash in opting out."

"Why?"

"Oh, you know, just to be present and observe you being schooled by a woman who is quite obviously your equal."

"And this is different from my everyday life, how? Last time I looked I am constantly surrounded by *three* women who are my equals!"

CHAPTER 57

Gaspard had been staring at the warehouse and motioned for us to join him.

He said, "I know this place."

I moved over to stand beside him. "What do you mean?"

"I mean that I think I have been here. Yes! I am sure of it." He was suddenly excited. "This is the place! This is where the cartel stores much of their cache of stolen art!"

Aaron looked around the area in total confusion.

"Okay, and where are we exactly?"

"France." Désirée answered. "Somewhere outside of Toulouse. The airfield where we landed has not been used commercially for decades. The cartel found it, bought the land and has been using it exclusively for the past five years."

"Wait a second," I said. "So you've only been flying the G6 for a year and you made a blind landing at an abandoned airfield? In the dark?"

She smiled.

"Well, I may have understated my experience by a just little."

"You think?"

Désirée turned and started walking toward the building.

I said, "Aaron, stay here and keep an eye on our guests."

"Roger that."

As Gaspard and I hurried to catch up, he gestured toward a door placed almost exactly in the middle of the building, saying, "There is the main entrance."

Walking quickly toward the door, we stopped when we got to within three feet or so. Moving a little closer, I squatted down to get a better view of the locking mechanism. Whoever had installed it had been a pro. There was no way even with my lock picking skills that I'd be able to defeat such a sophisticated lock. So, I did what any self-respecting locksmith would do when presented with an unsolvable dilemma. I stood, backed up, drew my pistol and shot the hell out of it. In case you are wondering what shooting the "hell" out of something looks like, in this case it required firing about fifteen rounds into the lock.

Désirée moved up to stand beside me.

"Subtle," she said with a sarcastic smile.

"I am nothing if not."

She approached the door to see if the barrage of gunfire had had any effect. It had. The lock was basically obliterated, as was the handle. She pulled on what was left of the handle and the door swung heavily outward. The three of us stepped through the entrance into an interior that was completely dark. Sniffing the air I could pick up faint but definite smells that immediately registered in my olfactory memory as being associated with automobile garages. Underneath, however, there was something else—something off-putting on a basic, primal level.

Using my weapon light, I searched the wall on either side of the doorway for a lighting panel and found it right where one would expect it to be, to the right as you entered. There were eight switches and I flipped all of them flooding the room with a warm glow.

I gestured upward.

"Do these lights have a filter or something?"

Gaspard said, "They are incandescent, Monsieur. The sun is not the only source of UV rays. Fluorescent lights are almost as damaging to art as direct sunlight whereas only about four percent of the light from an incandescent bulb falls into the damaging UV category. And once a painting is damaged from UV rays, it can never be reversed."

"But won't most of the art stored here be crated?"

"Some, but not all."

The first thing I noticed was a room situated in the exact center of the building. It was freestanding and constructed from large blocks of masonry that looked to be much older than the building surrounding it.

Désirée inclined her head toward the room.

"What is in there?"

"I do not know," Gaspard replied. "When I was given a tour of the facility, that room was not included."

I said, "I hate not knowing things," and started walking toward the room with the other two close behind.

I figured the interior dimensions of the warehouse to be roughly fifty feet by seventy-five feet, with the central room being about twenty feet square. Metal shelving stood in ordered rows against the far wall upon which were stacked numerous crates of varying sizes and shapes.

Désirée wrinkled her nose.

"What is that horrible smell?"

"I don't know." I paused and gestured toward the room. "But it's coming from there and I don't like it."

CHAPTER 58

The closer we got to the room, the worse the smell became. All of us made repeated attempts to identify what it was and came up empty.

All I knew was that it was bad.

Very bad.

Upon closer inspection, I could see that the room was constructed of blocks—thick blocks—with one door at the far end and no windows. Based on the look and feel of the blocks the structure definitely predated the warehouse. The door, which opened outward, was a bit wider than normal and appeared to be quite solid. After rapping my knuckles on the surface it confirmed my suspicion that it was constructed from steel, like a fire door. The only distinguishing feature was the slotted steel brackets on either side of the doorframe, like something that would have been used to hold a bar in place. And why would you need to have a bar thrown across a door if not to keep someone or some *thing* inside? When I knelt down to examine the lock I found it to be a very simple mechanism, like something that would have been used in the thirties and forties.

I pulled my gun and was preparing to fire a few rounds into the lock, when on a whim I decided to try the handle. It turned without difficulty and the door opened with a loud squeak reminiscent of a tortured soul crying out for mercy.

I triggered my weapon light once again and played it around the inside of the room before stepping through the portal. The smell was nearly overpowering.

I entered the room with Gaspard and Désirée following close behind.

"Can you identify that smell?" Désirée asked, plugging her nose.

I was about to answer when I saw it: Discolored and degraded bricks, layered with cobwebs and filth accumulated through years of disuse; thick, asbestos-backed metal doors hanging open like the gaping maw of some ravenous beast. Narrow rails protruded from the interior upon which a rusty sled rested, as if awaiting its next passenger. Arching overhead was a beam with a pulley system used to raise and lower a thick, guillotine-like inner door that was obviously meant to protect the operators from the extreme heat.

Gaspard whispered, "Mon Dieu! Is that..."

I walked toward the ghastly thing saying, "I believe that the Nazis had an interment camp outside of Toulouse."

As I shined my light inside of the oven, I was sickened and overwhelmed by what it most likely represented.

"Recebedou," Gaspard said softly. "The camp name was Recebedou. I studied about it in school." After a brief pause he continued, "Do you think that this was part of that camp?"

Backing up I swept the light around the room, not believing what I was seeing.

"I don't know, but I'm pretty sure what went on *here*."

Gaspard choked back a sob.

"The bastards are storing the art that they stole from the Jews here...in *this* room...by this...oven."

It was true. Placed in an orderly manner all around the perimeter were individual sculptures, half opened crates containing objects of silver and gold as well as chests that suggested the storage of jewelry and precious stones.

I shook my head sadly.

"That's cold! But it's like I've always said, once you become convinced that you need something, you can justify any action."

Désirée said, "That smell is the smell of death, but also

of something more."

I kicked one of the rusty furnace doors and it clanged shut.

"They stole their property, their individuality, their culture, their humanity and finally their lives. In that sense...I believe we are also smelling pure evil."

Gaspard spoke, "And the thievery continues through these horrible men in the cartel. They must be stopped at all costs!"

Désirée turned and hurried from the room.

"I have to go."

I understood completely. Through the door I could hear her retching.

Gaspard touched my arm.

"Promise me one thing, Jake."

"What's that?"

"Promise me that when you catch these monsters, that if it is at all possible, you will not bring them in."

I smiled humorlessly and said, "I'm not sure that is a promise I can keep, my friend, but I will try."

"That is all I ask. Now, if you will excuse me, I believe I will join Désirée."

Without another word, he hurried from the room.

I waited for a minute or so and then left, closing the door behind me slowly, almost reverently. The irony of what the cartel had done was nearly overwhelming to me. Hiding stolen Jewish art in a room where the Jews had been indiscriminately terminated—burned alive—gave me a picture of the level of depravity I was dealing with. It's easy to deny the existence of evil when you've never stared into the cold, fathomless depths of its soulless gaze. And while I had done so on numerous occasions, I had never encountered anything on this level.

Even the monster named Jones had more heart than these people. Hell, Paul Morgan had more heart than these fiends!

I turned and laid the palm of my hand flat against the door's surface. It was as if the collective consciousness of everyone who had died within that room's stygian depths simultaneously cried out for justice. It rocked me! I staggered back as though shoved by some palpable force. Of course I knew that was impossible.

And yet, it happened.

CHAPTER 59

Désirée and Gaspard stood by the warehouse entrance staring at me with concern etched into their features.

She said, "What happened to you, Jake? You look as if you've seen a ghost."

I nodded slowly, glancing back over my left shoulder.

"I don't know. Maybe I did." I turned back and found their eyes. "So many dreams and destinies died here. And while I realize that this represents a place of unspeakable horror, in some ways it's like being in a holy place."

Aaron approached and said, "You okay, bro? You don't look so good."

"I'm fine. Just found some nasty business inside."

He raised his eyebrows questioningly.

Désirée jerked her head toward the building.

"They apparently built this warehouse right over the top of a building from WW II." After a brief pause, she finished. "It...housed an oven."

I watched as Aaron worked out the implications.

"Sweet Lord Jesus! Are you sure?"

"Without question."

As he turned and looked in the direction of the warehouse, Gaspard asked, "What do you wish to do now, Jake?"

Before I could offer an answer—which was actually fortunate as I didn't really have one—two vans rumbled up the drive coming to a stop behind the sedans.

Désirée pointed toward the larger van.

"That van is from ELAC, and I'm assuming the other is a tactical team from INTERPOL."

Her speculation was proven correct as a group of six heavily armed men poured out of the smaller van followed by an officious looking, older gentleman from the ELAC vehicle who walked quickly toward where we all stood in a tight circle. While the INTERPOL team surrounded the car containing our bad guys, three more men and two women exited the ELAC van and began offloading various sizes of empty crates and slim, cardboard boxes.

I said, "Looks like our work here is done."

The man in charge walked straight to Désirée and shook her hand.

"You have done very well here, Désirée. Thank you for the additional call alerting us to the presence of the stolen art."

Gesturing toward us she replied, "I did very little, sir. These men are largely responsible for everything that has happened. Permit me to introduce Aaron Perry, Gaspard Ducharme and Jake Moriarity. This is Senior Field Agent Friederich Nussbaum with the ELAC—my direct supervisor."

He shook hands with each of us while saying in a thick, German accent, "I am pleased to meet you gentlemen. Désirée mentioned that there were people helping her. Whether you know it or not, you have done the people of Europe in general —and our Jewish community in particular—a great service in uncovering this trove of stolen art."

"Well," I explained, "it wasn't as if we set out to find this place. We sort of stumbled upon it when we were brought here to be executed."

Flashing a tight smile, he replied, "Even so, I thank you. Now if you will excuse us, Désirée and I have a few logistical items to discuss."

And with that, he took Désirée by the arm and guided her toward the entrance to the warehouse where they met up with the other members of the ELAC team. After a few moments discussion, she led them inside. Meanwhile, the tactical squad from INTERPOL had Chida and company out of the car and lined up against the side of their van. Chida and the fat man were directing a non-stop stream of verbal invectives at them in two different languages simultaneously.

Gaspard cleared his throat.

"As I was saying before I was interrupted, what do you propose to do next, Monsieur Moriarity?"

I checked my watch and was stunned to see that it was a little after ten p.m.

"Well, I don't know about you two, but I'd feel a whole lot better about life if I could wake up tomorrow morning at the villa."

"I couldn't agree more. I'll have Ph..." He started to say Philippe, before remembering that he was no longer riding for the brand, so to speak. "I guess we will need to wait for Désirée if we wish to fly back to Nice on my jet."

"Since ELAC assigned her to go back to Los Angeles with Jake to track down The Persian," Aaron explained. "That should work out just fine."

I said, "Maybe you should call the girls and let them know what's happening so they won't be worried."

"Yeah, *and* so they can have some food waiting for us. I'm so hungry my stomach thinks my throat has been cut! Any idea on when we can get out of here?"

Désirée exited the warehouse and walked quickly toward us, a tired smile playing around her mouth.

"Friederich has things under control and gave me permission to go."

That was a relief.

I said, "Assuming we can leave in the next five or ten minutes, how long do you think it will take for us to get back to Nice?"

"Well, the plane has adequate fuel, so we just need to drive back to the airstrip, file a flight plan with Nice air traffic control and take off. It'll take about twenty-five minutes to drive to the airstrip; fifteen minutes to prep the plane; a little over an hour flight time, so...call it midnight to be safe?"

"Add another thirty minutes to drive back to the villa from the airport. Aaron, why don't you tell the girls we'll be back around one a.m."

Aaron nodded his head and started dialing Muriel's number.

Désirée checked her watch.

"We should be going."

"You're right. Aaron, finish the call in the car."

He gave me a thumbs-up and climbed into the front passenger seat while I moved in behind the wheel. Désirée sat behind Aaron with Gaspard directly behind me. I started the car and drove away without so much as a backwards glance.

I was done with that place!

I never wanted to *hear* about it, let alone see it ever again.

CHAPTER 60

Désirée got me pointed in the right direction before sitting back, closing her eyes and dropping immediately into a deep sleep.

Aaron was staring at me.

I said, "What?"

"You know 'what', bruh!"

"Pretend I don't."

He glanced over his shoulder to make sure Désirée was still asleep.

She was.

He lowered his voice and asked, "You getting ready to stop this 'solitary man' nonsense?"

"What makes you ask that?"

While I couldn't see him, I could *feel* him rolling his eyes.

"Come on, dude! That little girl back there in Vegas has completely cut your legs out from under you."

"So, what are you saying?"

"I'm saying, ladies and gentlemen, that the oak has been felled!"

"Look," I said, trying to buy time, "While I feel that to be an obscene overstatement…"

"Obscene?"

"Okay…grossly overstated. However, I will admit that we do seem to share a certain, well, chemistry."

"So you sayin' that you hot for each other?"

I hated that he knew me so well!

"And again with the overstatement. I'm attracted to Gabi and she to me."

I glanced in the rearview mirror to see Gaspard grinning broadly and Désirée sleeping soundly.

"You've got to give me some space on this, Aaron."

"Okay," he replied. "And what, pray tell, would that look like?"

Good question!

"Well...maybe just back off a little and let this play out naturally without assumption."

"And what in *the* hell does that mean?"

"It means," I began, but then paused to consider what I wanted to say. "It means that it's been almost twenty years since I've had more than a platonic relationship with a woman. So, in many ways, I'm new to this, which is to say that I basically can't remember how to even *be* in a relationship with a woman. I've been—to use your term—solitary for so long, the thought of giving that up and inviting someone inside on any level is absolutely terrifying."

Aaron chuckled.

"Yeah, I get it. I'm just messing with you, man. I'm with you all the way, you know that." After a brief pause he asked, "You talk to Cassie about this?"

I found the thought terrifying!

"Now when would I have had time to do that?"

"I don't know. I'm just asking."

"Well...if you're asking if she knows about Ms. Marcus, then, yes."

"Ah, but something has changed, my man. Changed today."

He was right. It had, although I couldn't tell you why or when it had happened.

I said, "I really like her, Aaron. I like spending time with her. She's so...so...witty and undaunted by, well, me."

"That's a plus."

"And she's beautiful; refined; highly intelligent."

Aaron chuckled again.

"Dude, you gone. You good and gone!"

Gaspard leaned forward and patted my shoulder.

"Monsieur, we have a saying in France: *Qui n'avance pas, recule.* It means, 'who does not move forward, recedes.' In other words, there is no standing still, mon ami. You either evolve, or you devolve. I believe that nowhere in life is this more true than in love. Perhaps life is telling you that it is time to move forward."

Aaron whistled and said, "That's some serious wisdom right there."

"It is," I agreed. "It definitely is. Thank you, Gaspard."

"My pleasure." He paused and then added, "Now, if only I would take my own advice."

We all laughed.

Probably harder than we should have.

We had faced several potentially life-threatening situations and were understandably a bit punchy, and the laughter seemed to relieve the tension...at least for the moment.

But I had a feeling that things were going to get worse.

Much worse.

CHAPTER 61

The Persian stood in his lavishly appointed penthouse office staring through ceiling to floor windows that provided a clear view of West Hollywood, and the Hollywood Hills beyond.

Snatching his cell phone from the inside pocket of his camel hair sport coat, he punched in a number and waited for someone to answer.

"I thought you might be calling me," said Hayato Momotani on the other end of the line.

"And who else would I be calling? In case you have forgotten, the Russian and the German are dead! It is you who began this enterprise with me and together we shall finish it. Am I correct?"

"But of course," Momotani answered.

"The Scarred Man was unsuccessful against Moriarity and he was our best! It's not like I have an army of thugs at my disposal." The Persian's voice had risen in pitch to a ragged rasp. "Moriarity is one man! One! How is it possible that he can operate this efficiently?"

"I urge calm reason, my friend."

"Calmness when we are in danger of losing everything we have worked to attain? I want answers...no...I want solutions and I want them now!"

Momotani's own anger was close to boiling over. Who did this Persian think he was talking to?

He said quietly, in measured tones, "You would do well to gain control over your emotions, Persian, and remember that unlike you...I *do* have an army—not of thugs, but of highly skilled fighters. With a snap of my fingers I can end anyone's life...even yours!"

The Persian was stunned by the not so thinly veiled threat.

Drawing a deep, calming breath, he said, "I fear I have misrepresented my feelings."

Momotani replied coldly, "I believe your feelings were made quite clear."

The Persian laughed nervously, and then said something he had no memory of having ever said to anyone before, "I apologize. My anger temporarily got the best of me."

Silence.

He tried again.

"Did you hear me, Hayato? Can we now, please, move on and come to an agreement as to how we can eliminate Moriarity?"

Momotani despised The Persian. Had, in fact, always despised him. But he was useful. While the criminal organization under Momotani's direct control had vast resources, those resources tended to be perpetually tied up in one endeavor or another. And the one thing The Persian had that none of the others possessed was immediate access to vast reserves of liquid assets...an incalculable advantage to an enterprise that ran on cash.

"I agree that Moriarity must be taken care of," Momotani said. "And yet, I have no ready answers."

An associate entered The Persian's office unannounced and handed him a piece of paper, whispering, "You need to see this right now."

The Persian muttered, "One moment, please," into the phone and started reading.

A cruel grin pulled at the corners of his mouth. "It would appear that we have been presented with a gift from the gods."

"Oh?" Momotani replied. "How so?"

"I have had my sources tracking Moriarity's family and known associates on social media."

"Go on..."

"It seems that while Moriarity has lived a monk-like existence when it comes to romance, there has recently been a change."

"He has a woman? How could you possibly have found this out?"

"Simple. I employ only the best people on the planet and pay better than anyone else could even conceive of paying. As a result, they are fiercely loyal and work tirelessly to please me."

"And what did these 'people' find?"

The Persian replied, "They have taught me that anything you want to know about almost any person on this planet can be learned through their various social media accounts."

"I find it hard to believe that Jake Moriarity would even have a social media account let alone be posting to it."

"Not him...his lady friend."

Momotani was suddenly alert.

"Do you have a name?"

"Gabriella Marcus."

A Jew! Momotani hated the Jews.

"I will have her picked up immediately," he said stiffly.

"No! I want to do it myself. I wish very much to meet her in person. If she has Moriarity's heart, she must be a remarkable woman."

"Indeed she must."

The Persian paused and then said, "Now that I have had a moment to think about my earlier apology..."

"What about it?"

"My statement about not having an army was inaccurate. I *do* have an army. Yours is flesh and blood...mine is made up of money. More money than you can possibly conceive of. And I guarantee you that if it came down to it, you would run out of your 'soldiers' long before I ran out of mine. Good day."

CHAPTER 62

We rolled in to the villa about twelve forty-five a.m., too exhausted to do much more than assure Rémi and the girls that we were all okay and introduce them to Désirée. How tired were we? We're talking the big leagues of exhaustion here. Too tired to even eat, which has happened two, maybe three times in my entire life. And as far as Aaron is concerned, this may very well have been a first. The girls took to Désirée immediately and by the time they hustled her off to her bedroom, they were all chattering away like long-lost sorority sisters.

As it turned out, Rémi was not only a highly skilled tactical fighter, but also a trained EMT. He led me into the safe room, where Gaspard had assembled the equivalent of a small infirmary, and did an expert job of patching up my latest collection of wounds. He even offered a handful of pain pills that I politely declined. It's not that I'm that tough, and it's not that I am opposed to taking them in extreme situations, I just don't like the way opioids make me feel. "Muddle-headed" is the way Aaron describes the sensation.

By the time I got into my room it was nearing two a.m. and I decided that a shower would have to wait for the morning. I brushed my teeth—which, in the moment anyway, produced a level of pleasure that was nearly sensual in its intensity—re-examined my most recent injuries and staggered into the bedroom with the intent of throwing myself onto the bed and falling into an undisturbed, blissful slumber.

That's not what I did, however.

I checked the time differential and found that it was around five p.m. in Vegas.

So I called Gabi.

She answered on the fourth ring.

"Jake?" she inquired breathlessly. "You called me! Are you okay? Are you near death? In the hospital?"

I chuckled.

"Okay, okay. Point made, point taken."

"Well, you have to admit that it *is* a bit unusual for you to initiate contact."

"Yes, it is."

She was quiet for a few seconds. Long enough that I feared having lost the connection.

"Hello, Gabi?"

"I'm still here. I was just thinking."

"Oh? And what were you thinking about?"

"The same thing that occupies my thoughts most days and nights."

I said, "I need to tell you something before this conversation goes any further—something that won't really keep."

She sighed, "And am I going to want to hear this, Jake?"

"Well...I think so."

"In that case..."

"Here's the thing, Gabi...I like you. I mean I *really* like you. And I don't want to come off sounding like I'm special or anything, but it's very unusual for me to say that about a woman. It's been a long, long time since I've had any feelings at all for someone—like since my Abby died eighteen years ago."

I could hear her sniffing.

"I really like you as well, Mr. Moriarity. And just so you know, I was willing to wait for as long as necessary for you to come around."

"And how did you know I would come around?"

She laughed. I loved that laugh.

"Well, for one, I'm not exactly hideous to look at."

"Always a plus."

"And for another thing, I seem quite capable of holding my own with you on an intellectual, conversational level."

"I'm not sure I'd actually consider that a plus, but go on."

"And thirdly..."

"Yes?" I prompted.

"I pretty much knew you were a goner that first day in the gym."

It was my turn to laugh.

"Come on! There is no possible way you could have known that I—"

"Ah-ha! See? You were just about to admit it."

She was on to me.

I said, "Let's just say that you made an indelible impression."

"Merely 'indelible,' and not ineffaceable?"

"Okay, thesaurus girl. The impression you made was...ineradicable."

"Ooo. Well played, sir."

"Anyway, it's been a really long day filled with numerous ill-intentioned men who have sought to do damage to my person and—"

"Are you injured, Jake? Tell me the truth!"

"Okay. There's a difference between being hurt and being injured."

"And pray-tell what that might be?"

"If you are injured, you are physically unable to continue. However, if you are merely hurt, you just deal with your wounds and jump back into the fray."

"And, which are you?"

"Just a little banged up. Nothing serious."

"Would you even tell me if it *was* serious?"

I thought about it for a couple of seconds.

"Yes. I believe I would."

"Well, then...it sounds as if you should get some rest. What time is it there—wherever there is?"

"We're just east of Nice, France and it's about two-fifteen a.m."

"I just love France. Well, to be clear I've never been, but I love the idea of France."

I suddenly had visions of Gabi and me strolling through the quaint villages and narrow streets of southern France. It was a great vision.

"When do you think you'll be back in Vegas?" she asked hopefully.

"Honestly? I have no idea. You know enough about what I do for a living to know that there's really no time limit on these things. My hope is that it won't take more than another few days."

I suddenly had a wild idea.

"Listen," I said. "What is your schedule like over the next week or two?"

"Well, let me think...apart from that pesky part-time job of mine, nothing pressing that I can think of."

"Wait, that 'part-time' job where you basically control the lives of two high-powered executives?"

She laughed again, "That's the one. So, what are you thinking?"

"I'm thinking that you would love it here and the possibilities are very strong that I could arrange for you to fly back with me when this job is wrapped up."

"Are you kidding? I'd quit my job to do that. So, yes! Just let me know when it transitions from a possibility to a sure thing."

"I will, Gabi." I paused as I was overtaken by a yawn. "Man! Sorry about that. I assure you that it has nothing to do with you. It's just been a very long day and if I don't get to sleep within the next thirty seconds..."

"Hey, no worries at all." She was silent for a moment before adding, "So, what is the appropriate signoff for people at this stage of relationship?"

"Well, how about, 'I think you're swell and can't wait to talk to you again as soon as possible.'"

She laughed loudly.

"Okay. That works for me. And, like I said to you once before...take care, Jake. I need you in one piece when I see you again."

"I will endeavor to do just that. Good-bye, Gabi."

"Good-bye, Jake."

I hit the end button on my phone, tossed it onto the nightstand and was basically asleep before my head hit the pillow.

My last thought was of a very pretty face...Abby's face. Her lips seemed to be forming words. I could just barely make them out...

"Be free, Jake...be free."

CHAPTER 63

Somebody had let a wild animal into my room and it now stood just over my head, growling fiercely and blowing its fetid breath into my face.

I woke up only to realize that the "wild animal" had been me snoring and that the "fetid breath" was my own.

I rolled slowly to my right, and was shocked to see that the clock on the nightstand read nine-fifteen a.m. I couldn't remember the last time I had slept until nine.

I checked my phone and saw that there was a text from Gabi.

Good morning, Jake! I just had the most wonderful thought —it had to do with being able to say that to you face-to-face and breath-to-breath some day.

That's only because you can't smell my breath! I texted back.

Dear lord, it was awful. Since I had to pee like a racehorse—a simile that, once you've seen in person you will never forget—I eased myself out of bed and tottered to the bathroom. On the way, I wondered if there was a quantifiable difference between tottering and staggering. For the sake of positivity I chose to believe that tottering was preferable to staggering, which meant that I was doing better this morning.

After relieving myself in a toilet that had to cost as much as my first car, I brushed my teeth while reading the other text she had sent fifteen minutes after the first.

Anyway, I enjoyed our conversation last evening/this morning...whatever. You need to know that I'm not an insecure person.

You don't have to call or text me continually or even frequently for me to feel okay about this burgeoning relationship. Finish what you have to do, and if you have the time...call, text, whatever you can manage. Be well, Jake!

After wiping the excess toothpaste from my mouth, I thought about answering that one as well, but decided that it could wait. So I shaved—no small feat given how swollen my jaw was—and jumped in the shower where I stayed for a long, long time.

By the time I was dressed and headed downstairs, following the scent of fresh coffee, it was close to ten-thirty. Not exactly how I had anticipated this day starting. But, as I may have mentioned before, rest is a weapon.

"Well, he lives," Aaron said while pouring me a cup of coffee.

"I'm not sure how alive I am, but I'm walking upright anyway," I replied.

Gaspard and Rémi were in the breakfast nook talking seriously with Désirée while Aaron and the girls were seated around the kitchen island.

After I had given hugs to my girls, Vanessa said, "At least you look better this morning than you did last night."

"Yeah," Cassie agreed. "I thought for sure your jaw would be swollen, but it looks fairly normal."

Aaron touched the contact point gently.

"If Chida's punch had landed about a half-inch toward your chin, I'm thinking it would've broken your jaw."

I reached up and moved my jaw around, wincing at the pain and stiffness.

"You're right, and if Étienne would've clubbed me anywhere on the back of my head other than where he did..."

"Do we really have to talk about this, Uncle?" Cassie asked, as her eyes grew misty. "I mean it's bad enough knowing you go out and do dangerous things, but to listen to a blow-by-blow replay of how you could have died is just not my idea of a good time."

"I agree," added Muriel.

"Okay, fair enough. We will dispense with the telling of the tale until Aaron and I are alone in some manly place on a manly mission."

Gaspard, Rémi and Désirée stood and joined us at the island.

Gaspard said with a smile, "I was about to ask whether you had slept, but seeing the lateness of the hour..."

"I know," I replied shaking my head. "I didn't get to sleep until 2:30 or so."

Vanessa asked, "So, you took a shower last night?"

"Well, not exactly."

The girls exchanged glances with each other and then with Aaron, who shrugged innocently.

Cassie pierced me with a knowing gaze.

"You called her, didn't you?"

"I have no idea what—"

"You called Gabi. Come on, Uncle! You know you did and we know you did, so let's hear it."

Nothing like being nearly killed by bad guys the evening before and then being subjected to an interrogation not even twelve hours later.

"Okay! I called her."

Muriel pumped her fist in the air.

"I knew it! I knew you two would find a way to get together."

Désirée said, "I do not know who this Gabi is, but if she has your heart, she is a very fortunate woman." She paused and then added, "We have a development to discuss with you."

"Okay?" I prompted.

"My sources in the cartel who are at present unaware of my, how do you say...duplicity...called me earlier and it seems that all is not well between Momotani and The Persian."

"That could be interesting."

"Oui. Furthermore, the German and the Russian have vanished, and my associates at ELAC believe they have been terminated."

I said, "Purely from a survival point of view, that makes a lot of sense. From the very start it's been obvious that The Persian and Momotani are the true power behind the cartel. If I had to guess, The Persian controls the money and Momotani controls the soldiers on the ground through his Yakuza."

"That is exactly the way it has been. The other two were never mentioned by name and, from what I was able to ascertain at least, were in the cartel to provide distribution routes through their respective countries. It was, at best, an expedience."

Aaron said, "So if the German and the Russian are dead, that means that The Persian isn't going to be sitting still. My guess is he's in the wind."

Désirée wrinkled her lovely brow.

"In the wind? I do not know this phrase."

She turned to Gaspard and Rémi who just shrugged their shoulders.

I chuckled, "When a bad guy is on the run and you don't know where they are, we call it being 'in the wind.'"

"Ah, yes, of course. Well, then it is most likely true that both principles are, uh, in the wind, as you say. It is harder to hit a moving target, no?"

"So, assuming The Persian isn't just sitting in LA waiting for us to come and collect him, where do you think he'd be?"

She thought for a few seconds.

"While I am by no means an expert on this man's movements, he is a creature of habit."

Her face suddenly darkened and I could see fear spark in her eyes.

"Jake, this woman, Gabi...where does she live?"

As soon as she had voiced the question I was way ahead of her, grabbing my phone out of my pants pocket and stabbing clumsily at Gabriella's name and number.

Her phone started ringing.

"Come on, Gabi. Pick up."

It continued to ring.

And then it rang some more before finally being answered.

What I heard turned my blood to ice!

CHAPTER 64

A deep male voice said, "How nice of you to call, Mr. Moriarity. Then again, if I had a woman as lovely as Ms. Marcus for a companion, I suppose I would be calling her frequently as well."

I could hear scuffling in the background along with a woman's cries.

I put the phone on speaker so the others could follow the conversation while scribbling Gabi's address on a scrap of paper and shoving it toward Aaron with, "Jason Green!" and "Zack Hastings!" written underneath it and underlined. Detective Jason Green was a close friend who works with the Las Vegas Metropolitan Police Department.

Jason had been instrumental in Vanessa's original rescue from crooked politician Harry Olivetti and his late son, Collin —men who had conspired to make her life a living hell. Metro could dispatch officers to Gabi's house and hopefully catch The Persian in the act, so to speak.

"You listen to me, you son of a bitch! I know what you're thinking."

"Oh? And what am I thinking?"

"That who you are and what you have makes you safe. And if that is true, then you haven't done your homework on me. I will find you. I *always* find who I'm looking for. There is nowhere for you to hide. Now, if you let her go immediately, when I find you I will merely cause you a substantial amount of pain for troubling my friend. But if she is in any way harmed, you and everyone you care about will die horribly."

By now I was shouting, and out of the corner of my eye I could see the others in the room shrinking back from the force of my anger.

"Do you understand me, you piece of shit?"

There was a few seconds silence on the other end of the line.

"Those are serious threats, Mr. Moriarity. Are you certain you are capable of backing them up? After all, you are there and, well, we are here with Ms. Marcus. Which means we can do anything to her that we wish and there is nothing you can do to stop us."

"Correct. There is nothing I can do to stop you in this moment. But that isn't what I'm talking about. This moment will pass and you will do whatever it is that you are going to do. But then...there will be *another* moment. I can't say for sure when it will come, nor can you predict its arrival. But know that it is coming. And when it does, it will be terrible. And you know enough about me to know that I do not issue idle threats."

The man sighed.

"All this talk of violence. It is so unnecessary. I do not wish to harm your lady friend any more than you wish to see her harmed."

"Okay. Then put something on the table we can discuss."

"That is more like it. We are not animals here."

"Then, let her go and we'll talk."

He laughed long and loudly.

"Do you take me for a fool?"

"Actually, that is exactly what I take you for, because only a fool would poke the tiger." I quickly added, "By the way, we know that you killed the German and the Russian."

The man's sharp intake of breath confirmed that I had struck a nerve.

He said, "How very clever of you. It should tell you something."

"Oh, and what's that?"

I could hear him sigh deeply.

"I don't even know why I am having this conversation with you, given that you will be joining my former partners in death quite soon."

"That's not going to happen."

"Oh, but it will, Mr. Moriarity. And you will never see it coming."

Désirée stepped closer and said, "If you are still counting on me to carry out your evil, Monsieur, I fear you will be gravely disappointed."

We could hear the man breathing slowly as if trying to calm himself.

"Ah, yes...the lovely Désirée...our hidden asset."

"C'est moi."

He said slowly, evenly, "I will personally make sure that you regret this betrayal."

"What I already regret, Monsieur, is your very existence, which, if fortune smiles, I intend on ending quite soon."

Aaron had stepped into another room to place the calls and leaned around the doorframe, nodding his head and giving me a thumb's up sign.

In the background I could hear sirens approaching, passing and then fading. They weren't at her condo! They had to be in a vehicle.

The Persian laughed.

"Did you really think I'd be stupid enough to call you from Ms. Marcus' house, and then stay there while you called the police, Mr. Moriarity? Enough of these idle threats. Here is what is going to happen: you are going to tell the ELAC—"

"No!" I roared. "*Here* is what is going to happen! I already have the FBI looking for you. You know what that means, don't you? There is nowhere on this earth where you can hide. By now every airport—commercial and private—in Clark County, Nevada will have FBI, Homeland Security as well as Las Vegas Metro monitoring all outbound flights. And did I mention that there will be a roadblock at the border?"

Of course I had no way of knowing whether any of that were true, but neither did he.

He muffled the phone while he said something, I was guessing, to the driver.

Then, "It has become apparent that continuing this conversation will be a monumental waste of my time, and if I am being pursued as an International fugitive from justice, as you suggested, then I have no time to waste. Goodbye, Mr. Moriarity. I had so hoped that you would be reasonable. Alas, you are not."

And with that, the connection was broken.

"Dammit!" I shouted. "Aaron, tell me that what I said to him is actually happening."

"It is, bro. Zack *and* Jason got on it right away."

I stared helplessly at the faces gathered around the island.

"Are you okay, Uncle?" Cassie asked softly.

I started shaking my head slowly.

"I don't know. This is surreal...just, surreal." Locking eyes with Désirée I said, "Want to tell us what that was all about with The Persian?"

CHAPTER 65

Désirée smiled ironically.

"The cartel has believed for quite some time that there were two assassins in their employ."

"You and Chida?" I asked.

"Oui, Monsieur. As I mentioned earlier, Chida really did kill his targets while at the same time lying to ELAC about it to protect his cover. *I* am the one who put my targets into protective custody...not him."

Aaron said, "Forgive me if my trust level is running on empty, but with all this double-agent stuff going on, how can we even be sure you are who you claim to be?"

"ELAC will be happy to provide you with all the proof you need."

"But that's going to take some time, and time is what we don't have!"

On a certain level I shared Aaron's concern, but on another...I tended to believe her.

"I think she's telling the truth."

"As do I," Gaspard added emphatically.

Vanessa moved over and stood directly in front of Désirée.

"I may not know much about everything that's happening here, but what I *do* know about is liars. I can spot one a mile away." She gazed intently into Désirée's eyes. "And this lady is no liar."

Aaron and I glanced at each other.

"Good enough for me," he said.

"Me too. Now that that's settled...Désirée?"

"Everything you said regarding the tightened airport and border security would be daunting to most. But, the men we are dealing with are used to writing their own rules. Trust me when I say that The Persian has already made contingencies."

"Which means that it's highly likely they will escape before things can be put in place to stop them."

"Oui, Monsieur."

"So, what can we do?" Muriel asked in a small voice.

Désirée glanced at Muriel and then swept her gaze around the room making sure she had made eye contact with everyone.

"Even though he has made his plans...I know what those plans are."

I said skeptically, "How can you possibly know that?"

"Because, as I said, he is nothing if not a creature of habit, and...I know these habits well."

Cassie gasped, "You were with him, weren't you?"

Désirée dropped her gaze momentarily.

"Oui, Cassie. I was."

It felt like I'd been sucker punched.

"Wait...wait a second. Are you—"

"Saying that we were lovers? Oui. That is exactly what I am saying. It is not something I am proud of, except in the sense that it was what my cover demanded. So, I did it. And, yes...he is what you might imagine him to be—a pig!"

She spat the last word as if expunging something vile from her system.

I said, "That would explain his comment about betrayal."

"You can be sure he takes this quite personally."

We all stood in an embarrassed silence not knowing, really, how to get past Désirée's revelation.

Finally, Aaron said with a grin, "Well, this morning's just

full of surprises."

His lighthearted remark seemed to break the tension and Désirée laughed while I verbalized our options.

"Gaspard, are you willing to let us use your jet to get back to LA?"

"Of course, Monsieur. But on one condition."

"Okay."

"That I accompany you."

I started to protest but he waved me off.

"Oh, it is not that I wish to participate in the, eh, manhunt. If my plane is going to Los Angeles, I intend to see my Simone."

"Fair enough. Second question—can we fly non-stop, or will we have to stop and fuel."

All eyes turned to Désirée.

"At high speed, the G6 has a range of about six thousand nautical miles. I believe the distance from Paris to Los Angeles is around forty-nine hundred."

"So, theoretically we could do it?"

"Oui, Monsieur. And if we were to encounter severe head winds, we would simply drop into long-range mode, which would add about seven hundred miles to our range."

"How long are we talking here?" Aaron asked.

"There are many variables," Désirée replied. "But I would say nine hours is a good estimate."

I said, "Okay. Next question. How soon can you have that jet prepped and ready to go?"

She smiled.

"It has already been done. When we landed I told the cartel's ground crew to immediately ready the plane and have it standing by for long-range departure."

"Last question; you said you knew what his plans are. Care to fill us in on that?"

Désirée drew in a long breath and began, "While The Persian is incalculably wealthy and powerful, he, as is true with most people, has safe places where he retreats when he's feeling stressed. The urge to do so is almost entirely subconscious. Because this is a stressful situation, I am quite certain I know where he is headed with Gabriella."

"And is there any possible way you can up that level of certainty?"

"Oui. One of his personal bodyguards was, how do you say it...smitten with me? He would do anything I ask."

Aaron said, "So, you think you can reach him?"

She held up her phone.

"But of course. I will call, ask him where they are going and he will tell me."

Cassie scoffed, "How can you have that much power over him?"

Smiling conspiratorially, Désirée answered, "We women know when we have a man, as you Americans say, wrapped around our little finger, oui?"

"But doesn't he fear The Persian?" Cassie asked.

"Oui. It is true. But his desire for me overrides his fear. Trust me...he will do as I ask."

I said, "All right. You make the call and we'll get some things organized." As she left the room I continued, "We all need to be on that flight, so get your things together as quickly as possible."

Rémi had been standing in the background and stepped forward suddenly.

"Rémi will accompany you as well."

He put it as a statement and not a query.

Gaspard widened his eyes and began a rapid-fire back and forth conversation in French between he and Rémi resulting in Gaspard throwing his hands up in resignation and shaking his head.

I asked, "What was that all about?"

Gaspard sighed and shook his head.

"He is stubborn, this one. He insists on coming with us and I fear I cannot dissuade him."

Rémi stood rigidly almost as if at military attention.

"Have I not already proven my usefulness?"

I couldn't argue the point.

He continued, "While Rémi draws breath, Mademoiselle Cassie—all of you—will be safe."

"Boy's got a point, Jake," Aaron said around a wry grin. "I do believe this is gonna require all hands on deck."

Since I didn't have time to argue, I accepted Rémi's offer.

"Then let's get moving, people. The faster the better."

Désirée came back into the room smiling.

"So?" I prompted.

"My friend, Freddy, is not with The Persian. He is already at the location where Gabriella is being taken making sure things are prepared for their arrival."

My heart rate suddenly quickened.

"Where is it and when does he expect them?"

"Laguna Beach. The Persian had a helicopter standing by at a private airfield and they are already on their way. Freddy expects them in two to three hours."

"We need to get moving now!" I hollered, and watched as everyone scurried from the room leaving Désirée and me alone.

She put her hand on my shoulder in a sisterly fashion.

"Don't worry, Jake. I will not let anything happen to your Gabi."

I nodded my head. It was the only response I could make, given the large wad of cotton that had suddenly appeared in my throat.

CHAPTER 66

We made it to the airport in a surprisingly short amount of time and were actually on-board the G6 by ten-thirty. Since Désirée had filed a flight plan on the way in, the only thing left to do was to go through the preflight checklist, a drill that, to be honest, was torturous given the urgency of the situation. In a moment of frustration I asked Désirée whether she could speed up the process only to be politely, yet firmly, informed that there were things that had to be done and that she would take as much time as was needed to complete the list. A stupid man would have continued to force the issue. I am not a stupid man. So, having been thus enlightened, I found a seat in the rear of the cabin, settled in and resigned myself to this present, bitter reality.

I'm sure the entire process consumed no more than fifteen minutes, but to me it felt like an eternity! I kept imagining what was happening to Gabi at the hands of a monster like The Persian—a man with no scruples and an insatiable desire to possess and consume everything upon which his greedy gaze happened to fall. And I have a good imagination!

By the time Aaron sat down beside me I was, to put it mildly, in a state.

He said, "Listen, bro...I know you're worried about Gabi, but you got to just let this process play out. There's nothing you can do from this seat right here that will change the outcome in any way, shape, or form. Continuing to be as worked up as you are right now will just wear you out!"

I took a deep breath and started to reply in what I am certain would have been a dishonoring and dismissive manner. Instead I just blew it out and let my head fall back against the seat rest.

"I feel helpless, Aaron. Completely and utterly helpless."

"You're not helpless! You are one of the most resourceful and powerful people I've ever met."

I wasn't having any of it!

"But in the face of this situation, I am most definitely helpless."

"Look, I know it feels that way, but what if you approached it from a different perspective?"

"Okay, I'll play along. What do you have in mind?"

He paused momentarily to collect his thoughts.

"What if instead of looking at this delay between now and when we're wheels down in LA as something to be resented, you looked at it as much needed time to plan your strategy and to catch up on some sleep? 'Cause when you go up against The Persian, and whatever members of the cartel he deploys against you, you're going to have to be one hundred percent."

There was no arguing his logic.

"You make a very persuasive, salient point."

"Salient? Really, dude? I hate that word!"

"Why?"

"I don't know. Probably because it sounds too much like saliva."

"I assure you that the two words have nothing in common. Completely different etymology."

"Why, thank you Dr. Vocabulary."

I turned slightly so that I was partially facing him.

"Are you questioning the veracity of my contention?"

"The 'veracity of your contention?'" he replied with raised eyebrows. "Seriously, bro?"

"Okay, the reliability, the...uh...the legitimacy—"

He said, "So, you tellin' me that salient and saliva have

nothing in common?"

"That's exactly what I'm saying! I can't believe we're having this conversation."

He just grinned at me.

"What?" I prompted.

"French Kiss."

I stared at him like he was out of his mind.

"And what the hell does that film have to do with any-thing?"

He pointed out the window. All I could see were scattered clouds against a backdrop of blue sky.

He said, "That scene in the movie where Meg Ryan's character was freaked out about flying and Kevin Kline distracted her with some pointless chatter until they were off the ground."

"So, all this was just to distract me until we were airborne?"

He stood to return to his seat beside Muriel.

"See you in LA, bro."

I nodded slowly as a grin fought its way onto my previously scowling face.

"Love you too, Aaron," I hollered at his retreating backside.

CHAPTER 67

I know what you're thinking...that I spent the rest of the flight in intense planning and strategizing for how I was going to dismantle The Persian's criminal empire; that by the time we were wheels down in LA I would be totally prepared to engage in battle.

Well, you'd be wrong.

On the other hand, if you were thinking that I had about seven hours of restful slumber, you'd be quite right.

It felt good.

It felt *real* good!

I mean what else was I going to do from forty-one thousand feet?

Before dropping off into never-never land, I contacted Zack Hastings and told him what was happening and where The Persian was headed. He assured me that he'd do everything in his power to be there waiting for him.

And he was.

The only problem? The Persian never showed!

So he left a crew in place and when we landed at the John Wayne Airport executive terminal around ten-thirty a.m., he and his guys were waiting for us.

I know that Hollywood is fond of portraying FBI agents as the bad guys. And, to be fair, just as is true in virtually every profession you care to dig into, there *are* agents that are possessed of somewhat less than stellar character.

Zack's not like that.

Zack's one of the good guys.

I made my way off the plane and across the tarmac toward where he stood beside an agency SUV.

He met me halfway and shook my hand.

"He wasn't there, Jake."

I waited until my crew was gathered around me before answering.

"Désirée, Zack said that The Persian wasn't there!"

Her eyes widened in surprise.

"But, that is impossible. Freddy would not lie to me."

"Désirée," Zack began and then paused, blowing out a long breath. "We found a body in the residence. It was a male; approximately thirty to thirty-five years old; slender; blonde hair cut quite short—"

"Oh, mon Dieu!" she exclaimed covering her face with her hands. "That is poor Freddy."

I said, "So someone in the organization must've tipped The Persian off to Freddy's betrayal."

Zack nodded in agreement.

"Désirée, do you know of anyplace else The Persian might be taking Ms. Marcus?"

She closed her eyes, shaking her head slowly as if simultaneously attempting to deal with the horrible news about her friend, and realigning her thoughts so as to answer Zack's question.

"This is just...give me a moment, Monsieur."

She walked away, bowed her head and cried a little.

Zack jerked his head in her direction.

"I know what that feels like, you know...blaming yourself for someone's death."

"Thankfully," I replied, "It hasn't happened to me as yet, and I hope to never have to deal with it."

Désirée suddenly straightened, as if physically throwing off her grief.

"Okay, Monsieur Hastings. I am ready now. I believe the only other place The Persian would go—the only place where he'd feel safe and in control—is his office building in West

Hollywood."

"You got an address?"

"Oui, Monsieur. We will go together and I will show you."

"Hang on a second," I said. Sweeping my arm around our small assemblage, I continued, "We're not all going. You guys —Aaron, Gaspard, Muriel, Cassie and Vanessa—are going back to Carlsbad to Cassie's condo. And, Rémi, I want you go accompany them in case someone tries to get cute and attack my family again."

He nearly snapped to attention.

"Oui, Monsieur. It will be my privilege."

I turned back to Zack.

"How long will it take us to get into West Hollywood?"

"Well, if we drive, you're probably looking at an hour and fifteen to an hour and a half even rolling code blue."

I swore in a manner that surprised even myself.

"Too long! We're at the airport...what are the chances of co-opting a chopper?"

He grinned widely.

"In anticipation of just such an eventuality, I have one standing by."

I slapped him on the back and said to my family, "While I don't really anticipate anything, best for you guys to be on high alert from the time you leave here until you arrive at the condo. Even when you get there, keep someone on lookout until you hear from us that this is finished."

Cassie stepped forward and threw her arms around me.

"Be safe."

I returned her embrace tightly.

"You know I will."

Vanessa and Muriel were next. They both hugged me without words. Really...what was there to say?

Aaron and I did our customary bro-hug, which included an energetic and sincere knuckle bump.

"Be seeing you on the other side of this, my brother."

"That you will," I replied with more certainty than I felt.

Zack hollered, "We're airborne in ten."

Before I could respond, Gaspard approached me having just completed a call.

"I talked to Simone. She is going to meet us at Cassie's condo after today's sessions are over."

"I'm so glad to hear that, Gaspard. It's the best place for her to be at present."

He stepped forward and, with tenderness usually reserved for close family members, kissed me on both cheeks and then held me at arm's length.

"Jake, get this man...and the other one as well. They are a cancer on the soul of Europe."

"I will, Gaspard. It ends today."

As soon as I said it, I secretly hoped I could back up my boldness...the alternative was unthinkable.

CHAPTER 68

To Gabriella Marcus, the cruel, rough men who showed up at her condo were like something out of a horror movie where the heroine is abducted and carried away at gunpoint to face whatever horrible fate awaited her in the form of death or torture. Thus far, at least, she had experienced neither. The only thing lost was a bit of pride at being carried away in only her nightgown. When she had requested that she be afforded the dignity of at least putting on a robe, the men had leered at her near nakedness and coldly suggested that she keep quiet.

And then there was the man who was obviously in charge. The powerful, yet nameless one who spoke in low tones that simply reeked of refinement and elegance. And wealth. Don't forget wealth. She had been around wealthy men all of her life in her position as a highly sought after administrative assistant, so she knew—at least on a general level—how they thought, acted and reacted. But this man was different. His eyes reflected a certain something. Something largely unidentifiable, but she thought she knew. It was a conviction—a dead certainty on his part—that whatever he wished; whatever he even conceived would be carried out without even the slightest hesitation by those under his authority. She had worked for wealthy, powerful men all her adult life, and none had possessed what this man had. This transcended authority. This was raw, naked power, and power like that only came from possessing a level of wealth that was virtually incalculable.

She sat, not uncomfortably, in a room that, by any-one's definition, resembled nothing short of a war room. The harrowing escape from Las Vegas—the urgency of which she was absolutely certain had been driven by Jake Moriarity—resembled something out of a Hollywood thriller. The frantic flight through the streets, dodging police cruisers (all going the wrong direction); the wild and bumpy helicopter ride into Burbank; a second mad dash by car through the Los Angeles Metroplex eventually arriving at a high-rise somewhere in Hollywood by her reckoning. Had she not been certain that her life was in immanent danger, it would have all been quite exciting.

Somewhere along the way, plans had been abruptly changed and she was sure she overheard the directive being given ordering someone's execution. That alone brought the gravity of her situation to the forefront of her mind. And were it not for the fact that she knew beyond all doubt that Jake was coming for her, despair would have long ago interlaced its icy fingers around her heart and begun to squeeze piteously.

The man in charge, which is what she called him since they had not been formally introduced, now sat ten feet away staring at her in silent appraisal.

With a boldness she had always possessed around powerful men, she said, "Do you like what you see?"

He smiled for the first time.

"Why, yes. Now that you mention it, I must confess that I do. You really are quite extraordinary, Ms. Marcus. Quite extraordinary indeed."

"Thank you, Mister..."

The smile broadened.

"I am simply called The Persian."

"Ah, I see. What an odd name for parents to give their son."

The smile dissolved quickly.

"Do not speak of my parents!"

"Ooh, hit a nerve, did I?"

Sighing, he stood slowly and began to pace around the room.

"Let us get one thing clear, Ms. Marcus. Ours is not a cordial relationship. You are my captive. And you shall remain my captive as long as I deem it necessary for you to be so."

"Or, until Jake Moriarity arrives, as he most surely will."

"Jake Moriarity!" he fumed. "Why is this man even breathing the same air that I breathe? He is nothing! Nothing, I tell you. I could buy and sell him a million times over!"

"Ah, but that is where you are wrong, Persian. For Jake Moriarity cannot be bought."

He stopped pacing and turned to glare in her direction.

"And *that*, my beautiful Ms. Marcus, is where *you* are wrong. Transactions do not always involve money."

"You are, of course in your thuggish way, referring to my life, are you not?"

"Just so. It is a commodity I currently possess that Moriarity seems to place quite a high value upon. So, you see, he *can* be bought."

Gabriella thought about that for a few seconds, surprised at the conclusion she reached.

"No, you are wrong. Because if it meant sacrificing my life for a greater good, he would choose the greater good."

He took two quick strides and came to within a foot of where she sat, leaning over slightly at the waist.

"Even if it meant that you would be tortured to death cruelly, horribly, over an extended amount of time?"

She smiled sweetly.

"But you don't have an 'extended amount of time,' do you? In fact," she glanced at a large digital display clock on the far wall. "By my reckoning, he will be here momentarily."

"How is that possible," The Persian shouted. "He doesn't know where *here* is!"

"Oh, I think he does. And I suppose we will find out, shortly, who is right...and who is dead."

He raised his eyebrows comically.

"You are facing death and you quote the *Princess Bride* to me?"

With as much control as she could summon, she replied, "I just love that movie, don't you?"

He closed his eyes in effort to maintain control.

"Ms. Marcus, you are beginning to try my patience. I suggest that you cease before a line is crossed that you will, I assure you, regret crossing. Profoundly so!"

A burly man entered the room with a concerned expression on his face, beckoning The Persian to approach. As he did she craned her neck in an attempt to eavesdrop on the conversation. And while she couldn't pick up any specific words, body language alone was enough to tell her that Jake was getting near. In fact, she could almost sense his approach.

"Hurry, darling. Hurry," she whispered under her breath.

CHAPTER 69

I may have mentioned this before, so please forgive me if I repeat myself, but I hate helicopters! I hate everything about them, from the cacophonous noise in the cabin, to the inescapable reality that if even one thing fails in the chain of propulsion, you plummet like a boulder to a cruel and certain death below! At least with an airplane you have a chance—an outside one to be sure—but a chance to at least glide to safety on a public street or golf course, or something.

Zack hollered over the headset, "We have secured permission from a neighboring building to use their helipad."

"Their what?" I replied in horror.

"Helipad."

"So, we're going to set down on a postage stamp sized pad on the top of a, what, thirty story building and hope we don't blow off or that the pilot doesn't miss?"

He laughed.

"No, nothing like that. It's a sixty story building."

And then he laughed some more, like it was just the funniest thing ever.

I didn't share his humor and told him so in a manner that would've made a longshoreman proud.

Onboard the chopper was Zack, myself, Désirée and three agents plus the pilot and co-pilot. A Hostage Rescue Team, or HRT, who had already established a command post and secured a perimeter, was meeting us at The Persian's building. As such, there was virtually no way anyone inside could possibly get outside without crossing that perimeter. Unless, that is, The Persian had access to an underground garage/escape route of some sort that could be accessed via a private elevator. Which, the more I thought about it seemed highly likely.

"Zack!" I hollered.

"Yeah?"

"Do you have schematics available for The Persian's building?"

"Sure do."

"Can you have someone check to see if there was a private elevator connecting to some form of underground escape route or anything of that nature?"

"That's a very viable concern. I'm on it."

I felt the chopper slowing and beginning an initial descent. From my vantage point, there was no way in hell that we were going to survive setting down on what now made my earlier estimation of a postage stamp sized pad seem generous by comparison. Miniscule is the term that came to mind.

"Don't worry, Jake," Désirée said comfortingly.

At least I think she meant it to be comforting. Hard to tell when every syllable had to be shouted.

"Yeah? That's exactly what Terry Kath said before he put a gun to his head and pulled the trigger!"

"Who?"

"Terry Kath. The original guitarist for the band Chicago. He put a loaded gun to his head and said, 'Don't worry, it's not loaded.' And, of course, it was."

Staring at me with a worried expression, she said, "Are you always, as you Americans say, this random?"

"Pretty much. I find that it keeps people off-guard."

"Which, I'm sure, is a valuable tool in your world."

"At times, yes."

The chopper began shuddering as the pilot fought crosswinds coming in from the seaward side of the city, an experience somewhat akin to what I imagined it'd feel like were one to be suspended from a cork in front of a window fan. But, eventually he managed to land, much to the relief of one and all. Especially *this* one!

Climbing out was no picnic, let me just tell you! Haven't these people ever heard of guardrails, for God's sake! I mean just a few feet in every direction was the edge of the building, which seemed to beckon to me like a seductive, ghostly Siren luring me to my death. Man! I needed to get this over with and get back to a more normal routine.

We were quickly through the roof access, down a hall and crammed into an elevator that continued the day's thrills by plummeting at, or near, the speed of light, coming to a screeching halt just before splintering into a thousand bits against the basement floor.

Okay, I may have overstated that last part, but you know what they say...perception *is* reality.

Once out on the street, we were hustled into a waiting agency SUV and whisked away to the command center some four blocks away.

Zack turned in his seat and hung a detailed building schematic over the back.

"This is the original building plan we procured from the City of Los Angeles. There is nothing on here that indicates what you suggested was ever constructed."

"Which doesn't preclude the possibility," I said, "that a man with The Persian's wealth and influence couldn't have made it happen without anyone knowing about it."

"Right. But with nothing visible, we have no way of knowing if it's true or not."

Zack's earpiece seemed to crackle to life and he cupped his hand over his ear listening intently.

"Great! Well, so much for the element of surprise. Thanks."

Looking up he said, "They know we're coming."

"How is that possible?" I asked in astonishment. "I thought you guys were better than that."

"We are. But apparently his guys are as good as our guys. Makes sense. A guy with that kind of money must have his pick of the best mercenaries on the planet."

"So, if he knows we're coming, all the more reason to believe that rather than stand and fight, he'll cut and run."

Zack tapped his earpiece.

"I need a four square block area sealed off. No one gets in or out. No one! Got it?" Making eye contact with me he said, "Even if he does have an underground escape route, I seriously doubt even he has sufficient wealth to excavate further than four blocks in any direction."

Thinking back to my run in with Yves Barreau, I replied, "You'd be surprised what people can do given sufficient time and resources."

"Now that you mention it, I see your point." Amending his previous directive he ordered that the perimeter be expanded to six blocks with units watching every block in every direction. "That should do it. Don't you think that should do it?"

"Seems like it. Guess we'll find out soon enough." I paused and then added, "Of course, I could just go up by myself and stir things up a little."

"Absolutely not!"

"Why?"

"You know why!"

"Enlighten me."

He sighed as if in exasperation.

"Jake, this isn't the old west. You can't just go charging in there by yourself."

Désirée said, "He won't be by himself. I am going as well."

Both Zack and I snapped our heads in her direction so quickly that I heard the popping of bones.

"That's completely out of the question," we both said simultaneously each in our own way.

"And why is that?" she inquired.

I stared at Zack with no plausible answer. Apparent in his return gaze was the fact that he had nothing to say either.

Désirée continued, "I know this building inside and out —like the back of my hand—or whatever other clichés you wish to use."

"She's got a point," I said to Zack.

He replied hesitantly, "Okay. But if this even smells like it's going sideways, we're coming in."

"Fair enough."

"Okay," he said. "Let's get you two wrapped and strapped," and then climbed out of the SUV hollering orders to everyone within earshot.

Désirée and I looked at each other without speaking. There was nothing to say. What we were about to attempt was, by all logic, completely suicidal. But there was a monster to take down and a damsel to rescue. Melodramatic, I know, but it seemed to fit.

"Let's do this," Désirée said giving my hand a squeeze.

"One for all..."

"And all for one."

We both laughed.

I said, "That's a pretty stupid saying."

"You wouldn't say that if it had been your people that originated it."

CHAPTER 70

Upstairs in The Persian's safe room, things were getting a little crazy, at least from Gabriella's perspective. Orders were being shouted; men were running here and there, loading up with enough weapons to outfit a small army.

Through it all, The Persian sat behind a desk, like a king sending his soldiers off to war.

He suddenly stood and walked slowly toward her.

"Apparently your friend, Mr. Moriarity, is more resourceful than I imagined."

She smiled.

"That must mean that he brought the cavalry."

"Excuse me?"

"It's an American colloquialism originating during the pioneer days of the country when the US Army was called the Cavalry. Primarily horse soldiers of the frontier."

He screwed up his face.

"And that is apropos to what?"

"The fact that the FBI is with him."

He waved his hand dismissively and said, "Ah, yes. The much-vaunted FBI. Well, let me tell you something. They are no match for my mercenaries."

"Don't' be so sure of that. After all, they recruit from the best in our country."

"And I, Ms. Marcus my dear, recruit from the best in the *world!*"

"Then why are you so nervous?"

He widened his eyes as if in shock.

"Nervous? Me? That is preposterous. For I do not *get* nervous. I *make* people nervous."

"Uh-huh," she said slowly, drawing out the vowels.

"You scoff?"

"Yes, actually, I do."

"Well," he said with a chuckle. "When all this is over, I am the only one who is going to be laughing."

A thought suddenly came to her.

"You have a secret way out that no one knows about. Not even your men."

"Shhhhh!" he said, moving closer. "Be careful what you say."

She raised her voice, saying loudly, "What? You don't want your men to know—"

Suddenly his hand was clamped so forcefully over her mouth that she could barely breathe let alone speak.

Leaning in so his lips were no more than an inch from her ear, he whispered, "That will be quite enough of that. Hostage or no hostage, should you make the unfortunate decision to engage in a similar outburst," he tapped her larynx. "I will crush your throat like a cheap taco shell. Do you understand?"

All she could do was nod her head slightly, painfully.

"Good. And now that we understand each other, I will remove my hand."

She felt the air flow back into her lungs and reasoned that perhaps she wasn't quite as ready to die as she had at first imagined.

Sitting beside her, The Persian laid a hand on her knee, patting it as if giving comfort.

"That being said, yes. I do have a means of escape. But you will be coming with me, so you have nothing to fear."

"I was never afraid to begin with. Jake is coming. Remember?"

His eyes narrowed and she feared that she had, once again, pushed him too far.

"Richard!" he hollered.

A slight, well-dressed man came running.

"Yes, boss."

"Do we have eyes on the raiding party?"

"We do, boss. They are simply hanging back at the command station. Like they're trying to decide what to do next."

"Good. Good. Please inform me immediately should that situation change."

"You got it, boss."

Gabi said, possibly ill advisedly, "I can almost smell the fear on you, you know."

He rounded on her.

"It is not fear, my sweet, but anticipation. You see, even though I always win, I enjoy a worthy opponent."

"Always?"

He smiled, evilly.

"Yes. Always."

She held his gaze for several seconds.

"Until now. You have never faced a man like Jake Moriarity."

Breathing deeply, he replied, "Good. I have been needing a new challenge."

Richard came running once more.

"Sir, it is Number Two on the phone.

The Persian cursed and took the proffered phone.

"What is it?"

Momotani spoke quickly and harshly, "You fool! You have managed to plunge us into ruin with your pride."

"Plunge us into ruin? That's a bit of an overstatement, is it not?"

"Listen to me, you pompous, arrogant slime. If we survive this—and that is a big if—I will personally oversee your death. It will be exquisite. I will ensure that each and every breath, right up until and including your final one, will be filled with as much agony as a human being is capable of feeling. And you know me well enough to realize that I am a man who says what he means and does what he says."

It was true. All of it. The Persian knew it as surely as he knew that life as he had always known it was close to being over. But he couldn't crack. He *wouldn't* crack. Not for Momotani, and certainly not for Jake Moriarity.

"You are overreacting, my friend."

"I. Am. Not. Your. Friend! You would do well to remember that moving forward. I am now your sworn enemy. Should you be fortunate enough to prevail against the American FBI and Jake Moriarity, you will have me to reckon with. I find you detestable. Contemptible. And I am committed to calling upon every resource at my disposal to ensure your eradication."

"You forget one thing, Momotani."

"Oh, and what is that?"

"Moriarity is not only after me...but you are also in his crosshairs."

Momotani chuckled.

"Really? And whose building are the FBI surrounding as we speak. Certainly not mine."

"I have to go," The Persian said abruptly and terminated the call before turning and hurling the cell phone against the far wall.

Gabriella watched the outburst with barely contained glee.

"Looks like someone got to you."

Piercing her with an evil gaze, he said, "You would do well to concern yourself with your own well being, Ms. Marcus. For the time is drawing near when you will be of no further use to me. And when that time arrives, I assure you that I will not hesitate to end your life."

In her heart she knew that it was true. But she couldn't give up hope that Jake was coming. He would come for her.

That realization made her fall in love all over again.

CHAPTER 71

Zack, Désirée and I studied the site map for The Persian's building. It seemed that the top ten floors of the forty-story structure were devoted to his various criminal enterprises, while the lower thirty were leased to independent commercial tenants. Which, to be honest, complicated our situation immensely. Endeavoring to evacuate thirty floors of people when there was a legitimate emergency was hard enough. Trying to accomplish it without telling them why was, well, challenging if not downright impossible.

Complicating the situation was the very real sense Désirée and I both had that The Persian wasn't the type of man to back himself into a corner without a means of escaping said corner.

He was up to something.

I said, "What if he drew us all in, got our focus targeted on this building and the certainty that we had him cornered, when, in reality, he was just using this as a ruse—a misdirection and that his escape route was elsewhere?"

Zack ran stubby fingers through his thick hair.

"If you're asking me for a professional opinion, then, yeah...that's exactly what I would expect of him."

I looked a question at Désirée.

"I do not disagree...however...in all the time I spent there," She leaned over and tapped the penthouse office suite on the map. "I saw nothing to indicate the existence of a safe room, or even a secret, eh, stairway or something that could be used to get out of the building."

"Okay, look," I said impatiently. "When you are on the top floor of a forty story building and the FBI has the bottom floors and six blocks in either direction cordoned off, there are limited options. You can go out the window, which, as I am sure you will agree is *not* an option. You can come down the stairs or take the elevator to the basement—a basement that is completely occupied by our people, as I am sure he is well aware."

"Or...?" Désirée prompted.

"Or you can have a helicopter pick you up from the top. And since this building's airspace is completely shut down by Zack's guys, that option is out as well."

There was a commotion off to our left as dozens of people began streaming out of the building's main entrance; all with expressions that ran the gamut from terror, to confusion, to indignation at having had their plans disrupted.

I looked at the throng as something tickled the edges of my consciousness.

Something.

There and gone. There. Gone. Back again but as yet indiscernible.

"What are you thinking?" Zack asked.

I shook my head slowly.

"I don't know. Something about this..."

"This...what?"

I gestured at the people who continued pouring out of the doors.

"This."

He and Désirée turned to watch the spectacle.

Just then an important looking, well-dressed man in his fifties stalked in our direction, his gaze focused laser-like on Zack Hastings.

"Are you the son of a bitch in charge?" the man bellowed.

Before Zack could respond, two of his agents intercepted the man's forward progress and were, to his great vexation and utter displeasure, physically restraining him. He now stood fuming in their grasp about eight feet away.

"ADIC Zack Hastings, and, yes, I *am* the son of a bitch in charge!" Zack said with some heat. "What is the problem?"

The man shouted, "The problem is that your thugs interrupted a very important meeting and rousted us out of our building without apology and without explanation. I demand to know what is going on! I'm an American citizen and I know my rights. And when I get through making noise to your supervisor, you will regret this. Oh, yes, believe you me...you will regret this. I have connections in this town—connections that go right to the top!"

Zack grinned. I knew that grin for I had seen him use it on numerous occasions in our history. It was a grin that basically said, *"You are very close to pushing me over the line. And what I'd like to do right now is lock your sorry ass up for a couple of days just on the basis of the annoyance factor."*

Zack walked a step or two in the man's direction, stopped, stared silently for a few seconds and then sighed.

"What you are going to want to do right now, sir, is to shut the hell up. And let me tell you why that would be a good option for you. Because unless the next words that come out of your mouth are, 'Yes sir!' I am probably going to put you in restraints, throw your belligerent ass into the back of one of our cars, have you taken to our downtown LA field office and questioned at length regarding suspected terrorist activities being funded by subsidiaries of your corporation."

The man's eyes bulged, his face turned scarlet and he seemed to be having difficulty breathing.

"I..." he began and then stopped.

Zack said calmly, "Are we clear on the matter?"

The man began nodding his head.

"Yes...uh...sir. Perfectly clear."

Zack grinned and actually patted the man on the back.

"Good. You are free to go."

The man turned to leave but stopped and offered a quiet, "Thank you," before walking away.

I mimed applause.

"Impressive. They teach you that at Quantico?"

He laughed, "No. Learned that on my own. Teenagers, you know. Helps to know some mental Jiu Jitsu."

I looked past Zack at the people still streaming out of the building, and suddenly I knew what it was that had been trying to break into my consciousness.

"Plain sight!" I said forcefully.

"What?" Zack exclaimed.

I turned to Désirée.

"He's going to hide in plain sight."

Her head snapped toward the building's entrance and exit doors.

"You're right! He will try to come out with everyone else—he and Gabriella."

I started walking quickly toward the doors with Zack and Désirée trailing behind me.

Désirée said, "He will almost certainly employ a disguise of some sort."

Something suddenly occurred to me and I stopped walking and turned to Désirée.

"I just realized something: you are the only one who knows what he looks like."

"Oui. But I am confident that I will be able to spot him no matter how hard he tries to shield his identity."

I turned back toward the building's doorways and the throng of people still streaming out.

"Zack, you sure you have all possible exit points covered?"

"Without question. Street level, below ground *and* above ground."

"And this is the only available exit? Everyone is being funneled through here?"

"Yes."

I suddenly thought of something.

"Can your agents tell if people have come from above the thirtieth floor?"

"Stairwells are under observation as well as the private elevator bank that only goes to the upper ten floors."

I sighed in relief.

"Okay, we should be covered. So now we wait."

But I was still missing something. I had no idea what it was, but I knew it was there as surely as I knew my own name.

CHAPTER 72

The mood in the conference room was tense. The man with no name—The Persian—was issuing orders as quickly as a fry cook in Time's Square on New Year's Eve.

Gabriella Marcus sat where she had been planted on one side of an enormous conference table with two large men as her constant companions. How long had it been? Hours? It felt like days! At least she had been afforded the opportunity to use the restroom at the other end of the room...under close supervision, of course. Funny, it hadn't even felt all that humiliating to have both men leering at her throughout the process.

"Please remove your nightgown."

The order from The Persian had come so suddenly, and was so unexpected that she had to ask him to repeat it.

He leaned in, neither smiling nor leering and pulled her roughly to her feet.

"I said, remove your gown and be quick about it."

Her mind launched into hyper-drive. Surely he wasn't considering sex at this point. The situation appeared to be far too grave. What was he after, then?

"I would really rather not, if you don't mind," she replied with more calm than she felt.

Reaching forward with speed that belied his age and size, he snatched a handful of her nightgown and ripped it from her body in one smooth motion.

As she stood stunned, vainly attempting to cover her

nakedness with hands that seemed woefully insufficient in the face of what she was trying to accomplish, he snapped an order to a smallish man on the other side of the room.

"Raymond, take off your suit and shirt and hand them to Ms. Marcus."

Without hesitation or question the man began doing as requested.

The Persian sat beside her, his expression inscrutable.

"As beautiful as you are, my dear, it is not your body I am after...at least not now. We need to exit this place as quickly as possible. Therefore, I need you in disguise. The FBI is evacuating the building. You and Raymond are very close to the same size so you will put on his suit and we will simply evacuate the building with everyone else."

She thought quickly.

"But won't they know you have come from the top floors? Won't they know that anyone coming from this area has to be with you?"

His chuckle was devoid of humor.

"Very perceptive. But also, very short sighted."

Raymond stood before her clad only in his boxers, holding out his suit, shirt, tie, socks and shoes for her to take.

She reached for the bundle and couldn't stop herself from muttering a hasty, "Thank you."

The Persian said, "Put these on quickly. If you need help with the tie, Raymond will assist you."

He then stood and walked to the other end of the room to attend to something that seemed to demand his attention.

She had a choice to make. She could either allow modesty and humiliation to completely rob her of the dignity she had fought so hard to attain throughout her life, or she could just stand, get dressed and get on with whatever her captor had planned. Which is exactly what she did.

Maintaining eye contact with Raymond—who was putting on pants that were easily two sizes too big and shrugging into a long overcoat—Gabriella pulled on the still warm and slightly damp socks before inserting her legs into the slacks, surprised at how well they fit.

Fully expecting him to do something disgusting and dishonoring, he surprised her by saying, "My goodness, but you *are* lovely. Sadly, you possess the wrong plumbing for my persuasion, so you're safe with me, honey."

With a sigh of relief, she slipped her arms into the dress shirt, buttoned it up with slow efficiency and tucked the tails into the trousers. The shoes came next and then, holding the tie toward Raymond, she raised her eyebrows in appeal. With a slight bow, he took the tie and slipped it around her neck from the back, cinched it down and smoothed out the collar before stepping back around in front of her to survey his work.

As he held up his suit jacket, she stepped into it and waited while he buttoned it appropriately.

With a slight grin, he said, "One final piece," while slipping a dark fedora onto her head and tucking her tresses up underneath and then snapping the brim low over her eyes.

The Persian appeared, grinning in approval of the transformation.

"In a crowd, no one will be able to spot you."

"Where are you taking me?" she asked, surprised at the steadiness of her voice.

"Someplace that your Mr. Moriarity is certain to follow. And when he does...well...I'm sure you can imagine the rest."

"So, this whole thing is an effort to lure Jake Moriarity into following you into a trap?"

"This is true."

"But, why? Why go to all this effort?"

He stopped grinning and bellowed, "Because Moriarity has cost me everything! Everything! And I cannot get it back. My cartel. My enterprise. My career...my very life itself. And for that he must pay."

Once again, the boldness rose up.

"And, when you have accomplished your goals, do you intend to kill me as well?"

He seemed surprised by her question.

"That is...that is something that we can perhaps discuss and negotiate at some point, my dear. For now, just play your part and you will continue to draw breath."

She nodded.

Resolved.

Resolved that at some point, should the opportunity present itself, she would take this man's life as simply as she would step on a bug. She knew him, or, more accurately, had known others like him throughout her life. Narcissists! Men so blinded by their own power, wealth, self-worth and self-importance that other humans existed only within the context of the pleasure or value they could add to their lives.

Smiling as genuinely as she was able, Gabriella said, "All right, then I suppose we should be going."

The Persian smiled slowly.

"I can see why Mr. Moriarity is attracted to you. I find that am attracted to you as well. Perhaps I will need to rethink my plans regarding your future."

She stopped in front of him.

"Well, don't take too long. I sense that time is not exactly on your side."

His expression hardened and he jerked his head toward a door that was standing open at the far end of the room.

"If I didn't know better, Ms. Marcus, I would swear that you had grown a pair of balls to go with those trousers."

Smiling, she replied, "Yeah, I've heard that before," and then walked through the door feeling as if she were going to pass out from the stress she was valiantly attempting to conceal with bluster.

But bluster wouldn't save the day.

Only Jake could do that.

CHAPTER 73

We positioned ourselves ten or twelve feet from the exit doors, forcing the crowd to part and flow around us as if we were a large boulder in the middle of a stream. I don't mind admitting that I was stunned at the sheer volume of people the building contained and said as much to Zack.

Zack replied, "According to the city, this building's occupancy rating is set at three hundred and fifty people per floor. So, even without the top ten floors, and cutting that capacity in half, you're dealing with well over five thousand people!"

"I had no idea there would be this many. How are we supposed to keep eyes on everyone? And what if he somehow sneaked by before I figured out the possibility?"

"No way of knowing, Jake. We'll just have to make sure he doesn't get by us now."

And still they came. Old people; young people; middle-aged people; men and women in business suits; many in business casual, even a few children and teenagers. All in an unrelenting, frenetic stream.

Zack touched his fingertips to his ear bud.

"Say again? But that's not possible!"

"What?" I inquired.

"My guys just hit the top ten floors. They're deserted! Not a single soul anywhere."

Désirée and I stared at each other.

She said, "What does this mean? That he was never here

to begin with? That he slipped past us? What?"

"We need to get up there right now!" I replied dashing for the door with three of Zack's agents clearing a pathway for us.

Once inside, we headed for the four private elevators that serviced the top ten floors, piled inside and watched as the doors closed with agonizing slowness.

"What do you think happened?" Zack asked with genuine confusion.

"It's like Désirée said...either he and his people were never here, or he slipped past us." I thought for a second and then added, "Or, there's something he knows that we don't."

We rode the rest of the way in silence, each lost within a maze of thoughts; sorting and resorting bits and pieces of information in a desperate attempt to discern what had happened, when, and why.

The elevator door opened onto a vacant, opulent lobby. The large, brass logo behind the reception desk read, *"Masterpiece Collective—Selectivity Over Exclusivity."*

The three other elevators arrived, disgorging ten or twelve more agents who immediately spread out and began searching through the expansive space.

Turning toward Désirée I asked, "Well, anything come to mind?"

Without an answer she began walking to our right beckoning us to follow. At the end of that first hallway was a set of ornately carved double doors through which she proceeded without slowing down, as if she knew exactly where she was going. The doors opened onto another reception area behind which was a set of even larger and even more ornately carved double doors.

"His private office suite is through here," she said while shoving the doors open and walking inside.

I had been around some very wealthy people during my career. Many of whom were legitimate billionaires. And they all treated themselves very well when it came to appointing their private homes and workspaces. But nothing like this. The term "over the top" didn't even come close to describing the immoderate and excessive display of abundance. I found it truly obscene in every possible definition of the term.

"Gee," Zack said sarcastically. "It's a shame the guy had to exist in such squalor."

Désirée was standing behind the overly large desk and intently scanning the bookshelf that ran the entire length of the wall. Since I didn't have anything to do, I sat in the desk chair and began opening and closing drawers, feeling around for anything that may indicate a switch that would open the door to a safe room. Nothing!

One of Zack's guys ran in.

"Sir, you need to come and see this."

The three of us followed him out of the office, through the reception area and into a corner conference room. Once inside I immediately saw two things: a torn and discarded woman's nightgown, and a door standing open along one wall.

Gesturing toward the nightgown, I said, "Well, at least we know that Gabi was here."

Approaching the door cautiously, I nudged it further open with my foot and stood staring.

"I'll be damned!" Zack said, peering over my shoulder. "I wonder where that goes?"

He was referencing a wide stairwell that seemed to drop for many stories below us.

"Son of a bitch!" I said more loudly than intended. "I am willing to bet the farm that this stairwell ends up on a level lower than these top ten floors."

"I agree," Désirée remarked as she walked through the door and stood on the small landing where she peered over the railing. "It is not beyond reason to assume that he had all of his associates and employees assemble here, take these stairs down and simply blend in with the other evacuees."

"That's exactly what he did!" Zack muttered in agreement. "He had to have eyes on our movements, and before we had our vantage points set up, he herded everyone down to wherever these stairs terminate. Very smart. Very smart, indeed."

I started down the stairs.

"We need to see where these end up. If there is surveillance footage on that floor then we can take a look at and try to figure out what time he slipped past us."

It was a long way down. Maybe even farther than that. By the time we reached the twenty-eighth floor where the stairway terminated, my legs were burning and my chest heaving.

Throwing open the doorway I was somewhat surprised to see that it opened into another conference room.

"That's how they were able to blend in," I shouted while moving quickly across the room. "A bunch of people coming out of a stairwell could be a little suspicious. But people pouring out of another office suite would look perfectly normal."

Once in the hallway, we immediately began looking for cameras. We were in luck. Two were focused on the bank of elevators in the lobby.

Zack tapped his earbud and hollered, "Get me the head of security for the building." After listening for a few seconds he continued, "Good. Keep him there and tell him we're on our way."

"Is he close?" I asked hopefully.

"My guys have already got him set up in the building's security center."

Over complaints from a group of employees gathered around the elevators, we piled in to the first one that appeared with Zack's guys once again clearing the way. As the elevator plummeted toward the basement security center, it occurred to me that I should have been assigning some concern to Gabi's situation, but for some reason, I wasn't worried at all.

I hoped that I wouldn't eventually be proven wrong.

CHAPTER 74

Gabriella Marcus was in good shape. Very good shape. As such, the rapid pace she and the group of men surrounding her had kept while fleeing from the high-rise hadn't caused her a single second's problem. The Persian, however, was having serious issues. Sweating; gasping for breath; stumbling. She was certain that if they didn't stop soon, he would drop dead of a heart attack.

"You need to stop, sir," one of his men said with grave concern.

The Persian stumbled over to a bench in the shade where he collapsed with his chest heaving.

As his men set up a perimeter—looking to any casual passerby like a group of businessmen who were also being evacuated for mysterious reasons by the FBI—she sat down at the opposite end of the bench.

"Are you okay?" she inquired with feigned worry. "I'm not a medical professional, but you don't look so good."

Shifting only his eyes her way, The Persian replied, "I will be fine. Just need to rest for a moment."

Cupping his ear, the African-American man who seemed to be the head of his security listened intently.

Turning toward them he said, "They found the stairwell, sir, and are reviewing security footage."

The Persian waved his hand dismissively.

"They will never find us. No one knows what I look like, and Ms. Marcus' disguise worked perfectly."

The man drew a deep breath and held it, as if hesitant to

speak.

"Yes? What is on your mind, Antoine?"

"It is Désirée, sir. She knows your face."

The statement hung there for a few seconds.

Finally, The Persian replied with melancholy, "Yes, she does. She most definitely does. Well, it is of no matter. She doesn't know everything."

He stood with some difficulty and reached out his hand to help Gabriella to her feet.

She accepted his proffered assistance and stood, staring into his eyes.

"I meant what I said...uh...you know, about your condition. You need to take it easy."

The Persian closed his eyes and shook his head slowly.

"There is nothing easy about anything that lies ahead of me, my dear. It is all difficult. And do you want to know why it is difficult?" His voice rose in intensity. "It is because of your boyfriend!" He spat the word out as if it were foul tasting sputum.

"Riiiiight," she replied, drawing out the word. "You may have mentioned that earlier. But, you're not just dealing with Jake. It's the entire FBI. Their resources are limitless! There is nowhere on earth you can go where they cannot follow. How can you possibly imagine that this is going to end well? Oh, and besides whatever else you've done you can now add kidnapping!"

Drawing himself up to his full height, he replied, "I can see where a person such as yourself would find all you've just mentioned overwhelmingly daunting. Actually, I can see where almost anybody would find it so. However, I am not just anybody. I dwell on a completely separate plane of existence and have resources available to me that don't just level the playing field, as you Americans are fond of saying, it actually affords me a completely *different* playing field."

Her gaze remained unwavering.

"Must be nice to have that level of confidence."

He pretended to consider her statement.

"It is. It definitely is. Now, it is time to go and bring this little diversion to whatever conclusion destiny has dictated."

They began walking. Quickly, but at a much slower pace.

"Do you believe in God, sir?" Gabriella asked.

"God as in, Allah, Jehovah or as in one of the Eastern deities?"

"I don't know. Just...God?"

Linking his arm through hers he said, "I believe that there is something in the universe that keeps everything under control and operating on a certain level of order. As to whether that *something* is knowable or even desires to be known, I cannot say. I'm curious...why do you ask?"

"You referenced destiny a moment ago. Doesn't 'destiny' presuppose the existence of a supreme being, or, manager, as defined in your belief system?"

"What I believe in, Ms. Marcus...is me. *Only* me. I am the master of my own destiny—the master of my own fate. *I* decide what happens in my world...not God! The 'destiny' to which I made reference is the destiny that I, myself, have set in motion. For me. For you. And for your Mr. Moriarity."

The shoes were beginning to raise blisters on her heels and her throat was parched from the heat.

"How much further until we get to wherever it is we're going?" she asked.

The Persian raised his eyes questioningly in Antoine's direction.

Antoine said, "The residence is another block and a half. We can wait there until the FBI's perimeter is lifted."

"And what if they decide to do a door-to-door search?" Gabriella inquired.

He glanced at The Persian who indicated that he should answer.

"There is a safe room undetectable to anyone who doesn't know of its existence. Not even the FBI could find it."

In the next block she could see three casually dressed men standing on the sidewalk outside of an older home that looked as if it belonged on a historical registry. The men stood gazing toward The Persian's high-rise and talking animatedly on their cell phones as if concerned by what was happening a few blocks away. From The Persian's body language, and that of his men, she determined that this was the residence he had referenced.

It was at that point that her resolve nearly crumbled. What was to become of her, truly? Was Jake as good as she, in her somewhat fantastical mind, imagined him to be? Would he really come for her?

Drawing a deep breath she banished those thoughts by saying boldly, "You think a girl could get a bottle of water and a few minutes alone in a bathroom?"

Turning into the home's walkway, The Persian replied, "I am sure we can arrange something."

With a backward glance over her shoulder toward the circling helicopters she muttered under her breath, "Come and get me Jake. Hurry."

CHAPTER 75

There! Back it up."

Désirée was gesturing frantically toward the video monitor.

I asked, "What did you see?"

"I believe it is him."

The security technician did as requested and paused the frame when it came by again. A group of six men had hurried past a camera. One of the men, older than the others, could be seen in full profile with a much smaller man being almost drug along beside him. The smaller man was dressed in a business suit and wearing a fedora.

I leaned in for a closer view.

"Can you clear that up or at least zoom in?"

The technician wordlessly toggled a couple of levers and typed in few commands. Suddenly the image was larger, sharper.

"It is him!" Désirée exclaimed. "I am certain of it."

Zack pointed to the configuration of the party.

"Check out how they are arrayed. Two guys in front; the older guy and the one he's hanging onto in the middle; and two guys bringing up the rear. Looks like a classic security detail to me."

While I couldn't see the face, hidden as it was by the fedora, I knew it was Gabriella being dragged along by The Persian.

"That's Gabi with him. It's the right size and build."

Zack clapped his hands together.

"Okay. Now...see where they go from here."

The technician was good. Better than good. He was great. He was able to track their progress through the building and out the front entrance, where we got our first look at all of their faces.

"Definitely The Persian," Désirée said staring straight into the face of her former lover.

"And that's definitely Gabi," I added.

Zack was hollering into a handheld radio, "I want every traffic surveillance camera in the area focused on finding these guys. Let me know when you've got something." Turning toward Désirée, he asked, "Any idea where they might be headed?"

She thought for a few seconds and then her eyes widened.

"He has a home a few blocks away. It is old. Probably historical, or something. I remember when he bought it. He was so pleased with himself for owning a piece of Los Angeles history."

Zack said, "Do you have an exact location?"

"No, Monsieur. I was only ever driven there in the back of a limousine. The windows were blacked out and I could never see any street signs."

She paused, closing her eyes as if suddenly recalling something.

"I remember a number address. I believe it was, 8704. But that's all. No street name. Only numbers. And the house was enormous. Three stories at least and painted in a red brick color with lighter trim."

I asked, "Would you know it if you saw a picture?"

"I am certain I would."

"Zack, can your guys search for those numbers within our perimeter and see what comes up?"

An agent behind us said, "Already on it. Hang on."

We waited silently, impatiently for him to say something else.

"Got it!" He held up a tablet display for Désirée to see.

"That is it, Monsieur."

Zack slapped the tech on his back.

"Good job, Gary. How far are we talking?"

The agent pulled up a Google Earth map and did some quick calculations.

"It's...roughly five blocks east and three blocks north of our position."

Zack turned and hurried from the room yelling orders into his radio with Désirée and me right behind him.

"Assemble at the address, but don't do anything until we arrive on scene. Got it? And quietly begin evacuating the surrounding residences, apartments, whatever."

We jumped into a waiting SUV and from the front passenger seat Zack hollered over his shoulder, "The last thing we need right now is for one of my guys to go cowboy and start something that could potentially produce devastating consequences!"

I said, "How much of the interior layout do you remember, Désirée?"

"As I said, it is quite large. Although I never saw it, I am sure there is a basement."

She closed her eyes and gestured with her hands as she remembered.

"On the first floor, a vestibule that opens into a wide foyer. To the right there is a formal parlor; to the left a library; and then straight ahead a wide staircase that splits and then curves around in two directions. The dining room and kitchen are beyond the staircase to the right, and on the opposite side, the art gallery. On the second floor there are five bedrooms, each with a private bath. On the third floor is the master suite, and by that I mean that the entire third floor is taken up by the master suite."

Zack asked, "Any hidden rooms that you recall?"

"No, Monsieur. Then again, I was only there for one purpose. I hope I do not have to explain that statement further."

"No...no you don't. I get it."

We drove for a few blocks in silence, each lost within a private world of thoughts. Zack, no doubt, was thinking through the tactical aspects of performing a hostage rescue; Désirée enveloped in memories of a former time when her job required a sacrifice that had obviously left her deeply wounded. And me? Well, I was thinking that at this point, I would do whatever I had to in order to save Gabi. Along with that, came the inexorable thought that I cared for her far more than I had previously been willing to admit. And now having come to terms with my battered heart; having waited nearly twenty years to allow it to—if you'll allow me a moment of poetry—take flight, there was no way in hell I was going to give less than everything I had to bring her to safety.

Then again, that's pretty much what I brought to every case I worked on. I wondered, when it came right down to it, how this would look any different.

CHAPTER 76

T he SUV roared to a stop a block away from the house. Zack was basically out the door before the wheels had stopped rolling, jogging toward a hastily established command center.

As Désirée and I hurried to catch up, I heard him saying, "We have to assume that they know we're here. So any thought of doing this quietly is out the door."

A burly HRT commander replied, "Agreed. So how do you want to play it?"

Zack turned to me.

"Jake? Your thoughts?"

I watched the house in silence.

"We have to assume that along with The Persian, Gabi and the four guys in his security detail, there will be another four or five guys."

"So, call it eight to ten soldiers plus The Persian and Gabi?"

"I'd say so. Désirée, how many men do you recall seeing when you were here?"

"It is as you say. He would typically travel with no less than five and as many as eight men for security."

Zack looked through a pair of binoculars.

"I can't see any movement outside or through the windows, which isn't surprising. They're probably holed up watching everything we do on a bank of video monitors."

The HRT commander said, "Then we need to remove their eyes," as he toggled a handheld radio. "Joey, you got eyes on their security cameras?"

"Roger that," came a metallic voice in reply.

"How much damage can you do from your position?"

Zack turned and explained, "We've got three snipers. From their positions, we can see virtually every outside area of the house."

The radio crackled.

"I can take out...two...no, make that three. Junior, what are you and Adam seeing?"

Another voice came on.

"I've got two cameras visible on the north side of the house. Adam?"

"Yeah, I'm seeing three more from my position."

The HRT commander said, "Take them out. Do it now!"

We immediately heard pops as suppressed sniper rounds were fired sequentially, and then silence.

The radio again.

"Got 'em! That should severely hamper their ability to see us coming."

"Roger that," Zack replied crisply and then spoke to the HRT commander. "How do you want to proceed?"

The commander spoke into his radio.

"Joey, have your guys put some tear gas canisters through the basement windows. In fact, put a lot of them through. We don't want anybody even thinking about using that space."

"Roger that!" came the reply.

Just as I heard the spit of the sniper's rifles followed by breaking glass, my cell phone rang.

Stepping away from the command station I answered.

"This is Jake. Kinda busy right now."

"Mr. Moriarity."

I recognized the voice.

"What do you want, Momotani?"

"I will make this brief. I am calling to inform you that I am no longer associated with The Persian. The association has become, shall we say, unprofitable for me. I am telling you this because it may be helpful to know that whatever happens between the two of you will happen without interference from either myself or any of my associates."

"Okay. I'm not sure how you wish me to respond as 'thank you' seems a bit disingenuous."

"It is of no importance. I have done what I felt I needed to do. Now, good day to you, Mr. Moriarity. It is my wish our paths do not cross in the future, but I have a feeling that is a wish that will never come true."

And with that, he disconnected the call.

Zack tipped his chin up in question.

I spat, "Momotani."

His eyebrows rose in surprise.

"Really? What did that bastard have to say?"

"Just wanted to inform me that he and The Persian are no longer working together, and that as far as he was concerned anything that happened, would happen without reprisal from him."

"Okay. Good to know, but I don't see how that changes a single thing right now."

"You're right. It doesn't." I paused and then said quickly, "Listen...those guys are no doubt posted up in there. They could hold us off all day and night if it came down to a fire fight."

"Maybe, maybe not," Zack said. "Sort of depends on how aggressive we want to get. As it stands, I have plenty of horsepower right here to overwhelm just about anything they could throw against us."

"I'm sure you do, but at what cost? There's not a chance that I will risk Gabriella's life just to capture that piece of shit!"

He replied, "Nor would I ever ask or expect you to. So, you got something in mind?"

"Actually, I do."

"Okay, let's hear it."

As Désirée moved over to join our conversation I explained, "I'm going to just go knock on the door and have a little chat with Mr. Persian."

Désirée shook her pretty head forcefully.

"If anybody goes in, it will be me. I know the layout, you do not. I know where he is likely to be keeping Gabriella, you do not. I know most of his men, you do not. And his men like me. You, they would almost certainly shoot on sight."

Zack grinned.

"She makes a good point, Jake."

I said, "Not really!"

"And, why not?" she demanded.

"It would be too easy for them to overwhelm you. Then we'd have two hostages to worry about."

"And what about you? You are just one man."

"True, but—"

"No!" she insisted. "I am going in. It is settled."

"Hold your horses, there!" Zack replied with some heat. "The last time I checked, *I* was the ADIC...not you. Whatever happens will happen on my say-so and not on your decision. Are we clear?"

I suggested, "How about if the two of us go in together. Unarmed. Sort of a peace seeking mission."

"Peace is something I've never known you to seek, brother. What do you *really* have in mind?"

I explained my thoughts. Both of them bought in, and we began making preparations for what was coming.

Well, for what I anticipated was coming.

As it turned out, it was far different than anything I could have imagined.

CHAPTER 77

Inside The Persian's mansion, Gabriella watched as his security detail readied themselves for what they all believed to be a full-force assault from the FBI. The sophistication of the weaponry they had pulled from an armory off of the library on the first floor, was truly impressive. And although she hadn't spent any time at all around those with a tactical persuasion—besides Jake, that is—she knew a serious array of weapons when she saw one.

Even on the second floor, the fumes from the tear gas the FBI had lobbed into the basement were making her eyes water. It seemed to seep into the room from every corner, every crack and cranny. It was progressing beyond the point of irritation to being positively noxious.

The Persian suddenly appeared before her.

"Come with me," he said stiffly while offering her his hand.

She took it and allowed herself to be pulled to her feet.

"This way," he yelled and took off at a fast clip toward the stairs leading to the third floor.

"Where are we going," she asked while hurrying to keep up.

"Somewhere they will never find us."

"If it's inside this house, I think you're probably wrong about them finding us."

They had just started to climb the stairs, when she heard a commotion coming from the first floor.

"That sounded like gunshots," she remarked with a

knowing smile.

The Persian hesitated only slightly.

"It is of no importance. Now let us go."

She didn't know why she did it. In fact, for years to come she would ponder repeatedly why she had chosen that particular course of action.

"I believe I will go no further with you, Persian."

Her statement stopped him in his tracks, prompting him to turn on the stairs and stare uncomprehendingly.

"What did you just say?"

"I said that I'm not going with you to wherever you're going."

She could tell that the audacity of her statement was giving him some problems in cognition.

"But...this is not a choice that is yours to make."

"Oh, that's where you are wrong. We always have choices. And I am choosing to not accompany you."

The sounds of gunfire increased causing The Persian to hesitate.

Finally, he said, "At this point, you are largely worthless to me anyway. Very well. Stay. But I cannot promise that my men won't kill you."

He turned and ran up the remaining stairs toward the third floor, leaving her staring after him with her mouth hanging open in shock.

Since the gunfire seemed to be moving her way, she decided it would probably be a good idea to find a place that offered better concealment than the middle of a large staircase. Spotting a small antechamber off to the side, she quickly moved in that direction only to have her way blocked by a very attractive young woman holding two smoking guns in her hands.

The woman smiled.

"You must be Gabriella."

"Yes, but—"

"There is someone who wants to talk to you."

The woman then bolted up the stairs as a deathly silence descended, leaving Gabriella wondering what was going on.

She didn't have long to wait in order to find out.

CHAPTER 78

Désirée and I walked straight up to the front door with our hands raised over our heads. She knocked and we stepped back to await whatever was going to happen. Knowing that there was an FBI sniper somewhere behind me, covering anyone who would open the door, didn't do as much to calm my nerves as one might imagine.

The door opened.

The heavily outfitted African-American man who stood there started to smile and offer a greeting to Désirée, but stopped when he saw me.

"Hello, Antoine," she said.

"Désirée. I cannot say it's good to see you, although I am sure my boss will have a different reaction."

"And where is he...the boss?"

Antoine turned his head and stared hard, the barrel of his gun coming up and pointing in the direction of my chest.

"We're unarmed," I offered.

"Armed, unarmed, it matters not to me. I have orders to kill you on sight. So..."

Suddenly, a green dot appeared between his eyes.

"Can you feel that, asshole?" I said casually. "That's a .50 caliber sniper rifle trained right between your eyes."

What transpired next, happened so fast that there was no time to think.

Just act!

He tried to drop into a squat and bring his weapon up

to fire, but I don't care how fast you are, you will always lose against a highly trained and highly skilled FBI sniper. Suffice it to say that Antoine lost.

I retrieved his weapon, extra mags, and backup pistol that I quickly tossed to Désirée. Somewhere in the periphery of my vision, I was aware that people were moving up behind us, but I didn't have time to think as bad guys started appearing all over the ground floor of the old house. Once again, not thinking...just acting. As we moved through the foyer, and around opposite sides of the grand staircase, we both encountered resistance—resistance that was cut short due to some damn fine shooting from Désirée, and a bit of adequate backup from yours truly.

In the wake of our progress thus far, we counted five men either dead or suffering from wounds that were significant enough to take them out of action. We both confiscated bigger and better guns from the fallen, along with enough ammo to supply a small attack force, which, at that point accurately described the two of us.

We ran up the stairs in spite of the possibility that the rest of The Persian's security detail would be waiting for us.

They weren't.

And I found that to be utterly baffling. Were the five men below the only ones he had with him? Were the others hiding somewhere hoping to spring a surprise attack? We had no way of knowing.

Désirée said breathlessly, "I am going to the master suite on the third floor," and took off at a fast clip for the stairs that I assumed were somewhere toward the back of the house.

Thinking I had heard sound coming from one of the empty bedrooms, I held back to investigate. It was nothing. Just a television that had been left on. Which meant that someone had been in there. Recently. But where were they now?

Running after Désirée, I rounded a corner and saw...Gabi. She was standing with one foot on the carpeted stairs and one on the rich hardwood that covered all of the floors in the hall-way.

She looked at me.

I looked back.

Walking slowly toward her, I said, "Nice suit."

Glancing down dramatically, she replied, "Yeah, but they didn't get the cut right. It sort of binds between my shoulders, and the pants, well, let me tell you, they—"

She didn't get to finish. It wasn't her fault. I sort of grabbed her. Actually, it was more like a benign assault. I kissed that woman like I hadn't kissed any woman for twenty years.

And it felt great.

When we pulled apart, she batted her eyes and said, "So...would it be appropriate for me to assume that this means you've decided to like me?"

I didn't know what to say, so I kissed her again.

Longer.

Harder.

Hey, I had a lot of time to make up for.

This time when we broke it off, she didn't pull away. She laid her head against my chest and cried. It was a good cry. Pure and cleansing, as if the rivers of tears were washing away all the trauma of the past twenty-four hours. Me? I just stood there and held on to her knowing that to say anything, or even move would be detrimental to the process that was playing out.

Finally, she stood to her full height—which wasn't very tall—and looked me in the eyes.

"Well, Mr. Moriarity. You certainly know how to make a dramatic entrance."

I had just started to reply when Zack and the HRT team came charging down the hall behind me.

Zack wasn't happy.

"Are you crazy? That's the stupidest thing I've ever seen anyone do!"

"What?" I replied innocently.

"You know what! You and Désirée busting in here on your own and creating havoc!"

"It wasn't what we intended. It just sort of happened and we were forced to go with it. By the way, Gabi, meet Zack Hastings. Zack—Gabriella Marcus."

The tension broke and he shook her hand politely.

"I wish the circumstances were different, but pleased to meet you. Nice suit, by the way."

Désirée called loudly from the top of the stairs.

"You might want to come up here and see this."

CHAPTER 79

I grabbed Gabi's hand and started up the stairs with Zack in the lead and the HRT close on our heels.

When we arrived in the master suite, Désirée was sitting on the oversized bed, her brow knit in concentration.

"What?" Zack asked.

She swept her arms in a dramatic arc to encompass the ridiculously large room.

"This is what."

"But, there's no one here."

"Exactly!"

Zack called to the HRT commander.

"Scotty, fire up that infrared scope and see if there are any hidey-holes we're missing."

The commander did as requested, walking slowly around the room and scanning every square inch of wall space, and then doing the same thing with the floor.

After about ten minutes he said, "I don't see anything even remotely resembling a heat signature."

We all sort of stood in the middle of the room, scratching our heads and turning in circles.

I don't know why I did it, but it just occurred to me, so I had to check it out. Dropping to my knees, I peeked under the bed and saw a substantial pedestal holding up the mattress—a metallic pedestal.

"You got something?" Zack asked when I didn't say anything.

I stood.

"Think you can have your guys lift this beast off the pedestal?"

"Sure. Scotty?"

Scotty and the other HRT guys grabbed the edges of the mattress and on three tried to lift it off the pedestal.

It didn't budge.

"What the hell?" Zack exclaimed. "Is it screwed down, or something?"

Désirée suddenly slapped her forehead and swore in French.

"What are you thinking?" I asked.

She turned and looked at the ornate, bookcase head-board.

"When The Persian would have me over for a visit he would never let me touch anything on that headboard. One time I asked him why. He got very irritated and told me that my only concern should be pleasing him, and to not worry about anything else. But..."

She stopped speaking and crawled across the top of the mattress toward the headboard. Sitting back on her haunches, she surveyed various items that seemed to be arrayed in a completely random order.

"What are you looking for?" I said.

Holding her right index finger up as if requesting si-lence, she slowly lowered it until it was touching what ap-peared to be a small, men's jewelry case. After an unsuccessful attempt to open it, she closed her fingers around it and tried to lift it off the headboard. It wouldn't budge. Finally, she twisted.

It turned.

And with its turning came the sound of electronic motors being engaged and the mattress began to lift up to-ward the headboard like one of those old Murphy beds.

Désirée scrambled off of the bed and stood with her gun trained on what was now obvious to all of us: a hidden compartment of some sort under the mattress.

Zack muttered, "That right there is absolute genius."

I had to agree. Who would have ever thought to look for a safe room under the mattress?

When the mattress was fully raised, we could see a heavy, nearly seamless metal trap door set securely into the floor.

Désirée knelt on the door and put her ear against its surface.

Then she knocked.

My phone rang.

"Moriarity here."

"Congratulations, Mr. Moriarity. I was so sure no one would ever figure out my little ruse. But you continue to surprise."

I put the phone on speaker.

He continued, "Ah, but it is of no importance now,"

"I wouldn't be so sure. It would appear that we have you trapped in your own safe room."

He laughed. It was not a pleasant laugh.

"So it would seem. But, sadly for you, I am not here. You see, I have relatives in the Middle East. They have taught me well about, shall we say, home security. I not only own this home, but several others in close proximity—all of which are linked by connecting tunnels. My men and I have been gone for quite some time. I hear that poor Antoine didn't make it. A shame. I really cared for that boy."

Purely on a whim I said, "So, it won't matter to you if we just blow this house to hell and gone, right?"

"But, why would you want to do such a thing? It is a treasure. There is not its equal in all of Los Angeles."

"I don't really care much about architecture or antique homes and the like. So, it wouldn't bother me a bit to blow it up. Would it bother you, Zack?"

Zack winked at me as he finally figured out where I was going with the conversation.

"I wouldn't lose any sleep over it. In fact, I'd do it just because it means something to this sorry son of a bitch!"

There was silence on The Persian's end.

"Surely you cannot be serious. This is private property! *My* private property! You cannot—"

"Sure we can, " I said jauntily. "You are an international felon. We are in pursuit. Things sometimes happen when trying to apprehend dangerous criminals such as yourself. People die. Property is destroyed..."

Zack said, "Scotty, how much C4 will it take to blow this puppy to kingdom come?"

Scotty grinned.

"About as much as we have in the truck."

"Get it and begin setting charges. Oh, and start with this room. In fact put some extra around this trap door."

The Persian was muttering something unintelligible when suddenly the door broke free of its seals and started to open hydraulically.

With our guns trained on the ever-expanding opening, we watched as The Persian led a short column of four men out of the safe room and into our custody.

When he was finally standing with his hands raised in surrender, Désirée walked slowly toward him and stopped a foot away.

"You, Monsieur, are a pig! No, you are lower than a pig. It is unfair to the pig to compare you to him."

And with that, she kneed him in the groin. All the air whooshed out of him, and he fell to the ground clutching his damaged manhood and making little whimpering noises one would typically associate with small children.

Girl children.

"That," she said while kneeling down next to his writhing form. "Is for all the times you humiliated me in this room —on this bed, in your car, in your office. I intend to arrange it so you will never even *see* a woman ever again let alone *be* with one. In fact, where you are going, I can imagine you will be a popular fellow with the other inmates."

Then she stood, smoothed her clothes, held her head high and kicked him again.

"As you can imagine," she said calmly. "I have wanted to do that for a very long while."

"Understandable," Zack replied. "All right, boys. Cuff 'em and stuff 'em."

CHAPTER 80

While Zack and his guys rounded up their captives, Gabi asked, "What happens now?"

"Well, the FBI will take The Persian here into custody," I jerked my head in Désirée's direction, "and given *her* attitude I would hope for his sake it's protective custody. Then he and his accomplices will be transferred to INTERPOL and eventually tried for having brokered the sale of hundreds of millions, if not billions of dollars worth of Holocaust art stolen by the Nazis during the Second World War."

Gabi nodded her head slowly.

"My family is Jewish. Did you know that?"

"I sort of figured it was, given your surname."

She was quiet for a few moments.

"The Nazis were particularly cruel when they seized my great-grandfather's belongings in Vienna. He wouldn't let go of a violin he had made for my grandmother when she was a child. So they drug him out into the street and did terrible things to him before lighting the violin on fire and forcing him to watch it burn. And then, they put his eyes out."

A sob escaped her lips, and then another.

I pulled her close and just held her there, in front of all those tough FBI agents and HRT squad members. They had all heard what she shared, so it was almost like a holy moment... or something.

Zack finally said, "Okay, let's wrap it up here, fellas. Jake, we'll debrief outside?"

"Be right there," I replied.

They hustled The Persian—hanging between two agents —and his crew out of the room.

Désirée said, "Since it is my duty on behalf of the ELAC to inventory whatever we find here, I would like to get started. The safe room seems a likely place for him to have hidden the art pieces he deemed especially valuable.

I said, "We'll go with you."

We carefully descended the stairs and entered a room that, while having a fairly low ceiling, was the largest safe room I've ever seen. But that wasn't the most impressive feature. That designation belonged to an anteroom that seemed to be a remnant of the home's original architecture. Separated from the safe room by a solid, oak door featuring vintage brass hardware, its walls and floors were covered with too many art pieces to count.

We entered with a sense of awe.

"There is so much," Gabi said breathlessly.

I had just turned away to check out a small painting to the right of the doorway when I heard her gasp.

I spun around to see Gabi standing as if mesmerized in front of a color portrait of a pretty little girl in a red coat, sitting out of doors on a wooden chair holding a battered baby doll on her knee.

I leaned in to see if it was signed.

"I can't make out the signature. Can you, Désirée?"

Gabi said, "I know who it is by."

"But, how can you possibly know that?" Désirée asked. "Were you an art major in college?"

Gabi shook her head while wiping away tears with the backs of her hands.

"I know this painting because...it is of my grandmother when she was a young girl of seven or eight. The painting was stolen from my great-grandfather by the Nazis and then it disappeared sometime between 1942 and 1945."

Désirée stepped in for a closer look at the painting.

"That is remarkable. And you are quite certain it is the same painting?"

Gabi smiled demurely.

"The doll. I have it. It sits in my bedroom against the pillows on my bed. If I had my phone, I could show you a picture."

On a whim, I dialed her number and heard a phone vibrating and ringing in the main room. I tracked the sound and found it tossed carelessly aside and resting on the floor in a corner. The screen had one long and jagged crack, which did nothing to obscure the photo on the lock screen.

It was the doll.

Hurrying back into the anteroom, I held the phone up for Désirée to see.

She took it from me, shaking her head.

"This is most extraordinary," she said while holding the phone up to the painting so she could compare the image. "Most extraordinary."

"Is your grandmother still living, Gabi?" I asked.

She nodded her head, laughing.

"Yes, she is. Very independent, that one. At eighty-seven she still lives in her own condo on Coronado Island in San Diego."

Désirée handed Gabi's phone back to her.

"You are most likely unaware, Gabi, but the ELAC exists to reunite Jewish families with their stolen art pieces. I can't tell you how long it will take, but I promise you that I will do everything in my power to expedite the process and have this returned to your grandmother. I am sure she would love to see it once again."

Gabi wiped away more tears, nodding, "Yes, she would. Over the years, her stories about the painting have become almost mythological and we never knew how much of it was true. Not that we disbelieved her, but given the amount of time that has passed, coupled with her age..."

She let the sentence trail off.

My phone rang again.

It was Cassie.

"Uncle. Are you okay? Aaron just got off the phone with Zack. He called and filled us in briefly on what was going on."

"Yes, I'm fine." I glanced at Gabi. "*We're* fine. Some interesting things are developing that Zack doesn't even know about. I'll tell you when we get together later on."

"Can't wait to hear all about it. Do you need Aaron or me to come and get you?"

"No. I'm pretty sure Zack will get us down to Carlsbad just as soon as we finish the debrief."

"Okay. Simone is here with her dad. We've all been going a little crazy with worry."

I said, "We took The Persian and his crew into custody about fifteen minutes ago."

She chuckled, "I hear Désirée had a little message for him."

"That she did. And I'm pretty sure he'll remember it for a long time to come."

"I should probably let you go. I love you so much, Uncle."

"Love you too, little girl. We'll be there soon."

After I hung up, Désirée asked, "Was that Cassie?"

"Yeah. Zack called and filled them in a little on what happened. She was worried about me."

"I assume you will be leaving soon?"

"Just as soon as we wrap things up with Zack."

She stepped forward to hug Gabi, and then kissed me on both cheeks.

"I am so happy to have met you both and to have had the privilege of working alongside of you, Jake. It seems as if I have known you a long while, but it has been barely two days."

I laughed.

"That's hard to believe! So, now that the cartel is broken, will you go on to another assignment?"

She paused for a couple of seconds before answering.

"Of that I am not so sure. This business with The Persian was...quite unpleasant and not at all what I signed on to do. Monsieur Ducharme has made me a very generous offer to work for him as his full-time pilot. It is an offer worth considering. Besides, given his business, I would still be working with art."

"Take the offer!" I said. "Take it and don't look back."

She nodded slowly.

"Yes, I believe I shall. But first...I need to reunite Gabi's grandmother with her painting."

Gabi said, "She will be overwhelmed when I give her the news."

She hugged Gabi once again.

"I will bid you, adieu for now."

"Au revoir, Désirée," I said, with a surprising amount of regret.

"À tout à l'heure, Jake."

"By the way..."

"Oui?"

"Do you have a surname?"

She smiled sweetly and said, "A girl must retain some secrets, Monsieur," and then walked away.

Once out of the safe room and descending the stairs to the ground floor, Gabi stopped me.

"Tell me the truth...was there a little something extra going on with you and Désirée?"

"The truth?"

"Yes, please."

"I think that initially she was attracted to me—probably still is. But she figured out pretty quickly that my heart was not my own. She even said as much."

Gabi smiled slyly.

"And you weren't even slightly attracted to her?"

"Well," I said. "In another time and place—wearing different lenses—perhaps I could have been. But now? My vision seems to be suddenly myopic."

"Meaning?"

"I can only see you."

Her smile broadened.

"Have you been working on that, or did it just come to you?"

"Uh, it just came to me?"

"Hmm...you're very good."

"I've been told."

A aron and I were on the deck at Cassie's condo in Carlsbad grilling what would ultimately turn out to be the best burgers known to mankind. I'm not exaggerating. We do burgers better than just about anyone. It's an old family recipe. We infuse the ground beef with bacon.

Yes, I said bacon.

Now you know why I can make such a bold statement.

I know I said burgers, but every burger we make has cheese on it.

All of them.

Lots of cheese.

White, extra-sharp cheddar.

Basically, if you don't like *this* cheese on your hamburger, I question everything about you. It's *that* good.

And let's not forget the condiments. You see, in my world, burgers are simply a delivery system for condiments. Especially mayonnaise. I love mayonnaise! And onions. And pickles, tomatoes, lettuce. You get the picture.

A week had passed since our dealings with The Persian, whose real name, as it turned out, was Bahar Ghaznavi. He was now in the process of being extradited back to France where he would stand trial and eventually, hopefully, be sentenced to life in prison without parole. Rumor had it, that thanks to Désirée he still whimpered when he walked, sat, or basically moved even slightly.

Couldn't have happened to a more deserving guy!

"Time for the *Sweet Baby Ray's*?" Aaron asked hopefully.

He kind of has a thing for that sauce. If you want to know the truth, he's just as passionate about *Sweet Baby Ray's* as I am about mayonnaise.

"Let's give it another minute," I answered while lifting a couple of patties to peer at the undersides.

"Okay, but you know it's a timing thing, and if you miss it the whole batch will be ruined."

"Hey! How many times have we done this?"

He grinned.

"Not nearly enough!"

We fist bumped.

People were coming over for lunch, thus the grilling. I say "coming over" but some were already here. Earlier, Gabi and I had picked up her grandmother, Laura, on Coronado. "Nana Laura", as Gabi called her, was one of the sweetest people I have ever had the pleasure of meeting. And sharp! I was going to say that I hope I'm as sharp as she is when I reach her age, but actually, I wish I was that sharp now!

They were, at present, inside where Nana Laura was re-galing everyone with stories about Gabriella when she was a little girl. I must say that my girls—Cassie, Muriel and Vanessa —had developed an immediate fondness for Gabi, which, if you don't mind me saying, was surprising to me. I mean it's not like I'd had a parade of women running through my life. Gabi was the only one. So my expectation was that she would be intensely scrutinized and then either accepted or rejected. There was none of that! The invitation to become a part of the family had been immediate.

Brett Hansen, Vanessa's soon to be brother-in-law, her sister Laurie and niece Abby were also present along with Pete Tolles who was still on crutches following the horren-dous ankle injury he had suffered helping to rescue Simone Ducharme from Yves Barreau. Speaking of which, Simone, her father Gaspard, and her uncle Rémi were driving down from Los Angeles. Lonnie Falcon—Aaron and Simone's producer—

was already in town having spent the night in a nearby hotel. Désirée had called me earlier to say that she would be rolling in later on, after wrapping up a few final details in cataloguing The Persian's collection of stolen art.

The occasion of our gathering was to celebrate the completion of Simone's debut album. Lonnie had promised to bring a test pressing of the vinyl LP so we could all hear it in advance of the official release that was scheduled to happen in two weeks. So much had transpired in Simone and Gaspard's life since she began the project and we had been there with them nearly every step of the way. In that regard, today marked the end of a difficult season and the beginning of new day for their family.

"Now!" I said to Aaron who immediately and skillfully began to slather *Sweet Baby Ray's* over the surface of the patties. You might as well know that he considers himself an expert in its application. Now, I know what you're thinking: anybody could do it. You could say that, but he'd be quick to point out that you were wrong. Apparently, it takes a certain panache to get it just right, and according to Aaron...he always gets it just right.

As soon as it had become evident to Mr. Ghaznavi that it was, as they say, all over, he proceeded to throw Hayato Momotani under the proverbial bus in hopes of cutting a deal with the prosecutors. They gladly accepted the information, but I'm pretty sure Ghaznavi is screwed any way you cut it. In a perfect world, they'd wind up as cellmates in a nice, frosty gulag somewhere. In our profoundly imperfect world, however, it's anyone's guess as to what will ultimately be handed down in the way of sentencing. If you want to know the truth, I care way less about that than I do about the fact that those I love and care for are all safe.

For now, anyway.

As for Chida and company, the Spanish authorities rounded them up along with Étienne and Philippe, who, by the way, seem to be making a complete recovery from their poisoning. From what I have heard, they were, to a man, quite eager to assist the authorities in their efforts to put their former bosses behind bars, believing that said cooperation would reduce their individual sentences. I do think, however, that they are, well, screwed.

"Okay, flip 'em!" Aaron said loudly.

I started flipping the patties with a precision learned while serving as assistant manager of a *Jack In The Box* restaurant during my early college years.

Aaron intoned, "Looking good. Looking *very* good, my man."

"You definitely have the touch."

"Damn right, I do. That's why we make a great grilling team."

"Team Jake."

"What?"

"I said, team Jake."

"Huh-uh! No way, bro. Ain't no Jake about it. It's team Aaron all the way."

"Why should it be team Aaron?"

He seemed flabbergasted.

"Because...because all you do is flip the damn burgers. I'm the one who adds the magic."

"Dude, you pour sauce out of a bottle and spread it around."

"I do not *just* spread it around. It's a precision application—"

"That could be done by a third grader!"

Vanessa walked out onto the deck fresh from a shower with her hair up in a towel turban.

"You guys fighting again?"

"No!" we both said in unison, and then busted up laughing at the ridiculousness of the argument.

I heard a commotion coming from inside and turned around just in time to see Michael Harvey, Cassie's fiancé, being mugged by Cassie and Muriel at the front door.

Aaron said, "I always forget how good they look to-gether."

"Like they were made for each other."

Gabi walked onto the deck and slipped her arms around me...not speaking, just holding me. I had quickly learned that when you are with someone you truly love, there are times when words aren't necessary.

Vanessa pulled the towel off and started doing that girl thing where they run their fingers through their hair; shake their hair; run their fingers through their hair; shake their hair, etc., etc., over and over and over...you get the picture.

It made me smile.

Hell, everything was making me smile on that day. My family—the *entire* family—was all assembled together in one place.

The moment felt magical to me.

Almost as magical as the bite of cheeseburger I had just sneaked.

Almost.

EPILOGUE

Aaron and I were on the deck at Cassie's condo in Carlsbad grilling what would ultimately turn out to be the best burgers known to mankind. I'm not exaggerating. We do burgers better than just about anyone. It's an old family recipe. We infuse the ground beef with bacon.

Yes, I said bacon.

Now you know why I can make such a bold statement.

I know I said burgers, but every burger we make has cheese on it.

All of them.

Lots of cheese.

White, extra-sharp cheddar.

Basically, if you don't like *this* cheese on your hamburger, I question everything about you. It's *that* good.

And let's not forget the condiments. You see, in my world, burgers are simply a delivery system for condiments. Especially mayonnaise. I love mayonnaise! And onions. And pickles, tomatoes, lettuce. You get the picture.

A week had passed since our dealings with The Persian, whose real name, as it turned out, was Bahar Ghaznavi. He was now in the process of being extradited back to France where he would stand trial and eventually, hopefully, be sentenced to life in prison without parole. Rumor had it, that thanks to Désirée he still whimpered when he walked, sat, or basically moved even slightly.

Couldn't have happened to a more deserving guy!

"Time for the *Sweet Baby Ray's*?" Aaron asked hopefully.

He kind of has a thing for that sauce. If you want to know the truth, he's just as passionate about *Sweet Baby Ray's* as I am about mayonnaise.

"Let's give it another minute," I answered while lifting a couple of patties to peer at the undersides.

"Okay, but you know it's a timing thing, and if you miss it the whole batch will be ruined."

"Hey! How many times have we done this?"

He grinned.

"Not nearly enough!"

We fist bumped.

People were coming over for lunch, thus the grilling. I say "coming over" but some were already here. Earlier, Gabi and I had picked up her grandmother, Laura, on Coronado. "Nana Laura", as Gabi called her, was one of the sweetest people I have ever had the pleasure of meeting. And sharp! I was going to say that I hope I'm as sharp as she is when I reach her age, but actually, I wish I was that sharp now!

They were, at present, inside where Nana Laura was regaling everyone with stories about Gabriella when she was a little girl. I must say that my girls—Cassie, Muriel and Vanessa—had developed an immediate fondness for Gabi, which, if you don't mind me saying, was surprising to me. I mean it's not like I'd had a parade of women running through my life. Gabi was the only one. So my expectation was that she would be intensely scrutinized and then either accepted or rejected. There was none of that! The invitation to become a part of the family had been immediate.

Brett Hansen, Vanessa's soon to be brother-in-law, her sister Laurie and niece Abby were also present along with Pete Tolles who was still on crutches following the horrendous ankle injury he had suffered helping to rescue Simone Ducharme from Yves Barreau. Speaking of which, Simone, her father Gaspard, and her uncle Rémi were driving down from

Los Angeles. Lonnie Falcon—Aaron and Simone's producer—was already in town having spent the night in a nearby hotel. Désirée had called me earlier to say that she would be rolling in later on, after wrapping up a few final details in cataloguing The Persian's collection of stolen art.

The occasion of our gathering was to celebrate the completion of Simone's debut album. Lonnie had promised to bring a test pressing of the vinyl LP so we could all hear it in advance of the official release that was scheduled to happen in two weeks. So much had transpired in Simone and Gaspard's life since she began the project and we had been there with them nearly every step of the way. In that regard, today marked the end of a difficult season and the beginning of new day for their family.

"Now!" I said to Aaron who immediately and skillfully began to slather *Sweet Baby Ray's* over the surface of the patties. You might as well know that he considers himself an expert in its application. Now, I know what you're thinking: anybody could do it. You could say that, but he'd be quick to point out that you were wrong. Apparently, it takes a certain panache to get it just right, and according to Aaron...he always gets it just right.

As soon as it had become evident to Mr. Ghaznavi that it was, as they say, all over, he proceeded to throw Hayato Momotani under the proverbial bus in hopes of cutting a deal with the prosecutors. They gladly accepted the information, but I'm pretty sure Ghaznavi is screwed any way you cut it. In a perfect world, they'd wind up as cellmates in a nice, frosty gulag somewhere. In our profoundly imperfect world, however, it's anyone's guess as to what will ultimately be handed down in the way of sentencing. If you want to know the truth, I care way less about that than I do about the fact that those I love and care for are all safe.

For now, anyway.

As for Chida and company, the Spanish authorities rounded them up along with Étienne and Philippe, who, by the way, seem to be making a complete recovery from their poisoning. From what I have heard, they were, to a man, quite eager to assist the authorities in their efforts to put their former bosses behind bars, believing that said cooperation would reduce their individual sentences. I do think, however, that they are, well, screwed.

"Okay, flip 'em!" Aaron said loudly.

I started flipping the patties with a precision learned while serving as assistant manager of a *Jack In The Box* restaurant during my early college years.

Aaron intoned, "Looking good. Looking *very* good, my man."

"You definitely have the touch."

"Damn right, I do. That's why we make a great grilling team."

"Team Jake."

"What?"

"I said, team Jake."

"Huh-uh! No way, bro. Ain't no Jake about it. It's team Aaron all the way."

"Why should it be team Aaron?"

He seemed flabbergasted.

"Because...because all you do is flip the damn burgers. I'm the one who adds the magic."

"Dude, you pour sauce out of a bottle and spread it around."

"I do not *just* spread it around. It's a precision application—"

"That could be done by a third grader!"

Vanessa walked out onto the deck fresh from a shower with her hair up in a towel turban.

"You guys fighting again?"

"No!" we both said in unison, and then busted up laughing at the ridiculousness of the argument.

I heard a commotion coming from inside and turned around just in time to see Michael Harvey, Cassie's fiancé, being mugged by Cassie and Muriel at the front door.

Aaron said, "I always forget how good they look together."

"Like they were made for each other."

Gabi walked onto the deck and slipped her arms around me...not speaking, just holding me. I had quickly learned that when you are with someone you truly love, there are times when words aren't necessary.

Vanessa pulled the towel off and started doing that girl thing where they run their fingers through their hair; shake their hair; run their fingers through their hair; shake their hair, etc., etc., over and over and over...you get the picture.

It made me smile.

Hell, everything was making me smile on that day. My family—the *entire* family—was all assembled together in one place.

The moment felt magical to me.

Almost as magical as the bite of cheeseburger I had just sneaked.

Almost.

AUTHOR'S NOTES

While "The Secret Of Gaspard" is a fictional narrative drawn in its entirety from my own imagination, and the ELAC a fictional organization, the Commission for Looted Art in Europe is very real. Since its inception in 1999, it has been instrumental in recovering over 3,500 paintings, drawings, silver, books and manuscripts, stolen by the Nazis between 1933 and 1945, and returning them to their rightful owners.

Also very real is the monumental theft that occurred during the Nazi occupation. There is no way of knowing exactly how much art the Nazis stole. Some say six million objects, however, that figure is not inclusive of the millions more that they deliberately destroyed.

I derived considerable inspiration for The Persian's stash, from the actual discovery in November 2013 of twelve hundred and eighty paintings, drawings, and prints in a Munich apartment owned by the son of a prominent art dealer. The total stash was valued in excess of a billion dollars. Unbelievable!

If you would like to pursue further study on the topic of stolen art and the Commission for Looted Art in Europe, please go to: lootedartcommission.com.

Books do not happen by inspiration alone. It takes a lot of very hard work by many amazing people.

I am, as always, deeply indebted to my advance readers, Steve Betz, Sharon Walling, Bob Book and Sarah Wagner, as well as Rob Weidenfeld, my cover designer, Captain Sean

Archer for expert aeronautical expertise, and Sarah Wagner, my art consultant.

My prodigious editor, Cheryl Gollner—who will actually take exception to me using that word—was once again on top of her game, thus saving this mad scriblerian from public humiliation.

Thank you for reading. My hope is that you enjoyed this novel enough to follow Jake and Co. in their next adventure, *"The Haunts Of Cruelty."*
R.G. Ryan
Las Vegas, Nevada
July 2017

ABOUT THE AUTHOR

R. G. Ryan

 R.G. Ryan is the author of the Jake Moriarity series of thrillers, The Voices In My Head (the biography of late Las Vegas entertainment icon, Danny Gans), and the popular Snapshots At St. Arbuck's series. He lives with his first wife on the coast of somewhere beautiful. Can sing a little.

BOOKS BY THIS AUTHOR

Watercolor Dreams

Eighteen-year-old runaway, Vanessa Phillips, knows a secret...
and the secret knows her—knows where she sleeps and where
she eats on the streets of Pacific Beach in San Diego, Califor-
nia.Crooked Las Vegas politician Harry Olivetti is willing to
kill in order to protect this secret, and his two hired assassins
are closing in leaving Vanessa nowhere left to run.To a city by
the sea—where the world flocks for sun, sand and surf—comes
legendary FBI missing persons consultant, Jake Moriarity...a
lost soul in a desperate search to find this lost girl. Moriarity
can save her, but first, he has to find her. And the only thing he
has to go on is like a watercolor painting that has been left out
in the rain with all the colors running together.

Finding Wonderland

Simone Ducharme is poised to be the next big thing in the
world of jazz. In fact, according to industry insiders, it's
almost a sure thing. Twenty-four, exotically beautiful and
blessed with the kind of voice that seems to come along only
once in a generation. But to stand where she now stood, in the
live room of a legendary Hollywood recording studio—a studio that had been home to some of the most famous recording
artists in history—required more than looks and talent. She
also had an understanding of the music industry in general
and the Jazz genre in particular that transcended her age and
experience. In short, Simone was the whole package.

Her producer, Lonnie Falcon—also jazz great Aaron Perry's producer—is confident her debut album will surpass one million units in sales and be the crowning jewel on his already illustrious career. But while polishing up her vocals on the album's final track, she simply vanishes while on a five-minute break from recording. But is her disappearance voluntary, or has she been abducted? Falcon only knows one man who can make that determination—Jake Moriarity.

When Jake agrees to take on Simone's case, he has no idea that his search will uncover a secret past, a vengeful former enemy and lead him through long forgotten, subterranean ruins into a violent encounter with Yves Barreau...an honest to goodness dead man walking and the toughest man Jake has ever faced.

"Finding Wonderland" takes the reader on a fast-paced journey from the pristine recording studios of Hollywood to the gritty sands of Ocean Beach in San Diego where Jake is running out of time in a place that time has forgotten.

The Secret Of Gaspard

2:00 a.m.
Just outside of Toulouse, France, an obscure warehouse sits in the middle of a forgotten orchard. A monstrous evil is hidden away within its musty interior where four men have gathered in secret conclave. Powerful men—and ruthless beyond comprehension—they comprise the core of a multi-national cartel dealing in Holocaust art stolen by the Nazi's during World War II. The purpose of their nocturnal gathering is to determine the fate of one of their own.

Six hundred kilometers away, in Villefranche-sur-Mer, Jake Moriarity is enjoying blissful days and balmy nights in Gaspard Ducharme's Mediterranean family villa while he recovers from serious injuries suffered as a result of his conflict with Yves Barreau. Surrounded by his best friend and family, life is good and worries are few, for Gaspard Ducharme is a kind and generous host...who will be dead by morning unless Jake Moriarity can fight his way through more twists and turns than an Olympic Giant Slalom and save his friend.

The fast paced action takes the reader on a frantic journey from the Côte d'Azur of Southern France, to the Costa Brava of Catalonia, the deserts of Las Vegas and finally to the high rises of West Hollywood. And in the end, Jake Moriarity will be left wondering if he can trust anyone...including himself.

The Haunts Of Cruelty

On the trail of his most hated enemy, Jake Moriarity is deep in the Amargosa Desert. He is cut off from the FBI team that inserted him, severely wounded, running on empty and apparently hallucinating, because he just shot Paul Morgan in the head with a 12-gauge and then watched him get up and walk away.

Paul Morgan, the man single-handedly responsible for causing Jake's niece Cassie, to become addicted to heroin and then setting her up as his main girl in a Seattle escort service.

Paul Morgan, who has now kidnapped Cassie and is threatening to kill her while forcing Jake to watch.

Paul Morgan, whose life Jake should have ended when he had the chance, but didn't—a decision that has now come back to haunt him, cruelly.

The Wood Between The Worlds

An obscure and ancient Turkish church where, if legend is to be believed, thousands have been healed of all manner of disease and injury by simply walking through a door and into a small, candle-lit chamber.

A renowned archeological team from a prominent Pacific Northwest university who have uncovered an ancient manuscript claiming to lead its possessor to a relic, the discovery of which would be the single greatest archeological find in history.

A clandestine conclave of nine incalculably wealthy men ensconced in an obscure Swiss chalet. Their focus is also consumed with unearthing this selfsame relic. For in their possession, the geopolitical, financial and ecumenical global landscape will be altered...shaken to its very core, with everything falling into their avaricious and diabolical hands.

And Jake Moriarity in a desperate life and death race to secure the relic before The Nine. What's required is a clear-cut strategy. What he has is nothing more than a faint reflection of riddles. But even if he has to kill in order to bring it about, the relic must be protected...for it is The Wood Between the Worlds.

The First Stone

Bartholomew Bennet hadn't planned on living on the streets of the Burnside Triangle, addicted to heroin and pimping himself out. Far from it. A newly minted MBA in hand and a job with one of Portland, Oregon's most promising tech start-ups, Bart had arrived with hopes and plans for the future.
And then, it all fell apart. The once bright, engaging twenty-two-year-old hipster was now a skinny, desperate, dying drug addict who would do anything for twenty bucks. And the saddest part of all? No one would be there when he died...not his mother, or his grandfather...Father Jack Mahoney.

A thousand miles away in San Diego, Father Jack turns to his good friend, Jake Moriarity to find his grandson. What begins as a favor for a friend becomes a life and death dance with a master of the game as Jake stumbles headlong into a web of intrigue involving prominent members of Portland's wealthy elite, the judicial system, and the Russian mob.

At the center of that web Jake finds Bart hopelessly ensnared, but he's not alone. Adolescent and pre-adolescent girls—some kidnapped, some sold by families, but all trafficked for sex— are also there, hidden in plain sight in the City of Roses.

With action that is both taut and terrifying, this fast-paced thriller follows Jake Moriarity on a journey through the dystopian darkness of Portland's underworld where he comes face to face with a foe as formidable as Jake is fearless.

Snapshots At St. Arbuck's Volume 1

Socrates once said, "An unexamined life is not
worth living." Well, R.G. Ryan would make Socrates smile. This
little book will make you think about every part of your life: your childhood, important adults (like parents, grandparents, aunts and uncles, relationships) your career, your future—you name it, it comes to life under R.G.'s observant eye. Let R.G. Ryan put your life
into perspective. I am a raving fan of R.G. and this book.
—Ken Blanchard, co-author of The One Minute
Manager® and Leading at a Higher Level

Snapshots At St. Arbuck's Volume 2

I started to read Snapshots on a plane ride from Amsterdam to Barcelona and couldn't put it down. When I got to my hotel, I had to finish it. Socrates once said, "An unexamined life is not worth living." Well, R.G. Ryan would make Socrates smile. This

little book will make you think about every part of your life: your childhood, important adults (like parents, grandparents, aunts and uncles, relationships) your career, your future—you name it, it comes to life under R.G.'s observant eye. And does he
express his observations well! I was jealous of his writing as I was
reading. I am a raving fan of R.G. and this book.

—Ken Blanchard, co-author of The One Minute Manager® and Leading at a Higher Level

The Voices In My Head

Danny Gans poured his energy intoeverything he loved, from his family tohis faith, from baseball to his career inentertainment. Whenit came time todocument hislife story, he poured hisenergy into this project as well.Sadly, one day after this manuscriptwas completed, Danny died. Hisinspiringstory remains, offering a compelling mixof touching tales and life lessons. Fromthe baseball diamonds of his youth to hissold-out stardom on the Las Vegas Strip,Danny charts the struggles and successesof his life. Along the way, he tells us ofthe heartwarming courtship of his wife,Julie, and his close relationships with hisfather and mother. An uncommon giftas an impressionist lifted "The Man ofMany Voices" to the pinnacle ofthe LasVegas entertainment industry, where hewill be long remembered as a much-lovedperformer and a generous man. Here isthe story ofDanny Gans, told in his ownvoice, and from his own heart.

www.ingramcontent.com/pod-product-compliance
Lightning Source LLC
Chambersburg PA
CBHW030402180626
46812CB00005B/1903